The Dancing Other

THE FRENCH LIST

The Dancing Other

SUZANNE DRACIUS

Translated by Nancy Naomi Carlson
and Catherine Maigret Kellogg

LONDON NEW YORK CALCUTTA

www.bibliofrance.in

The work is published with the support of the
Publication Assistance Programmes of the Institut français

Seagull Books, 2018

Originally published in French as *L'autre qui danse*

© Suzanne Dracius, 1989, 2007

First published in English translation by Seagull Books, 2018

English translation © Nancy Naomi Carlson and Catherine Maigret Kellogg

ISBN 978 0 8574 2 479 2

Typeset by Seagull Books, Calcutta, India
Printed and bound by Hyam Enterprises, Calcutta, India

For Pierre Pinalie
and grandmother Germaine,
in memoriam.

CONTENTS

*África de selvas húmedas
y de gordos gongos sordos . . .*
Nicolás Guillén
'Balada de los dos abuelos' (1934)

For I is another.
Arthur Rimbaud
Letter to Paul Demeny (15 May 1871)

This is a novel. Any resemblance to persons living or dead would be pure coincidence. 'But there are no coincidences. There are only correspondences, in the Baudelairean sense of the word' (author's own quote from *Climb to the Sky*).

A glossary, sorted in alphabetical order at the end of the book, provides an explanation for Creole or African words that are not readily understandable within the context.

Thanks to Curtis Louisar for his magnificent song 'Aganila, the Revelation Personified' (3A Productions).

Promonologue

I DON'T WANT ANY OF THIS AFRICA OF COERCION, this false Africa, this fabricated Africa, this Africa that maims, demeans, disfigures. I am smothering in these boubou robes.

You cannot be Africa, a grimacing mask solely guided by evil, only imposing oppressive rituals, only embarking on overseas trips of disgrace, just like in this cursed trunk.

Rehvana is suffocating among the insipid boubou garments in garish African colours.

She really wants to be his wife, she wants to be one of them, but not at this price!

He had led her, willing, in love, seduced, into this decrepit building in the fourteenth arrondissement, where his pals shared a squat house.

The friends were pleasant and talkative; they'd eaten dried fish seasoned with manioc flour, and millet pancakes they'd somehow managed to cook; they'd drunk sorghum beer, made fun of Babacar, who was hankering for a Coke, and they'd smoked lots of yamba, sitting on the floor and listening to the rhythm of the calabash drums.

And all the girls had purplish marks on their cheekbones.

'I don't want to be marked!'

But I am awake: their drug had no effect on me since I can hear them, their muffled, worried voices, through the dirty wood;

I am breathing, I am outside the trunk, I am tall, my true face revealed, I leap out of the trunk!

They are saying I'm dead, that my forehead hit the edge of the table, that they don't know what to do with my body . . .

No! I am not a prisoner, I got out, I escaped—was that a magic spell of the real Africa?—because I was there, prostrate in that worm-eaten box of wood from which I still feel the cramps in my body and smell the stench of death. I was there, enclosed, when Aganila appeared, huge and black, draped in a long sabador of indigo and scarlet lamé—a mannish feminine figure and taller than all the others, a large woman standing quite strong and straight-backed, with a wide form and immobile curves—and then the goddess liberated me.

Massive arms stretched wide, released from the heavy folds of the ceremonial robes—with these she set me free. Mother Africa, her ample sleeves pointing out other routes to me, stood up, full, unique, for my salvation and for my life.

I was allowed to flee, and here I am running in the city streets, and the mulatto from Pantin guides me through a familiar labyrinth. Hieratic, sovereign, in all its functional formality, the Montparnasse Tower soothes me, seduces me and swaddles me in its glow.

People on cafe terraces, and passers-by with peaceful looks. Then suddenly the boulevard, the pavement flaming with neon and incandescent lights, and the tower again, over there, raised on the night sky in a nebula of spangles.

From now on, Rehvana is far from everything she's just discovered in that horror. The goddess' flying takes her leagues away from the black building with blind windows turned towards the cemetery, and where, two streets further down, grovelling humanity swarms, ensnared in the aberration of a false deliverance.

FIRST SONG

The Initial Alliance

They are two men of flesh and bone;
there is one who reads and another who dances;
I see nothing else in it.

Alfred de Musset

On ne badine pas avec l'amour

'YOU KNOW I WAITED HOURS FOR YOU AT LE MAHIEU—don't you even remember you had a date with me? Anyway, I hung around without much hope. I had a feeling you wouldn't show, or if you did, you'd be so aloof, so disdainful, so cold . . . '

Rehvana barely captures the words that dance and buzz around her. She nevertheless consents to confer a half-closed eye, puffed up and blazing with contempt, on the pleading young man who timidly offers the strong support of his arm. Her slender legs, outlined and exposed in places by the torn pantyhose, boldly grab hold of the lifesaving asphalt, limping but proud.

Furious, she's just noticed that one of her heels has been lost in the battle, and she's quite simply beginning to wonder if it wouldn't be better, yes, quite simply, to walk barefoot.

Barefoot . . .

Wide feet from 'Over There', wide as gum-tree trunks, devoured by elephantiasis or hookworm—the 'dog's worm'? And her mother who'd said, the day after the hurricane, not to go around barefoot in the streets of the city, that other city, after the hurricane was over, teeming with cockroaches and rats, the ones that died in the storm, floating with paws and pointy muzzles grown stiff, exposing their bloated bellies on the sea waters spread throughout the city—the city dazed in the morning and defiled by all the filth carried by the destructive winds of the night—and the living, daring ones who see in the city's distress an immeasurable godsend.

'Don't go around barefoot, I tell you, you'll get big feet.'

And she, filled with the exalted desire to go back to a tradition of women who cut the sugar cane—though these women who tie down the canes in the fields wrap their feet and their entire bodies in several layers of old clothes to escape the bites from the cane—that warrior woman, tall and sly, bristling with barbs that sought to pierce their black flesh—a tradition of the poor, coarse bitako Negress, of the servant (though her mother's servant arrives perched on twelve-centimetre-high heels from which she agrees to only descend to put on flip-flops, strictly reserved for housework).

But Rehvana liked to think she was authentic—more authentic than the ones who never left for the 'Other Side'—and she strutted insolently on the pretty, fine feet of a historic mulatto woman with fragile aristocratic ankles on the unsympathetic macadam of her native, yet foreign, Fort-de-France.

'I was sure you'd gone to meet up with that guy, so I went to wait for you in front of the squat house. I would've waited hours for you, you know, but you also know that it was better for me not to try to go inside . . . '

A fleeting smile stretches across Rehvana's lips: it was true, it was wiser not to do anything about it . . . One evening, on the subway, she was joking around and flirting with one of Abdoulaye's vague acquaintances—a Senegalese man who was flirting in return—and she simpered, whirled, laid it on thick to taunt Abdoulaye, to tease him without really knowing why, to see how far she could go . . . And suddenly violence erupted: with one leap, the man was upon her, and the slaps came crashing down. Slaps? No, blows, massive fists were bruising her face, heavy hands crushing her limbs. Gasping, stunned, she didn't even have time to react. Her pride, her refusal of the injustice with which the brutal mass was crushing her body, commanded the young woman to defend herself but she could only try to dodge and gather the last-ditch strength to protect her face by deploying her arms.

She didn't suffer as much from the blows as from the humiliation, and the unbearable discovery.

She who abhorred violence, she, so delicate, a fragile flower, the object of attentive courting, even though that was no longer in style—but so refined, so precious that no suitor ever dared approach her without taking on the role of a small marquis of Molière—she was lying there in a second-class Métro car, almost unconscious, under the mocking eye of a delighted pseudo-Guinean.

A sharp thunderbolt split the air with a dazzling flash; the steel gleamed, furtive, and under her distraught eyes, a scarlet thing gushed, on fire, dreadfully real and yet dreadfully unbelievable in this unreal scene, with a savagery she would never have believed could exist.

Blood pours from an unknown flesh, from a throat that appeared suddenly from who knows where, and she staggers again, flooded with nausea, crushed by her bruising and the pointless horror, the distinct, senseless and bizarre horror of those afro-comb teeth stuck in that throat, very near her . . .

My God! How she'd like to be elsewhere! She'd like to scream at them that she doesn't belong here. What's this 'good little girl' from the Saint Joan of Arc school—that haven of peace that butts up against the Orantes convent—what's she doing in this vulgar farce? She's embarrassed—simultaneously, of being embarrassed—to be there, under the gazes of the peaceful travellers, terrorized jellyfish clutching their bags on their knees, and she's red from confusion, red from contusions, swollen from punches and shame.

'Nothing is more certain!' she spat, while quickening her step. 'It was better, indeed, not to show yourself.'

And this reminder brought to Rehvana's lips a fake, icy smile, because she is angry at him for having alluded to that other horror, and for being there, and forcing her gratitude with his stitches in his neck, and having still been there that night, and seeing all that, and still being there, just having met her a short week ago, a mini *deus ex machina* that watches over her and always appears with impeccable timing to see her emerge from her muck and receive her in the beauty of his strong, open arms, and for which she has no use.

He'd started to worry, for a different restlessness had seemed to reign in the squat house when he saw her—a sudden appearance of wild wings—disdainful flight of the beloved woman.

A shape shot out from the grimy door; with long arms driving back long tentacles of cotton fabrics bought at the bazaar, and with an infuriated vehemence, she'd gone past without seeing him—oh delirious look of the beloved woman! What unfathomable hatred, what inexpiable evil spell compels you, pitiful, to these savage descents into a hell not your own? Rising from the idolized mouth—full lips, a pomegranate smashed under inexplicable blows, mauve membranes violated—towards them all my kisses are offered, my soul!—rises a husky refrain with strains of terror.

What can he make out from this appalling appearance, this repeated lament that bursts from the lips of the beloved, the ravishing woman, the Gorgon with great, rebellious hair, in the incongruous, ferocious outburst?

Africa vera verissima
Africa Rehvana vera
Aganila!

'What did you mean? You were screaming things that made no sense! But what have they done to you? Why did you rush outside, tearing at your clothes as if they were burning you?'

'Leave me alone, will you?'

Rehvana has finally deigned to answer him, with a tired and exasperated tone.

'They've simply invented a new, ridiculous system to keep so-called tradition alive, but more strictly interpreted than ever— a story about tattooing, I think, or some such thing. I thought I saw some sort of crude incisions on the girls' faces, some swollen scars. I don't know too much about it. I didn't have time to get a good look; at a point, I understood they'd decided to do the same thing to me, and I didn't go along with it, that's all. Then they wanted to do it to me by force, and what's more, you're now getting on my nerves with your questions! . . . They'd drugged me with some sort of concoction they'd put together, or at least they'd tried—Diop had made a weird preparation from an ancient recipe given to him by the marabout from Belleville, and had offered it to me by saying: "Here, drink this, you'll see, it's the absolute best."'

'The best for what, I wonder! And you drank some, evidently, always too happy to steep yourself in all the bogus plans of that band of lunatics!'

'Yes, I drank some, to do as everyone else had, believing they all had got high on it before my arrival. They all looked so odd when I came in, I thought they were under the influence of their magic potion, and I drank some to join them on their "planet". Since I still didn't know where they were headed, I was convinced that it was some of their bullshit psychedelic stuff . . . But their recipe was certainly not up to snuff, because I remained completely conscious, and when I finally realized what they wanted to do to me, I struggled like a crazy woman and started to howl and break everything—so they tried to mark me by force. Abdoulaye insisted, though the others wanted to give up and were starting to get fed up. I even felt they were a little scared, but I think it was Abdoulaye who didn't want to let it go.'

The great black man full of arrogance, the chief, was superbly offended.

Profoundly wounded in his honour as a so-called great male of Africa, he could no longer back down.

'*Kité ti salop-la pati*! *Nou pé ké rivé ayen épi'y.*' ('Let that little slut leave! We won't get anywhere with her!')

'*Tjébé'y, man di'w*! *Sé madanm mwen, man ja di'w I madanm mwen, i té dakò, atjolman i pè, mé i ké obéyi, ou ké wè, man ka di'w I ké obéyi*!' ('Hold her tightly, I tell you! That's my wife, I've already told you she's my wife—she agreed, and now she's afraid, but she's going to obey, you'll see, I guarantee she's going to obey!')

She felt it was a bad sign: they were suddenly taking shelter behind their clumsy and garbled command of Creole, a lame Creole learnt as best they could on the pavements of Barbès, in the eighteenth arrondissement of Paris—for they had never set foot in the Antilles, not a single one of them—and they were trying to draw from it the necessary strength to continue.

As for Abdoulaye, it was out of the question for him to lose face in front of his friends—be someone who tolerates a rebellious companion.

'If he'd been alone, if the others could have gone away, I'm sure he would've stopped everything.'

And the women in brightly coloured boubous, they themselves already marked, and more or less voluntary accomplices to this sinister farce, these women exhorted Rehvana with their shrill screams growing more and more hateful, for she had to be like them, there was no reason for this little bourgeois woman—too light-skinned—this pretentious young madam with supple curls, to have won the favours of their most handsome male and be allowed to refuse to do what was necessary to be wholly one of them.

But she really wants to be one of them! What else has she been trying to do, for so, so long, that she makes herself, to please them, eat unspeakable things in insane postures, and to 'make the saroual pants beat and imprison her legs', as she is fond of saying, even when the heat of the continental summer encourages her to put on a miniskirt rather than ape the Tuaregs from some factitious desert?

Rehvana is full of love for Abdoulaye, drowned in the fascination of those large, long-muscled limbs, and stirred to trembling by his mahogany eyes with their tawny, imperious, darting irises in two almond-shaped orbs muddied with small, yellowish specks; yes, to the point of convulsion, she loves the minuscule yellow puddles that stain the corneas of his eyes.

God, how she is transported by these small specks of negritude—yes, for her, such emotion, before what she calls the specks of negritude: she has anxiously scrutinized the way-too-white blue of her own eyes, until ferreting out, oh triumph!, a minuscule trace of pale ochre that instantly filled her with pleasure.

Oh! She's tried everything, followed all the excessive paths that could lead her back to her roots, including the never-ending sessions of hair braiding, when she would have her hair ruthlessly pulled, one by one, eight by eight, although it was too straight to remain braided for long. Against all odds of comfort and reason, she patiently stayed seated an entire afternoon to obey, to the point of euphoria, the deft hands of Josépha, the swift Haitian hairdresser with the bearing of a Bambara princess.

Rehvana gets lost in faraway daydreams, as little by little her scalp appears, all pale in the winter sun, made naked by even rows separating a multitude of long, long braids, thin and tight, that will have to be held together with cords that are themselves extremely tight, for Rehvana's hair is not sufficiently coarse for the braids to stay put on their own. Oh! We never get what we want: to her right, a young African woman with a good complexion, who has everything Rehvana dreams of having, is busy choosing hair extensions. Skillfully interlaced at the end of her very tiny, curly braids, they will produce, finally, almost the same effect as Rehvana's real hair; however, one of them will be in agony, when she will have to endure the nocturnal assault of four hundred bamboos and the countless multicoloured pearls, rings, balls and garnets that decorate the end of each braid, while masking the maintenance rubber bands. Each night Rehvana will try everything to contain this invading flood: the ridiculous hair-net, adventure-seeking ties, elusive hairpins . . . In vain! Nothing will ever prevent this crashing wave, so splendid by day, from doing its best each night to fiercely bite her cheeks, its stubborn groundswell digging into her flesh. And the other will tremble at the slightest gust of wind, will be compelled to follow a thousand and one precautions, a thousand and one tricks, to preserve the expert architecture of her hairdo and contain the vague desires for independence of her fake locks.

Back there, in the muck of pungent smells, in front of faces that were sometimes jeering, sometimes cruel and grinning from ear to ear, Rehvana could only refuse.

Why not female circumcision, while they were at it?

'That's it! So you feel the "vibration", and I'm supposed to swallow whatever you spit out! The goddess Africa came to your rescue, and magically made you come out from the trunk where you had died and start speaking in Latin through your mouth! No, but you're taking me for a fool. You agree to drink any old demented drug that makes you babble deliriously, and then you find it normal to let yourself be banged up by a band of macaques who want to make God only knows what kind of idiotic markings on you, you let yourself be stuffed into a trunk like a bag of dirty laundry, you're forced to escape half-naked into the streets of Paris, and you have the gall to tell me it's nothing, it's your fault!'

'I was the one who panicked, I'm telling you. It was nothing at all: a little nothing of a tattoo. I was simply annoyed. Their whole staging had impressed me, and at the time, it truly seemed horrible to have marks made on my face. I've always been overly sensitive to pain . . . I didn't want to be marked, I was afraid, scared of hurting, scared of being disfigured . . . But maybe it doesn't even hurt . . . that could be the case! The other women had these marks; I'm the one who's just a chicken!'

Rehvana resumed her limping walk; there's something a little ridiculous in her strained, lopsided gait, the result of her pitiful broken heel.

'I should have put on slippers once and for all!' she grumbles without conviction. 'Anyway, Jérémie, you can't understand this kind of thing. All that interests you is living your little, petty, assimilated, gulped down, digested life. You therefore don't see you're nothing but a bleached Negro—salvaged and hopeless!'

Enough is enough, and Jérémie explodes.

'Listen, I really want to play devoted admirers and bashful lovers, I really want everything you want, but don't start insulting me again! You get hit in the subway: I run, I fly, it's me, Zorro, I rescue the tearful beauty, I take an afro pick in the throat, but no problem, to hell with the cost! And what's more, the beauty is so pretty . . . You hold my hand on my hospital bed, you coo, you make goo-goo eyes at me, and as soon as I have my back turned to surprise you (because I love you, idiot that I am, because I had a surprise for you!), as soon as I leave you for one minute, you dash back to this guy's house!

'But what do you see in him, in this moron? Abdoulaye? Abdoulaye, my eye! No more Abdoulaye than I'm the pope! But what are they smoking to come up with all this nonsense, your operetta Africans, your sect of idle fanatics who aren't named Babacar or Abdoulaye any more than I am! And you, what do you want with this gang of would-be Mandinkas? Real madmen, yes siree! Don't tell me you really take seriously this gloomy crew of weirdos and lazybones who live off all kinds of sleazy dealings in the name of triumphant negritude, convinced that stealing from whites is not stealing! What can a girl like you find but trouble with this band of riffraff who got mixed up in a cycle of idiotic rituals for the simple reason that they really don't have anything else to do! But you don't see they are incompetents, a dysfunctional bunch of half-imbeciles, obsessed with a maniac who finds it quite easy to dominate them! . . . But what can you do in the kingdom of the blind . . . Ah, he's a piece of work, your Abdoulaye! All you'll get with these little gangsters is to end up in prison, or in a thousand pieces in a vacant lot. In any case, I'm getting really tired of playing the forgiving and cuckolded Good Samaritan!'

He can't contain himself any longer and grabs the elbow of the young woman who keeps walking straight ahead, hobbling along, without appearing to listen to him.

'No matter what, I'm letting you know this is the last time I stick my nose into your nonsense.'

But Jérémie, saying this, knows all too well that this time can't be the last, and if his voice wavers and wanders, it's not from rage—it's from feeling he'd rather stop talking.

'The Ébonis-True-Sons-of-Agar!' he enunciates in an affected grandiloquence, shaking his head from right to left and sadly shrugging, as if confirming his refusal of this strange sorrow, surreal and crippling, which plunges him, despite his best efforts, into a world which in other times, other places, would have evoked in him nothing but disgust and amused disdain. 'I can tell you they're odd birds, your "Ébonis", your neo-Maroons, anachronistic Negroes in the middle of twentieth-century Paris! If you want my opinion, they should all be locked up!'

He maligns, vilifies, makes fun of them; and he shrugs and shrugs, and angrily throttles this crazy love that numbs him; sceptical and scornful as he may sound, he's undeniably crippled with heartache, he gets agitated and loses his composure, and he spouts insults and sarcastic remarks to better fend off the ineffable tenderness that binds and entwines him to this woman.

She gently extricated herself, a long time after he had placed his hand on her, as if she hadn't immediately felt his fingers' touch nor understood his words.

She seems reluctant to pull herself away from some broken dream he can't fathom.

Jérémie is what people call a *négropolitain*, just like Diop, Abdoulaye, Babacar and the others, who were baptized in the Catholic church with names of Jean-Loup, Marc and Thierry. Born in Paris in the nineteenth arrondissement to parents who had emigrated from Guadeloupe to France, he only sees the Antilles through rhythm, Malavoi and Kassav, codfish fritters and rum punch. For him, Guadeloupe and Martinique only represent a pleasant folklore—nothing to renounce—but he struts his dark skin of the most beautiful black, without hang-ups and bitterness, in the streets of Paris and the halls of the École des Hautes Études Commerciales, France's top business school. His life consists of brilliant studies that are almost finished, that open up a beautiful future for him, and he feels at ease in what Rehvana calls 'the system', where he has his place and refuses to let anyone have the right to step on his black toes. His life also consisted of his parents, kindly and well-to-do civil servants so used to France that they only return to Guadeloupe in the summer, on holidays, on subsidized breaks, and now this little calazaza from Martinique has suddenly appeared, disconcerting, erratic, with her litany of heresies, and has thrown him into a universe of violence.

As for Jérémie, he hears neither the clinking of slave chains nor the voice of Africa.

A child of mulattos from the main island of Grande-Terre, bizarrely born black-blue, a shade of night darker than father and mother, as sometimes happens—middle child between an older sister with soft and milky russet tones and a little gingerbread brother—a peaceful childhood in Pantin, with healthy scuffling under the centuries-old, large chestnut trees in the playground, honour awards in elementary school and perhaps, most

13

importantly, loving progenitors, strangers to criminal activities, undoubtedly upright and unique in having no axe to grind, who had spared him from the hang-up of not having 'saved' skin (in other words, miraculously light-skinned, evidently a survivor of black servitude).

Jérémie has known neither fear nor shame from his midnight-blue skin, nor self-loathing in front of his mirror, nor a frizzy head downcast to the world, nor furore, rancour or feelings of injustice, it seems, nor irrational camouflage to hide the stench from a ship's hold and from exile that neither oceans nor centuries would have washed away from his skin.

Quite the contrary, when a smile reveals to prying eyes the white of his perfect set of teeth, inflating and parting his full and fleshy lips—brown-violet and moist—he is neither revenge nor renunciation, he is smile.

He is not crossing any line; he exists. Could this just be for appearance's sake?

'You're too serious, too solid, too patient and too full of future to get involved with someone like me. Leave me alone, Jérémie—there's nothing to expect from me,' she argues, emerging, as if in reverse, from this crumbled dream where Jérémie has no place.

'That's exactly what I think, imagine!' he responds, almost shrieking. 'And I'm even asking myself what I'm still doing here with you, dwelling on pointless anger. I'd be better off letting you go,' he adds, raising his voice even louder.

'You're quite right, my prince—better to let her go, maybe you'll have more luck with a blonde,' a stumbling vagrant blurted out, sententiously. 'Hey, speaking of blondes, would you have a little one for me, my prince?'

With pestilential breath, the drunkard plunged towards Rehvana to get a better look at her, then veered, reeling, towards Jérémie. In high spirits, he insists and begs for a cigarette; then, managing with difficulty to find his centre of gravity, since the simple gesture of lighting a Winston had been enough to drain

his meagre reserves of concentration and had dangerously compromised his balance, he gets back to boldly looking the young
woman up and down; with a flaccid mouth, cigarette plastered
to his flabby lip, he is ecstatic. Tufts of greasy hair become visible
from his ears and nose as he comes still closer, and his rheumy
eyes insolently examine the young woman in tatters, covered
with bruises, tottering, miserable little swindled woman, broken.

Rehvana has always had a holy hatred of people who come up
as close as possible to speak to you, nose to nose, but this is too
much; what is Jérémie doing, just standing there like a big fool?

What is she doing there herself, half-naked on this public
pavement, dazed, bruised from blows, forced to endure the all-
too-real, close-up view of a bunch of blackheads?

Rehvana violently recoils, irate, crazy with rage.

Aside from gagging in disgust, what infuriates her the most
is something she reads in the drunk's glassy eye and in Jérémie's
frozen stupor: she's enraged to find similarities between herself
and this ragged drunken wreck.

Rehvana resumed her walking—increasingly hurried, chaotic and
painful—not knowing the destination. Not even turning to face
him, she blurts out: 'Where do you think you're taking me?'

And Jérémie answered in that pacifying tone, mushy with
compassion, though slightly hypocritical and terribly irritating,
the tone people use to soothe the hiccupping sobs of a child who's
fallen. 'It's not that far now: that was my surprise . . . I found a
studio in the Latin Quarter and, like a big schmuck, I was so
happy to be closer to you. I just moved in—ciao, Pantin!—and I
was dying to tell you the news while you were holding your black
masses!'

Jérémie really couldn't tell if he was trying to make the girl smile,
make a fool of himself or avert something dreadful.

Abruptly she stopped to take off her shoes, stooping first to the right and then to the left, in precarious balance, with no means of support. She coiled an index finger around each strap and started walking again, barefoot, belligerent, swinging her stilettos with fake nonchalance; once or twice for fun, she twirled the straps around her fingers like the stiff trapeze artists of a small imaginary circus, and that brought a smile to her lips. While walking by a telephone booth, she paused, looking puzzled, as if she were suddenly remembering something, then in one swift move, she threw her shoes. The sad acrobats of fine kidskin crashed against glass and metal, in a short salvo of dull thuds.

The One

'YOUR ARSE IS AS SOFT AS AN APRICOT—an apricot, I'm telling you!
A peach! A mango!'

'You should stop—you're laying it on too thick!' Rehvana
interrupts, laughing loudly.

Rehvana surrenders and yields to the emollient flattery of this
tenacious love. This bliss, however, feels criminal, deceitful and
despicable. Cuddled, coddled and surrounded by a surfeit of
cloying tenderness, she feels out of place.

She has gradually begun to hate his crab-like, troublemaker
fingers between her thighs, and the gluttonous tribute paid to her
proud breasts.

She's infuriated at finding herself there, dehiscent and tepid,
showered with enveloping embraces, smooth moves, forgiving
caresses and anaesthetized by the scent of desire. Despite his
broad forceful hands accustomed to making themselves gentle,
not to mention the soft and appealing hair on his chest, she's
screaming inside that she doesn't have the right to indulge in this
conventional and sweet Parisian live-in arrangement among students. She doesn't care about a reassuring ideal of assimilated,
brainwashed *négropolitains*, and she abhors all Jérémie has to
offer: the prospect of a well-to-do life after meritorious studies.

She tells herself that she really likes the sweet rasp of his
broad and smooth belly with its strip of taut flesh that rubs and

presses against her, teases her with its steady rhythmic beats, makes her vibrate, lifts her and makes her erect. She tells herself that she likes all this too much: the man's weight on her chest or the small of her back, the way her knees go numb and even the way the man roars when he makes himself fluid, ocean, African sea deep down within her, liquid life, African God dissolving deep inside her.

And also that she gets way too much pleasure from it.

And still his strong and secure arms encircle her, these long arms taut with honeyed tenderness pull her towards a comfortable future, a warm home, three beautiful children, or two, who knows?—'the king's choice'—she convinces herself. His large, loving hands found a way to capture her heart through gentleness.

Imperceptibly, she yields to the intoxicating temptation of a haven of peace, of a serenity which she can decide to turn into joy.

She would love to weld her living flesh to this vigorous bronze body and allow herself to cling to him—to be set ablaze in all the heavens.

But she senses she's losing control; indeed, she senses she's foundering in forbidden depths, exhilarated and besieged by the blue-black Negro's pulsating skin and the heat of his scent. She has a vague feeling that something is missing; she's cognizant of a growing awareness that her destiny has not yet been fulfilled.

Rehvana can't linger with Jérémie any longer. Rehvana is restless and listless; she doesn't have to give in.

She must distance herself from him.

She persuaded Jérémie not to file a complaint for the second time, though he was really insistent today: this time it was about her.

To tell the truth, the first time, on his hospital bed, he had quickly yielded to the silent petition cast by the almond-shaped eyes of that beaten mademoiselle, as if he were also detecting another invitation, other promises.

This time, it had been about her, and he had insisted, protested, pleaded, rebuked; he'd tried, at length, but in vain, to force her to go to the police precinct, file a complaint, initiate an efficient, disciplined, civilized process; her consent to do so would have proved she was healing, symbolizing her return to safer values and more solid morals, and a rejection of the diabolical disorder and foolish danger into which she'd thrown herself.

After that, he might have been able to hope for everything, to believe everything.

Yes, he'd tried all he could think of to make her come around, moralizing and tender, ironic and grim, in turn. She was spared no taunting, no ridicule, no prayer. With all the energy of despair and the resentment of the aggrieved lover, Jérémie had desperately clung to the hope for an act of faith, a token, a final absolution.

He'd played all his cards to win her back, and had lost.

The Other

JÉRÉMIE HAD FOUND AN ALLY IN THIS VENTURE: Rehvana's older sister, healthy and tall, with Caribbean or Viking high cheekbones, who stood firmly on long, shapely legs like an ancient Greek caryatid, comfortably inhabiting her unusual polychrome skin— a shade of Ivorian ebony—with smooth, cinnamon arms and apricot-stained satin face, and never-ending hands ending in long, rounded fingernails.

Never had Jérémie seen such a being so splendidly and decisively variegated; he stood speechless before this creature who was, at once, diaphanous and marmoreal; the moire of her temples and her neck lent a matte translucence, pleasing to the eye, to the games of light and shadow. At first he hadn't known what to say to this young woman—undulating river, both climbing vine and cork oak—this unimaginable new beauty at the crossroads of many centuries, this sumptuous harmony of all races converging.

Simultaneously imbued with suzerain rainbow reflections and virgin-island perfumes, urban refinement and tropical torpor, she faced the world with sharp features straight from the banks of the Ganges—a proud, perfectly Indo-European nose, the impetuous, rippling waves of her long, unbridled hair and the soaring callipygian stature of a Yoruban princess.

She was a splendid illustration of history's peregrinations. And without having uttered a single word, the métisse was leaving *him* speechless.

It was as if each race, each people had invested their best in her flesh; as if some alchemist, some visionary genie, had had the power to concentrate all the beauty of the universe into this being, distilling and blending it into a perfect symbiosis.

She was there, out of his reach. A free Pandora, she was solidly planted in the intermingling of her many bloods.

Through the half-opened door, Matildana stood before him.

WITH FIERCE WILLPOWER, Rehvana has extracted herself from this false Eden, this deliquescent love—so far from all this boring beatitude. She no longer wants to hear about the room in the Latin Quarter, this furnished room suited for hard work, where Jérémie studies for exams and still finds the time to love her, to sweetly buy groceries, do the dishes, cook, clean and lavish her disdainful laziness with attention.

Rehvana wakes up at noon, wanders like a lost soul throughout the tiny studio and gloomily contemplates the roofs of Paris.

She's been dragging around like this for days.

After the bloody episode with the afro comb, a single vision had remained stuck in her memory: Abdoulaye and his friends scurrying away after their crime, disappearing into the labyrinthine Métro corridors, leaving her there, alone with the unknown wounded man.

She had only been able to find the strength to call her comforting and charitable big sister, just like when she used to shake her awake in the middle of the night, when they shared a room in their parents' house, and insufferable nightmares would besiege her sleep.

And Matildana had soon come to her aid, dazed but lucid, knowing, as always, whom to call, where to go, what to do.

Matildana had led her through the hospital hallways, and had answered some questions and sidestepped the most inconvenient ones; she'd given the necessary explanations and had preserved the peace; in short, she'd saved the honour of her fallen younger sister and the mysterious saviour.

She can't identify the assailants; she doesn't know them from Adam or Eve, nor does her sister, of course; otherwise, she would have already told them. Yes, she has no idea why these people got into a fight, why they assaulted her sister, why they attacked this young man who apparently was just trying to intervene.

They are only there to render assistance to the injured young man.

No, they don't want to file a complaint. What for? Against whom? It should be the young man's decision when he wakes up.

No, she doesn't know his name or address: it's the first time she's laid eyes on him. Her sister, too, for sure. Doesn't he have some form of identification on him?

She's really sorry she can't be more helpful.

As she is talking to the young police officer, he can see unbearable flashes of fear in her eyes, so he quickly jots down his notes and beats a hasty retreat.

Matildana had remained at her sister's side in this world of suffering, with its acrid and antiseptic smells—that other sinister city within the city—when the unconscious young man had been taken away on a squeaking gurney, when the felled archangel had disappeared behind swinging doors, between a foul-smelling drunk and a humble old Arab bearing the noble, emaciated features of an ancient shepherd from the Tinrhert Plateau, injured in some illegal night job, maimed far from his sun, in the cold confines of some morally corrupt construction site.

Staggering, on the verge of nausea, dazed from the blows, the little sister leant on the older sister, the irreproachable Matildana, armoured with audacity—it was on her shoulder of tender rock that the little sister had rested.

It was to her that she had clung, for days, before the archangel, healed, would unfurl the sanctuary of his arms— before he would plunge his wondrous midnight-blue Negro eyes, stippled with jasper and gold, into the deepest part of her being.

Matildana has strong shoulders, broad shoulders, and is slender and sturdy, free, naturally maroon, and freckled with a fleur-de-lis pattern. (Yes, she bears on her shoulder the fleur-de-lis mark of the slave convicted of running away, she herself not having been branded by a burning hot iron but by a triumphant melanin before birth; at the same time, in the small of her back, the blue Mongolian spot was outlined, made by those who ventured from Asia's yellow lands to the confines of the unmapped Land, *Incognita*, before the white man named it—long before the white man called it America by mistake.)

Warrior woman, supreme to all markings of infamy, subject of neither king, nor master, nor malediction—tall, strong, unbound Matildana—noble, grand woman freed from all chains—Matildana, great immortal, better version of Rehvana's self—indomitable and lively, intrepid and complete, impeccable and flawless—superior big sister already formed when Rehvana's frail being was still in limbo.

Indestructible Matildana, why is she still coming to her rescue?

Solemn Matildana. Laughing, immortal Matildana, faithful big sister, the Eternal goddess.   .

She who carries the little sister on her back when trails are steep; she whose hands are torn by brambles because the little sister likes blackberries; she whose legs braved the nettle sting when, brothers and cousins all vanished, the baby sister was there, sobbing and numb.

Paris

REHVANA IS STILL ASLEEP WHEN JÉRÉMIE LEAVES for class each morning, and even if the sound of the coffee maker rouses her, despite the extreme precautions Jérémie takes, she pretends to be in a deep slumber.

When they see each other each evening, they make love, speak little; she reluctantly eats the succulent food—having eaten nothing all day—lovingly prepared by Jérémie upon his return, between two theorems and a handful of statistics.

Jérémie tenderly protests, comically rants or theatrically pleads, but for all his efforts, he is unable to rid her of the strange dietary habits, taboos and draconian rules which she learnt in the sect and which, sometimes unconsciously, she still follows. For Rehvana—and it has become second nature—anything not associated with the Sons of Agar's traditions are disgusting and distorted. She keeps quiet, out of weariness, but picks among the foods for anything boiled or from overseas, pushing aside everything else or moving it around the plate, so that Jérémie believes she's eating. She makes up excuses and then, as soon as his back is turned, races to the garbage can to toss out the steak she has unenthusiastically cut into mouth-sized bites.

She does nothing all day, and has no desire to either visit her sister or go out to enjoy the smell of spring flooding the city.

Rehvana sometimes tells herself she's taking the time to rest, that this life is filled with peace; she even tells herself that she feels good.

And yet, she is languishing in such a dreary life, and unwittingly puts up with the hopelessly optimistic, whirlwind company of Jérémie's neighbours: the entire exuberant and studious seventh floor, and Marie-Aude, a sweet blonde who is always sunny; at times she lets herself be led across the hall to the room that looks like a veritable aviary, where a swarm of smart, busy, spirited, friendly female students flutter about, laughing and talking—Jérémie's female friends, thanks to whom he was able to find his studio apartment.

Rehvana bristles, ready to attack, when carefree and idle conversations between these educated, Third World–fascinated women bring up the formidable great themes of negritude, racism, identity, roots. They speak grudgingly, from a distance, as if it were some kind of dirty business. Do they want to please her or tease her, or perhaps heal her?

Jérémie is behind this . . . And they try to analyse, minimize, simplify . . . They set boundaries, they surrender and they dissect . . .

In Rehvana's mind, they have all, unawares, become part of a deliberate servitude; anyway, these annoying jokesters are driving her crazy, and day after day, the industrious, insipid seventh floor seems increasingly like a mental institution.

She feels more and more uncomfortable among these drudges full of drive; she can no longer bear how they dismiss Africa and only see in the Antilles a gang of amateurish, immature, bomb-happy islands for whom the zouk is the only medicine.

She usually plays dead when they knock at her door; more and more often, she holds her breath, concentrating with all her might so that those coming to get her for 'a quick bite among friends' believe she's not there.

The laughter retreats into the stairwell.

In this jovial, cordial and hospitable student cacophony, Rehvana is bored to death.

SQUATTING ON A MAT OF DRY, ROUGH RAFFIA PALM, her entire body propped on bare feet, straight-backed and stiff, in the noble manner of the proud warriors of the Beginning, Rehvana affectedly laps up the scalding mint tea. The fact that her body is in full African posture is proof that she has forgotten nothing, said nothing, revealed nothing of their secret. Hiding behind a cautious silence, they move as if in slow motion. After all, she isn't their woman, and it's not up to them to settle her fate.

Abdoulaye isn't there.

No account has been cleared, nor dirty linen aired. From a distance, their gaze falls onto the frail, penitent figure—the fearful little sister begging for forgiveness.

At first, surprised and stunned by the rebel woman's return, they had welcomed her, the undeserving sister, who could not live up to her faith.

She had followed them, back stooped, unable to see, along the fetid, sour-smelling, dark tunnel that led to the cellar where meetings were held. Then, without a word, they had intimated the order to sit in the midst of the putrid cesspool, in the middle of indeterminate, musty smells, facing the heatless brazier whose twirly flames tormented her eyes. Did they do this to see her more clearly, to confuse her or to read in her features her humiliation and her appeal?

Fingers crossed, placidly, they await Abdoulaye's return.

A pair of eyes, laden with rebuke, rimmed with swollen, hostile fat, has been watching her since she entered the room.

Voluminous Fassou sits apart, sulking. She picks abstractedly from the bowl of dates or dried figs placed in front of her and gloomily gobbles them down. Ever since she became Diop's wife, the huge, milk-chocolate-skinned métisse has swapped, without regret, her native eighteenth arrondissement (where, for twenty years, she endured not being either black enough or white enough), her first name (Monique) and her baggy blazers, in exchange for a squat, a pseudo-Guinean name (Fassou) and an extra-extra-large boubou. She banished for good the store-bought pastries and other sinful baked treats from her bulimic life, and if she keeps putting on weight, it's now in full compliance with the rules, the community's resolutions and without breaking their laws. No Brothers have ever caught her doing anything wrong: nothing she eats all day is European or chemical (though it's true they have yet to notice that fat Fassou recently has begun to discreetly seek privacy in order to make herself throw up). While she had never felt truly at peace with her body, even when living in her colourful Barbès neighbourhood, now she was absolutely convinced at last: she knew she was perfectly obese and had the self-confidence of being completely *something*. She had met the Brothers one night when she was in a deep, half-reggae, half-samba funk, in a club on the Right Bank—an Afro-Antillean disco (or Afro-Cuban, depending on the night)—and they had given her love and understanding. Even if, from time to time, she sensed to some degree that Diop was just going through the motions, out of respect for rules or tradition, and that he didn't find her superabundant flesh particularly superb; even if she sometimes caught him sneaking a few peeks of longing at the chief's wife—that skinny little thing, that insignificant zibicrette of a girl who would eventually get what she deserved.

When Rehvana makes a sudden movement to stand and stretch her legs that have now gone numb, the gaunt, gleaming muzzle of the German Army Luger, for which they'd bartered at the Clignancourt flea market, suddenly slides, like a grass snake, out of Amin-Diouf's long sleeve.

They order the girl to be silent as she opens her mouth to protest, to proclaim her innocence.

They shouldn't treat her like an enemy, despite the other night when she had wavered for the first time.

They look at her like a pariah; but what are they thinking? How can they believe for one second that she, Rehvana, the chief's wife, is no longer Agar's Daughter, and that she betrayed her faith?

They should know, for sure, that Rehvana has always helped them, always acted like them, kept quiet, been there to carry out their projects—even the craziest ones—that she has never talked, never disobeyed, never backed out, even when it came to doing ridiculous, difficult things.

She has never failed in her duty, never refused a mission, no matter how dangerous; she has, once and for all, turned her back on her family's principles and her conservative Catholic education; she has renounced her virtuous habits, her childhood integrity, and has given the Brothers the full amount of her parental allowance, initially intended for her studies.

For them, she had sold her furs and the Creole jewellery inherited from her grandmother: the enormous spider-brooch and the earrings shaped like tied bales of sugar cane. For them, she had even wangled from her sister unbelievable sums of money, making up all sorts of lies, at a time when wise Matildana, highly respected as a right-minded person within their sacred family circle, could still obtain cash from their parents' pockets, until the day when the suspicious kinfolk, having guessed where their generosity was being funnelled, categorically put an end to these inexplicable and illegitimate money transfers.

No! She was neither a nasty little bourgeois ninny nor a renegade!

She had faithfully followed them, down to their most obscure delusions. She had compromised herself and become an accomplice to their crimes, and had been there, with them, until the fateful evening when, curled up beside Abdoulaye in the stolen car parked on rue Saint-Merri, she found herself dreading the highly explosive outcome of their ambitions, and had no idea what chain of events was to be triggered that night, together with their bomb.

Ten kilos of plastic split between several fruit juice cans were hidden in the boot, destined to blow up Beaubourg, 'that colourful factory distilling the arrogant knowledge and bigoted culture of whites behind the garish pipes of a monumental, allegedly artistic, refinery.'

Tomorrow it would be smashed to pieces, that fortress of Western intellectual heritage which tames and enslaves Negro culture by gutting out its substance, like removing bile from the gizzard of slaughtered chicken before roasting and devouring the meat.

'And they call *us* cannibals? They consume Afro-Negro literature—that's how they eat it—culture-robbing, cannibalistic masters of the world, but only once it's made edible, bleached, cleaned of bile and brains . . . '

In this fashion, Abdoulaye lectures a reluctant Rehvana, to convince her of their expedition's legitimacy, of the need to give the universe a warning.

'Tomorrow morning, when ex-president Senghor begins his commemorative visit to pay tribute to his late friend and classmate, Georges Pompidou, the Ébonis will swallow the impostor whole, the alleged apostle of triumphant negritude—he who agreed to "shed his blackness", to wear the green uniform of the Academy, to become white, since he was, perhaps, unable to fully bleach himself in order to enter the Academy of Whites, this racist bastion once ruled by Richelieu, and today still impervious to the cries of Agar's Sons . . . '

So speaks a fuming Abdoulaye, boiling and foaming with hate, eager to slaughter the abhorred whiteness—those who were coming to preen and pose for photographs in front of the Centre Georges-Pompidou. His conscience won't rest until he places the bomb but Rehvana's won't rest for far longer, after the deed is done.

She is starting to doubt herself and truly fears they've gone too far this time; she has all sorts of qualms about the bomb. So she timidly asks Abdoulaye if he's fully certain that this mute and blind violence will be well understood, and if the fiery, rather terse message he prepared for the press will be enough to convince the masses—enough for them to accept the carnage, with innocents maimed for life and children's bodies blown to bits . . .

Will they understand what's going on? Will they understand the Sons of Agar's message when the terrible blast is unleashed?

She's fanatical—she swears it's undeniably so—but she's not bloodthirsty.

'Yes, we have been disembowelled, decerebrated and enucleated!'

Her head is suddenly spinning: great masses, peoples, sovereign states, races, heads of state, bombings, cascades of blood . . .

She feels small and beyond all hope.

She declares defeat and gives up: Abdoulaye is certainly right. He examines it all, analyses, dissects, theorizes, puts into practice: he knows what he's doing.

The next morning, around ten o'clock, all hands were on deck: on port side, half of the sect had their eyes riveted to the television screen, while on starboard, the other half heeded the order to keep ears glued to transistor radios so they could catch every crumb of the ceremony's broadcast—or, rather, be on the lookout for the prodigious collapse of which they would be the heroic authors.

Souleïmane, who never did anything like the others, although he was a faithful observer of the rules and a servant of the cult beyond reproach, had a hard time hiding his emotions under the headphones of his Walkman (which the French insist on calling 'baladeur', but Souleïmane doesn't really care about the French language). Metal headset haloing his head, he was concentrating—a lonely, lanky, bellicose and high-strung anchorite.

He noisily snapped his fingers to a beat no one else could hear. He moved to and fro with a catlike gait, and, at times, his endless lean muscles sketched a strange dance step, a languid but self-possessed calypso—his narrow, swaying hips rolling to the rhythm of an impossible merengue, and his supple spine and arched back waving under the lascivious surge of a lafouka beyond reach.

And Souleïmane was making the squat's dilapidated parquet floor creak under his weight, ready to absorb the blast of the formidable explosion that would instantly blow away this masquerade into a jolting jumble of white skins carousing with black faces.

There was no mention of it on the radio nor on TV.

They only heard speeches. They waited until evening, until all the nightly news programmes on every single station had aired; they were half-heartedly hoping for a delayed detonation, and in the end, to get it over with, Abdoulaye angrily crumpled the message intended for the media and, with the hand of a sickened mulatto, pulled out his gold Dupont lighter and ignited the grand declaration of dignified Negroes, now totally devoid of meaning.

Rehvana was maintaining her composure; she found it hard to hide her relief and she was pretending to console the big chief; she wiped away the tears of defeat surging into the almond-shaped eyes drowned in liquid sienna and kissed the thick, well-defined lips contracted by furious contortions.

Abdoulaye probably had been given ineffective, expired materials or maybe none of the Ébonis had really known how to use them. Maybe the bomb, hidden in the restrooms, had been discovered, disarmed, maybe still, the detonator, which was connected to the unreliable movement of a clock radio, had failed due to weak batteries?

Perhaps the plastic, stolen from a construction site where it was being used for caulking joints, wasn't really explosive?

In any case, the vengeful load—bearer of all their pride as great Negroes, of all the obvious dignity of black people and of the cry of the real sons of Africa—the bomblet fizzled out in a mouse's whisper.

Neither acknowledging the likely dishonesty of their suppliers nor their own probable incompetence nor possible clumsiness, the Brothers summoned sceptical suspect Rehvana—the one who on many occasions had attempted to get them to forgo the attack—to appear before the elders' council—the sect's original founders, Abdoulaye, Diop and Babacar.

All had seen this move as an opportunity to get rid of the outsider—this spy who was not living with them on a permanent basis, and who regularly returned to her clean little flat near Place Maubert to take luxurious showers whenever she had enough of the uncomfortable lack of privacy of the squat.

After a strenuous, indecent, almost obscene interrogation— a harassing line of questioning that Rehvana had been able to deflect with no sign of emotion—the Brothers fell silent. They had been unable to find any flaw in the young woman's profession of faith and, as if to better meditate on her fate, they smoked a huge quantity of yamba for a long while; in fact, it was common hashish from North Africa or, worse, marijuana from Latin America, since the shipments from Senegal were lately unreliable and the real hemp from Dakar was a lot harder to come by. But they kept calling everything they smoked yamba, in accordance to the rule, for the sect had its language, its key words—an actual code—and it also had its own beliefs and customs.

The best yamba supplier, once he had completed his studies, had returned to the palace of his minister father, and the young man from Zaïre who'd taken over had cut off all relations with the Ébonis as soon as he'd gotten wind of the sect's main activities, and especially of its terrorist tendencies. So they'd had to resort to shopping wherever they could.

Gradually a falling-out had developed with those of pure— not mixed—descent, of African extraction, and who held authentic passports from a compromised Africa. The least aggressive of them were content to utterly and contemptuously ignore the crazy Ébonis, and the most ferocious were using any excuse to start bloody brawls against the alleged 'Real Sons of Agar' whom they thought of as this 'badly bleached' gang of great-grandsons of slaves. These fights would take place on rue Au-Maire and most often on rue Cujas, after leaving the nightclubs which they shared with Abdoulaye and his clique in a new kind of apartheid. Rejected by the ones they believed to be their allies, their brothers, the Ébonis had been forced to vow vicious hatred against these undignified bearers of the African identity and passport.

The only African of 'pure descent' who'd been won over, God only knows how, to the obscure Éboni cause, was Aganila, Babacar's magnificent concubine—the one who would, weeks later, deliver Rehvana from the trunk. In vain, she'd deployed her ample lamé boubou in an attempt to deflect these clashes, but all she'd done was to make the scuffle more venomous and almost had her arms and legs torn off, a modern-day Sabine ripped apart between her Guadeloupean man and her Fulani cousins. She'd been called names—'arse-for-cash' and manawa—and was accused, among other pleasantries, of having become the whore of these dirty, degenerate Antilleans.

Cruelly cast out by their fake brothers, considered pariahs by Africa, the Africa found in geography atlases—not mother Africa, their Africa—the Ébonis had turned that egotistic Africa into the beast to kill, the ultimate traitor, the enemy bigger to them than the whites themselves who at least left them in peace.

It was war.

They were fighting with knives, with fists, with kicks, and it was not a quadrille the Antilleans were dancing in Paris: this was serious fighting. The holders of the undeserved green passports were beating up the 'real sons of Africa'; in these fratricidal fights, and thus, without mercy, unrelenting because unreasonable, and in fact highly messy, the blood was flowing from black and métis skins alike, until, to separate them all, the French police would send agents who themselves hailed from Lille, Brittany, Martinique or Guiana; the navy-blue uniforms of the disciplined servants of the Republic would charge into the multicoloured heap, and the Ébonis, welcoming the new arrivals with sore and bloody fists, would yell at them, calling them 'traitors' too, as well as 'corrupt, assimilated, rotten!' At the end of the day, it was the same police van that would contain this melting pot of enemy colours, and the henchmen appointed monthly by the state-controlled colonialism would confuse, in the same crackdown, the bearers of black or mango-green passports and the reluctant holders of the French blue passport. The lackeys of white capitalism, dressed in blue broadcloth livery, paid no attention to colour and took this as an opportunity to arrest and lock up all the undocumented.

How many times had Rehvana gone to wait for Abdoulaye (all the while cursing the Pantheon, the so-called Great Men of this decadent nation, the unjust order of the French State, and the sins of the heretics) at the fifth-arrondissement precinct where the peacekeepers, venal officials of the Bureau of Migrations for Overseas Territories, had had the gall to send him and, what's more, insult him by keeping him there—a broken-down Abdoulaye who emerged half knocked out, gait shaky, but more certain than ever of his faith.

With what religious respect did she hook her arm into his to help him walk and lead him, through good times and bad, back to the squat, half carrying her hero who was swollen with blows and glory.

After the Beaubourg disappointment, Abdoulaye, the tall, black mulatto—having concluded that they had badly served Agar and, having done everything he could to exonerate his soft-skinned lover, as president of the council and leader of the proceedings—retired to the most remote and warmest recess of the squat, alone with only one candle and three grains of sesame for a solitary nocturnal consultation with the divinity.

As soon as he came out of his retreat, Abdoulaye immediately imposed upon himself and the Ébonis a seven-day, seven-hour, seven-minute penance to appease the wrath of their God. As spiritual, temporal and undisputed chief of the sect, Abdoulaye himself set up the purification programme, which consisted of a strict fast, abstinence without exception and purifying collective ablutions.

For seven days, seven hours and seven minutes, the Sons of Agar neither ate nor had sex. They drank the stagnant water of their own baths and gave the gift of their nakedness to the God of true Negroes, as they collectively sprayed their bodies with the water from their macerating flesh, standing in a row of small ironbound tubs, to the great dismay of fat Fassou who was thus condemned by the implacable rule to a diet under duress and to display her elephantine cellulite and considerable pendulous breasts which seemed to her even less fit to be seen when compared to the small, perky tits of the chief's wife who had unfortunately come out unscathed from the great council. The tall tubs made of hundred-year-old oak filled the air with an aroma of wine, urine and faeces of mixed vintage; these were, in fact, old recycled barrels that Abdoulaye had had a hard time obtaining and that had to be cleansed of their sticky sediment before proceeding to the purification of bodies and souls.

They washed themselves inside as well as outside, and they thoroughly washed their epidermis and their bowels with tepid waters that smelt of vinegar and the perfume of sacred herbs; the elated Ébonis were pleased that this aroma might reach their God's nostrils.

At the eighth minute of the eighth hour on the eighth day, fat Fassou, who couldn't hold on any longer, rushed as one woman, with all the weakened strength of a starved pachyderm, onto the sacrificial mutton, devoutly garnished with aromatic herbs for the benefit of Agar's nostrils, and devoured it raw.

As soon as the Ébonis, emerging drunk from their pious ethylic state, regained their composure, they were in for a bigger shock: Fassou's notorious impiety caused her to be the subject of an exemplary public flagellation. Since she was already naked and had just jumped out of the expiatory tub in a colossal splash of foul-smelling spray, the famished fasting ones enjoyed an unparalleled treat: the spectacle of the giant woman's wet trembling flesh, gradually reddening, blow after blow, streaked with stings unleashed by Diop's wrathful right hand.

Fat Fassou first starts squeaking like a mouse, then turns to a horrible husky mooing, her insufferable foghorn voice made hoarse by the extended immersion and the imposition of the rule of silence (because it was without a word that the Ébonis had to take their long purifying herb baths). With a wide, imperial gesture, and without uttering a single word from his cold, chapped lips, Abdoulaye had shown Diop the instrument of torture, the cat-o'-nine-tails with eighteen knots. Diop had immediately understood and set to work right away, grabbing the ivory handle with both hands. Huffing and puffing, straining and sweating, in a spectacular frenzy, he'd lashed Fassou's massive flanks with the raw leather strands.

But since her scrawny lover, a puny Negro skinny by nature, had, during the votive week, additionally lost the little strength which Agar had bestowed upon him at birth, all the able Brothers—those not too weak or too stiff after having been crammed in a tub for a week—were designated to relieve the valetudinarian hobbit, with the exception of Abdoulaye, who, as chief, had the privilege of choosing the executioners but who, notwithstanding, had much better things to do. He left the execution of lowly tasks to the inferior Brothers, having covered his august, albeit sexy, nakedness with a large ceremonial boubou, and had put on his goatskin leather sandals with dignity and left on an emergency run to the halal butcher of la Goutte-d'Or to get a second consecrated mutton (one that had been bled), but not before heaping curses from a pasty mouth reeking with hunger on the obese, sacrilegious mammal who was keeping him from a well-deserved ritual barbecue—a prospect that during these eight days had largely contributed to making his macerations tolerable—and setting a limit of seventy-seven lashes that the huge, now satiated, gelatinous fat folds should receive, so that the inconceivable sin of the intemperate famished Fassou would not fall back onto the Ébonis. The number matched the gravity of the sin, for they needed all that to shield the Brothers from the wrath of Agar, who had been denied his feast, and the offering of a bloody female in torment would placate the God in the interim.

Although they were quite far from being as sickly as Fassou's master, most Brothers had caught a cold during their prolonged marinating, so coughing and spitting, they took turns to administer, more or less, the punishment to the insatiable woman in the geometric centre of the wise men's assembly. They were squatting in the consecrated enclosure which represented the huge trunk of Agar's baobab (the emblem of the God, the symbol of the breadth and circumference of his mighty power) in a perfect circle of solemn severity but, released from the cold waters, and out of necessity, from the obligation of silence, they were sneezing and blowing their noses incessantly.

The whip lashes Fassou's bound flesh in the centre of the magical ring where everything is by Agar and is done for Agar.

Since their chief had left so quickly, not taking the time to allow them to put their clothes back on, they were still naked in the heatless cellar. Only Abdoulaye communicated directly with Agar; thus the faithful, who did not know if they, too, would be deemed guilty if, in a fatal haste, they hid the nudity commanded by the God, actually preferred, in their doubt, to wait naked for the return of their Guide.

Their wet skins did not want to dry. Dazed by the heady vapours released by this grand fermentation, either feverish or frozen between the humid leprous walls, the Sons of Agar dedicated their destiny to their omniscient steersman; nonetheless, the law of silence was broken by the loud clanking of their teeth and the guttural trumpeting of the gluttonous sinner.

The women, as well as the skinny men who were not lucky enough to be designated as officiants, were inwardly envious of the chosen ones who could warm up a bit as they whipped.

Abdoulaye had glanced worriedly at his Submariner Rolex and left the squat, cursing under his breath, praying that the butcher in rue de la Charbonnière would not yet be closed and that behind the peeling paint of its gates, the carmine-glazed tiles would not yet be emptied of their piles of skinned beasts.

He was also imploring the heavens that Ahmed had a whole mutton in store—not cut up—because he'd had to order the other one several days in advance.

Otherwise, he would have to invent a variation to the rule he had himself decreed two weeks ago for the occasion and get the Ébonis to agree that the sacrifice of an ordinary chicken or a modest rabbit was enough to satisfy their God.

What's more, as he swiftly stuck his high priest boubou into the waistband of his boxer shorts in order to jump over the Métro turnstile, he remembered that he had not paid the Arab; he wondered anxiously if Ahmed would allow him to buy on credit again and if, like last time, he would be satisfied with the promise of a hypothetical delivery of cameras not yet stolen and a paltry down payment of yamba which was not even of high quality.

Dazed with hunger and rage, Abdoulaye ruthlessly jostles the Fatimas, the Mamadous, the Mustaphas, the Mohammeds and the Sékous, the Raïssas, the Manuelas packed together on the pavement and in the street; in a blind kick, he even topples the overflowing bag of a poor Kabylian woman, and a set of panties from Tati and one-franc-ninety socks spill onto the muddy pavement from the pastel-pink-and-blue striped fluorescent shopping bag. It doesn't really matter to him.

Barely missing a beat, Abdoulaye resumes his mad dash, salivating at appetizing baklavas and gooey sweet cheese pastries, kanafehs, halvahs sassily dripping with shiny honey, and Turkish delights, delicious temptresses taunting him behind their shop windows. But the ritual solemnly instituted by the chief forbids him to eat anything before Agar has feasted on a victim sacrificed according to the rules . . . And he sticks to it, despite the fact that his sacrilegious stomach, his profane intestines in great danger of blasphemy, and his adrenal glands, relapsing into heresy, are starting to recklessly renounce Agar and together commit this remarkable crime, shouting to him that he's the chief, after all . . .

If Ahmed, the only purveyor he knows who is greedy and naive enough to do business with him and provide the specially prepared meat, has closed shop—if he cannot or does not want to give him and his insides satisfaction—he swears he'll strangle Fassou himself!

The Roots of Stone

What is there implausible?
Roots of stone.

Fulani proverb

STANDING IN THE NARROW CORRIDOR that passes for a kitchen, poring over a bilingual Latin–French book from the Budé collection, Matildana is making a chocolate mousse, her speciality, while translating *De rerum natura* by Lucretius.

Her endless brown hands break the eggs with a smart blow to delightfully separate yolks from whites.

'Me want to see how you do,' Rehvana implores, using the language and small voice from their Fort-de-France childhood to make the older sister laugh.

Matildana steps aside and hands her the small bowl; Rehvana applies herself, concentrating and absorbing herself in these wholly simple gestures: a swift movement to crack the shell, then fingers spread to slowly let the egg white slide, ever so slowly, delicately, without breaking the fragile circle of yolk.

The pain in her arms, her legs, her entire body gradually dilutes itself in the humid and fluid caress that emanates from Matildana's presence; why bother telling her about the crisis and the tears, the pointless denials and the unbearable distrust?

Why bother telling Matildana about the insanities, the hard words and especially the unfair suspicions, all the torments, all the trash and all the slaps, the hatred from others, their obscene laughs, their scorn and the brutal return of that man?

In any case, she feels Matildana's gaze on her. She was never good at making up things and she knows that Matildana will ask no questions, will not blame her for anything; she knows that she's here, quite simply.

'Hurry up, you're too slow! I have friends coming for dinner in a bit; they'll soon be here. You should stay with us tonight; in any case, we won't go to bed late, as I've got midterms tomorrow morning.'

Matildana pretends to be upbeat and acts nonchalant, twirling around, busy; she wants to hear nothing, see nothing of these unusually red cheeks, these strangely sunken eyes.

Self-possessed, clear-sighted, providing good counsel, she suggests in her distinguished voice, though slightly ironic, that Jérémie would make a good catch, as their parents would say, for the kooky younger sister.

'Hold on to him, Rehvana, I beg you,' she whispers, her long brown-bronze hands joined together, gleaming with all her gold rings, cradling the stubborn chin of the younger one, who recoils, brusquely retreats, rebels and mutinies against so much misunderstanding.

But Matildana makes herself soft, caressing, unctuous, and she imperiously sweeps aside everything Rehvana would want to say about Abdoulaye, poisonous loves and this rough lowlife world about which she doesn't care to know, for she feels neither the strength to censure, nor the power to proscribe. She boils with hatred for the sacrilegious hands, the big stupid hands, but for now she can only attempt to erase the unbearable tears with the soft warmth of her fingers. Sunset has turned Matildana's fragrant hair into a warm halo of molten gold, and the little sister buries herself in it, and Rehvana loses herself in it, and Rehvana is drowned in this wave's suspended time. Weak and defeated, Rehvana has made herself heavy in her sister's arms and has nested her battered body deep into her sister's chest. She feels good enclosed by this smooth flesh and she is lingering and losing herself, drunk on the idea of betraying the brutish one and the placid one, of betraying them both! Matildana is all voluptuousness and peace: betray them all to better find herself and escape into the brown gold that is pouring over her.

Within this lush mane, each highlight is never quite the same—tawny black or red, copper-tinted amber—depending on how the light hits it.

Still drifting, languid, full of love for her sister, Rehvana calls Jérémie on the phone, reassures him, smothers him in the kisses which Matildana lavishes upon her and promises him she'll be back the next day.

And Jérémie is surprised at this halting voice, these groans, these unusually tender words interspersed with heavy silences and sighs.

THE GENUINE BAMUM PRINCESS, laughing joyfully, has fried up some plain beignets—not like cod-filled fritters—and she imperiously hands the platter over to Rehvana.

The young woman has come to the kitchen to assist this stranger of a princess—effervescent force of nature—in order to put on a brave face and flee the confusing magnetism of the tall mulatto.

With one hand, the princess pushes her into the hallway, motioning for her to go offer the dish of hot beignets to the guests; she unwillingly has to leave the soothing smell of grease and the steamy shelter of the kitchen and return, stumbling under the weight of the enormous tray, to the huge living room filled with strangers and mingle with the buzzing, colourful crowd, where all her contradictory wishes keep bringing her eyes back onto the young man they call Enryck.

Rehvana is really sorry she allowed herself to be dragged by her sister to this rowdy party—after the small student dinner that was supposed to end so early—where she is bored and doesn't know anyone, hosted by a PhD in philosophy from Cameroon married to a woman from Martinique who is an assistant in linguistics.

'You've got to have fun,' she said, 'and get out of that funk. You'll see, the world doesn't revolve around the Ébonis!'

It's true, all sorts of people are here, from France, Spain and all over—*le gai Paris*—Africans, Domiens, Tomiens, interracial couples, a Pakistani woman without a veil or sari, with her French-German husband, the woman from Les Abymes in Guadeloupe with a preppy-looking guy who is standing there, pale and dignified, listening knowingly and cheerfully to the banter of two Antillean laundry workers who are calling each other escapees from the Planet of the Apes, doing a thousand crazy antics, both irresistible, grinning from ear to ear, tall and handsome, healthy and strong. They announce with a great laugh that they are vacationing in Créteil-Soleil, a shopping mall. All are tipsy from the free-flowing whisky, red wine, champagne and rum punch. Rehvana and Matildana's brother was very well received with his assortment of white and aged rums drawn from their parents' ample reserve.

The Bamum princess, finished making her beignets, bounds straight for the middle of the dance floor, but not before taking a swig of heartwarming liquid—the rum that grabs you by the throat and spits fire in your gullet.

She unfurls, grabs and bewitches, flags down a partner for a second, then immediately pushes him aside for another; they bend as one, to the left, to the right, waists pressed together, with a serious demeanour.

Matildana enters the dance; moves she's never learnt anywhere come twirling from her belly.

All the bodies are dancing (or almost: there are two who are not); a snaking circle has formed where they smile and clap hands. A random body breaks away, led by an invisible force emanating from the dance music or pushed by the other bodies, and this body chosen to be in the centre spins, stretches, fills the space revered by the other bodies and, for a moment, reveals to the other bodies the magic of pelvic thrusts, jumps, leg lifts, pirouettes, skirt swirls, wide steps, somersaults and funny faces. When she enters the circle, Matildana discovers her body has taken on a life of its own and has found itself there, knowing when to go, when to leave and what to do.

Slowly, bodies career, heat up and erupt, reaching a true climax.

And the sweat beading their faces brings back the tropics with African heat dripping along the disjointed bodies that leap, raise their arms high together and yell the same obedient OUÉÉÉ, subject, without rules, to the same understanding, in the same voice, men and women, boys and girls, in shrill harmony when the beat of the big gong extols the muted cry of Africa or the land of exile. For they feel they're nowhere, swaying in swirling waves, seigneurially simian, emotionally moving and literally moving to the edge of a dizziness never reached because nothing is lost in the wonderful whirlwind—not self, not balance—nothing to lose and everything to regain.

The festivities are beautiful, because children and old women are finding the truth of the dance. Soon, male and female dance partners feel unbridled, jostled, liberated by the children's toad-like leaps, beautiful beyond the calibrated, self-centred science of mainstream dance steps. The daring moves of old women, bending their knees until their bottoms almost graze the ground, freed from concerns about posture, drooping breasts or pro-truding bellies, propel the dancers towards the truth. A short man with a handsomely sculpted face and upturned nose soon aban-dons the measured, mechanical dance steps coupled with conven-tion, and his contortions sweep the other bodies along, as in a wave. A circle forms around him—no more hoochie coochie, no more partners: with suggestive swaying, duck waddling, comical mimicry of cutting sugar cane—knees flexed, buttocks boldly bouncing—they let it all hang out, they get revenge and take what is owed, they belong to themselves, I say they *belong to themselves*.

Why do you call it a 'release'?

You simply don't get it. (Maybe you've never wanted to get it.)

Did you at least take a look?

But it's not by watching that you'll learn, you'll have to enter the high-sea wave of the dance.

I'm talking about a cutting-loose-great-wave-of-a-dance where Negroes can redeem themselves without a machete. I'm talking about a deliberate sweat that cleanses the infected wounds of alienation, for now and for always. I'm talking about the nightly revelry.

It's the same kind that used to shake the plantation's chains at night; they don't teach that in the academies, and Matildana knows it. It's the same kind of celebration the master used to bless and ban, depending on the circumstances. (It sounds dan-gerous but serves a useful purpose.)

No, it's not just a release!

It's a bubbling and fusion, it's vigour, I tell you! Movement of souls and communion.

It's not to be danced alone.

When it becomes neither sexy nor flirtatious, in the sudden impulses of prepubescent bellies and the unyoked ecstasy of old women, with neither obscenity, modesty nor compulsory moves imposed on slow-moving couples—when it becomes grace and perfection, through ape-like antics, slapstick gesticulations and disorderly positions—when it's the absolute, because no one would dare take it seriously—that's when Matildana loves the dance.

When Matildana lives the dance.

And Matildana dances, and Matildana dances and dances and dances.

Carried away, captivated by an unknown ritual, but to which she feels she was effortlessly initiated ages and ages ago, Matildana, dazed and transported, dances and twirls in unison, in the ease of the dance and echoes of lascivious steps that come from an ancient memory, accented by loud hand claps.

There she is with her wings spread, tall and brazen, in the exaltation of her own self; there she is, flooded to her inmost depths with her being; there she is, riding an imaginary mare, back arched, hurled into a gallop, wild with being everywhere at once.

A sight that can't be missed! Handsome devils, free and unchained, and Matildana with them . . .

They have to know how to disengage, decelerate, 'de-shackle', twirl until the madiana, dance until daybreak.

A sight to be seen, kicking and doing backflips . . .

She's steering clear of him.

He's laughing his head off, standing on the other side of the living room, a glass in hand.

She's not looking his way but she knows he's there.

She's sure she's escaped from him. He's not paying attention to her. He hasn't even noticed her. The pains she's taking to avoid this guy are annoying her no end. What does he have that the others don't? And Rehvana is angry at herself for this unusual shyness that hunches her over, forbids her from meeting these eyes, for this stupid attraction which irresistibly brings her back towards the stranger, for this odd emotion coming from beyond herself, which makes her pay attention to him against her will, tells her where he is and what he does and his slightest moves, when all her efforts are aimed at avoiding watching him.

He's not really a stranger. They've already seen one another in the squat. Yes, it feels like she's met him before. Yes, she believes it was at the squat where she had caught a fleeting glance of him.

But then a strong brown hand reaches over her shoulder and plunges into the half-empty platter. She doesn't need to turn around to be certain, to know to whom this blue-black palm belongs, this muscular forearm, this fine-grained, even-coloured black skin. She bites her lips until they bleed, feels herself blush quite involuntarily, freezes, her fingers clutching the tray.

He asks if she made the beignets. Her face is flaming red, her eyes well up, she knows she's getting even redder under the fire of this gaze.

She stutters bluntly that yes, well no, not exactly, she was only helping. She stammers, mumbles, squirms and is dying to slap him because he's asking her something else and she doesn't really know what to say. An unbearable redness is burning her face; she hates and blames him for it.

Rehvana doesn't know where to stand. Never has she known such agony, such shame, such confusion. She's embarrassed to be there, blushing, numb, so dumb with her large tray of oily beignets, for only God knows how long.

She hates him because he keeps towering over her with his height, his haughtiness, overwhelming her with a self-confidence so criminal that it makes her all the more ridiculous. She unintentionally hides her face while dreaming of setting him ablaze with an all-consuming glance.

Her blushing bites her cheeks and overpowers her forehead, and the young man's eyes on her exacerbates the kindling of her flesh.

She senses she has something melodious and marvelous in store for him; she blushes knowing he's watching her blush once more.

She senses she has, for him, the harmonious voice of a sorceress, opera singer or temptress. But her voice, when she manages to reply, sounds more like a croaking than a diva vocalizing. Far from a Circe or Siren, she sees herself transformed into a creature more dimwitted than the most primitive corpuscle.

She'd like to take revenge on him and his swaggering allure, his degrading magnetism, and get him to swallow his words and his beguiling smile back into his square jaw. Instead, she stands there, blushing and passive, as if left on a silent auction block.

She's longing to vamp him but her lips dispatch a sort of quivering grimace in his direction, as if triggered by nervous twitches. She doesn't need to look in a mirror to know that his impression of her is closer to that of a bovine, starry-eyed girl than a femme fatale.

Why does the pack of inanities he reels off sound so supremely intelligent, when all she manages to put together in her stammer, as soon as she attempts to reply, sounds inexcusably stupid? What lack of fairness has given him this resolute look, this composure, which leaves her with no willpower, defenceless and even soulless, which delivers her to him?

He asks her what she thinks of the party—why she doesn't seem to be having a good time. The more innocent the questions that emanate from the young man's virile and cavernous throat, the more insipid, imbecilic her responses, and the more she curses the inexplicable injustice which is responsible for her not being able to emit more than shapeless, babyish gurgles when she'd like to zap him with something witty and biting.

Her ears are buzzing, and her entire body feels unpleasantly itchy. What are the others doing?

What's Matildana doing? Why don't they come to her rescue? Why don't they deliver her from this infuriating show-off who is bullying her and won't let go?

And now she's laughing at his nonsense. Without even understanding what he's talking about, she can't contain a nervous trembling that shakes her, a disharmonious cascade, inept, a fake uneasy laugh making her feel even more uneasy, a kind of stupid, sickly, unflattering hiccupping she's never experienced before. She would never have thought herself capable of cackling in such a vile manner, and she'd never noticed how cacophonous her laugh could be and how unladylike. It had never dawned on her that it was possible to laugh without thinking, to be ashamed of one's own laugh, of the sound of one's own laugh and even of showing too much teeth and gums, ashamed of the way lips twist when laughing, all the while harbouring, deep down, this hatred and desire to kill. No, until this very minute, she'd never have agreed that laughing could be so disagreeable. She'd like him to leave her alone, to quit hanging around, to cease to exist; she'd like for him to go back from where he came and to stop destroying her.

For the first time in her life, Rehvana feels as if she has enormous teeth—oversized, unsightly, rabbit teeth—an off-key voice, a smile like Carabosse, the wicked fairy godmother, maybe even bad breath, because of that disgusting salad dripping with garlic. Inexplicably, she remembers an old Egyptian story of a pharaoh's wife with garlic on her breath; she doesn't know the ending and doesn't remember how it began, and now her canine teeth are noticeably overlapping and turning yellow, then separating like never before to reveal her improper dentition, and if she laughs, everyone can see her gums; she'd better stop laughing; she pulls in her suddenly conspicuous incisors; how did she not realize this before? And earlier, why didn't she pause before the mirror near the front door to check for bits and pieces of lettuce stuck to her teeth? She can't wait for him to look away so she can slide her tongue along her teeth—inelegant but necessary—in order to get rid of anything that shouldn't be there, anything that might detract from her laugh, and yes, it can only mean one thing, she can read it in his eyes, he finds her ugly and he's making fun of her, and, for sure, she smells bad.

Ah, what a smart thing to do! What was she doing in this kitchen? Her body, her dress and even her hair reek of hot oil and grease. She's sure of that. Every pore of her skin exudes the fear of displeasing him.

It's better to talk to him than to just sit there, ankylotic, smelly and gawky; out of nervousness, her lips begin to twitch left and right, paying no attention to what she's saying, as if in a badly dubbed movie.

Because she's thinking about these things for the very first time, because in this unavoidable minute she would have wanted to be full of grace, mystery and charm (oh! make him see me this way!), she finds herself incredibly naked and awkward. Her worthlessness and utter clumsiness hit her with cataclysmic force; she feels her joints creak as if she were a rusty robot. Why did she need to uncross her legs and let the deafening suction sound overpower the party's music? That's it, now he's heard it; her skin is clammy and sticky, say goodbye to glamour!

To hell with him!

She turns purple with anger and tenses up even more, because she thinks she sees, in the young man's tepid eyes, what was betrayed by the tremendous sound of her epidermis coming unstuck, and what he irrevocably guessed—the stickiness of her aroused thighs. He had to be deaf not to hear.

Suddenly, the presence of the others around her interrupts her train of thought and she's overcome with unexpected shame. She doesn't care about this kind of shame and she can't stop staring at the bent, brown head smiling at her.

She shrinks back a bit more into her chair. Nothing prevents her from getting up and putting an end to her torment, and yet the young woman remains there, without daring to move, smile or speak, without defences and a will of her own, but certainly not without desires.

Rehvana is not dancing.

When Jean-François, an acquaintaince, made a vain attempt to drag her into a cha-cha-cha, Enryck's large brown hand firmly landed on his extended forearm. More explicit than anything the young man had been able to say or do until then, the gesture disdainfully rejected the suitor and sealed Rehvana's fate. The lips were still smiling but the fingers' quick pressure didn't permit a retort.

Small, hollow shell filled by this grand gesture, she had let him do this without putting up a fight, granting him his manly rights over her being without conditions and without a word of excuse to Jean-François, whose retreat and crestfallen look she'd enjoyed. An instant later, outraged by the impropriety of the dismissed suitor, she expressed surprise that someone had dared interrupt her life's greatest hour. She hastened to explain that the unfortunate one had no rights to her, so afraid was she that the stranger might misunderstand.

She said it badly, got tangled in her explanations and fell silent. And so she found in her fear the necessary resolve and audacity to get up from her chair on her own, and although she felt tense and frightened, to face the living God, waiting for him to carry her off through the city in his car.

Two hundred forty kilometres an hour on the peripheral boulevard surrounding Paris.

It's an intoxication that's bracing and wild, not a drunkenness that makes you drowsy. Bursts of air bite into her cooling cheeks and her hair flaps in the wind. Enryck is taking her away.

Going two hundred forty kilometres an hour on the peripheral boulevard to reach the eighteenth arrondissement: the young man hates driving through Paris. It's an obsession with him to not only avoid red lights but overall to drive very fast, as fast as possible, taking huge risks, as if playing a game of Parisian roulette, in memory of the weekend speed races in Fort-de-France.

He has gradually slowed down and is now driving at a leisurely speed.

'I don't remember your first name,' he blurts out, as he stops whistling a reggae tune and tapping his steering wheel to the beat of the music. His fingers pick up the rhythm again as he adds, 'I'm Enryck.'

She knew it already, she remembers. She knows him already. She's seen him a few times in the Éboni squat: he's an outsider, a non-believer who deserved the scorn of the entire gang, scornful towards the sect and scorned by it. She'd seen him from time to time, had run into him once in a while when he'd swing by to pick up some equipment, do some bartering . . . He took part in the Agars' trafficking from a distance and conducted business with them without sharing their beliefs. Somewhere along the line, when the sharp night air lashed at her face, she seemed to remember that this so-called Enryck had something to do with bartering plastic, but she had been too preoccupied then by the grandiose bombing business which had led the Ébonis on the warpath to worry about a playboy type like him.

Rehvana was utterly unable to explain how a guy like this could attract her for a minute.

A powerful intrusion of Eau Sauvage cologne had invaded the inside of the car and irritated her nostrils; Rehvana shrugged in secret but curled up in the leather seat. Catlike, domesticated, she quickly sunk into the half-darkness, neither voicing taunts, nor mentioning any tenets of the sect's catechism that aggressively and disdainfully stigmatized the use of commercial fragrances or any other consumer products aimed at diluting the Negro essence.

She was silent.

At most, Rehvana regretted somehow that the heady eau de toilette he had splashed on his body would, for the moment, drown Enryck's authentic smell.

This damn guy had made no impression on her when she'd seen him in the squat. Not so long ago she would have laughed in the face of this artificially perfumed, would-be Don Juan, and she would have given him a shower and put him back in his place in a jiffy. She would have laughed even harder if someone had told her then that one night she would get into this guy's car and let herself be driven all over the place.

Yet tonight, inexplicably, one single look, one single second had been enough for Rehvana to make Enryck the man of her life.

To *see* in him the man of her life.

SECOND SONG

Second Alliance

One would say a snake
dancing on the tip of a staff.

Charles Baudelaire

'Spleen and Ideal', *Flowers of Evil*

IN THE FETID BAGGAGE CLAIM, Rehvana is delighting in her sweat. She stubbornly wraps herself in her heavy sweater, made from raw wool, which scratches her throat and bathes her in a sweltering dampness, but which she refuses to remove—not so soon. Under her saroual, the thick, woollen tights she's deliberately kept on are voluptuously grazing her skin. Rehvana revels in the beloved, suffocating heat; it would be too easy to strip off sweater and tights, to take off all warm clothing, winter wear, clothes from France, as she'd been tempted to do as soon as she stepped off the plane, like everyone else, including Enryck, and as she'd planned on doing before the trip. She'd even given considerable thought to the kind of clothing layers best suited for the crossing; with a feverish and strange jubilation, she'd chosen the thin cotton tunic to wear under the hefty, coarse wool, and which, with one simple gesture, she could quickly remove.

Yes, it would take one simple move, arms over head, and she'd find instant relief, but she delayed this act out of dogged masochism. She was eager to be hot—very hot—for as long as possible. Not satisfied with having soaked up, panting, the feverish fragrance rising up to her from her native land, she was standing still—hieratic, fervent, expectant—at the centre of the tarmac while the bustling travellers skirted, with some surprise, this tall woman frozen in place in an obscure offering, until her companion—annoyed, aloof, almost hostile—dragged her along with a shrug. A few minutes later, momentarily released from Enryck's mocking presence as he kept an eye out for their luggage, Rehvana was now savouring the scents *sui generis* of her rediscovered, native island—an orgy of rich and penetrating perfumes.

From the scent of ylang-ylang, the caress of frangipani, the wantonness of red wild plantain, the exhilaration of the Creole and the universal quivering infused with sweetened sweat, Rehvana was piously gathering the gift . . . the legacy . . . the long-awaited dream.

And, as a sacred, delicious fever was slowly seeping into her skin, she felt the beat of her entire life, a surge deferred for so long, her entire body revealing the ancient being in the enthusiasm of all her pores, in her veins, chanting the victory cry, in her blood beating her flesh and in the ecstasy pervading her entire skin, in the elation of her restored being.

Trembling with anticipation, she can't wait to return outside and deeply inhale the fresh air. She fears neither neon signs, noisy baggage carts, taxis, blaring announcements nor the garish billboards of the modern world; she pushes forward, Enryck's strong arm placed once again onto hers, Enryck's handsome smile vanquishing her ridiculous thoughts—intoxicated by her land under her feet. She's ready; she's finally agreed to pull over her feverish head the absurd tangle of wool which now lies, ludicrous, at the bottom of the trunk.

And there in the airport car park, at night—just like when she was born in the little house in Terres-Sainville—rebirth comes to her as promised, at last.

Martinique

THE YOUNG WOMAN TOOK HER PLACE in the back seat of Enryck's friend's brand-new BMW. There she must remain; men sit in the front.

Long gone is the exhilarating, wished-for elation of the beginning.

As the dreary road unwinds, Rehvana is surprised by the display of so many carcasses of run-over dogs, cats and opossums, stiff legs splayed on the asphalt. But Chabin builds a case against dogs, sworn enemies of the Antillean people—dogs that used to ferociously chase criminal runaway slaves—carnivorous beasts fed inside the master's quarters with rich, red meats while the Negro had to make do with his tub of cod, and his salted pork tail ration meant to last a week—mastiffs whose vicious, bastard descendants still growl today at the smell of a Negro. Cats probably perish from drivers' myopia, perhaps killed by mistake by motorists inadvertently wreaking vengeance on the small, innocent felines. As for the opossum—small, drab, short-haired mammal, half wild rabbit, half field mouse, with the tail of a domestic pig and exquisite-tasting flesh (for locals eat them, according to Chabin)—their albino eyes render them almost sightless, leaving them defenceless at night against the blinding headlights of murderous speedsters.

The mongoose, however, hardly ever falls victim to road hogs; this snake killer is disconcertingly handsome and possesses magical speed: it cleaves the air and rushes across roads—russet lightning flash, triumphant over space, quick and dazzling like a red squirrel.

Once, however, Rehvana saw one, or, rather, two of them—a couple in fact—in the middle of the road: perhaps the pregnant female, weighed down by her belly, had been struck by a car, and the distressed male couldn't bring himself to abandon his companion's corpse. It miserably circled the small, inert shape, then withdrew towards the bushes, only to quickly return to try in vain to pick up the scent of the lifeless body.

She's never been car-sick in her life, and yet she's feeling increasingly nauseated; later she'll remember this unexpected motion sickness—this queasiness that makes her gag and which she attributes to the unbearable vision of half a dozen crushed animals.

When they drive past the heights of Canelle, past the Lheureux neighbourhood, and before getting to Presqu'île where the river crosses the road in a spattering geyser, Rehvana scowls and wonders why Chabin is making another detour and in whose kitchen they'll make her wait while the men hold a secret meeting in the living room. The road twists more and more, and the river gushing onto the road has frightened her, although Chabin has calmly driven the BMW across the water; the car has slowed down quite a bit in order to ford the flooded area, but Rehvana, who doesn't recall ever feeling so sick in a car, is overwhelmed with nausea and it worries her.

On the highway, more fresh air, more speed. Chabin is going on and on about something and Enryck smiles at her. She's draped her arm on the back of his seat and Enryck, without turning to face her, has picked up her hand and pressed it to his chest.

She can see his face in three-quarter view; uncomfortable, arm numb, her hair lashing her face, she lays her cheek on the head rest. An incredibly intense wind is racing through the car . . . Eyes half-closed, Rehvana is feeling better and Enryck is holding her hand.

The rain of warm dawns silently draws a spatter of cat paws on the car windows as if a squadron of small felines, invisible and crystalline, had settled there to stare with vacant eyes at the occupants of the vehicle. This drizzle will hardly get you wet if you playfully wave your arm outside; this rain is sly and sassy, with nothing in common—heavens no!—with the triumphant, torrential rains you hear swelling from far away, preceded by thunder that grows and growls—deafening—leaving you under the spell of that ponderous cavalcade foreshadowed by the sign of a flying cockroach, led astray at dusk into the strangely lit human circle, clumsily landing at your feet and, if it tries to flee, destined to die there, under the disgusted, half-irritated, half-irate, perhaps dogged and spiteful sole of your shoe. They say this repulsive bug only flies when rain's coming; its foresight is quite striking, since fear keeps it stuck to the ground, while fending off danger makes it fly to its death.

On the outskirts of Sainte-Thérèse, the gridlock is horrendous, and the heat is hellish. Rehvana is dying to get to the relatively cool shade of the shop where Enryck dropped off the clothing he's sewn himself. One of his old buddies had jumped at the opportunity to hire a lowly paid saleswoman to liquidate old inventory no one cared about: that's how he ended up lending Enryck a little haberdashery, hidden in a remote section of Terres-Sainville, passed down from his mother, dead many months ago, and where strips of yellowing lace, dusty ribbons and faded fabrics blanched by the sun still hung. The so-called friend had never known what to do with the poorly situated, hole-in-the-wall store, far from downtown's bustling commercial streets, and soon after her arrival, Rehvana had been charged with overseeing the shop. Enryck had painted the old, wooden facade as best he could, installed meadow-green carpeting over the damaged floor, whitewashed the crumbling walls and posted Rehvana below the useless, rusted fan. Each morning Chabin would pick them up whenever it pleased him—most often at dawn, when pipiris were singing, but sometimes after eleven—and the two men would drop her off at the kerb and leave for God knows where.

From the moment he stepped foot off the plane, Enryck and his best friend from way back—a towering chabin and former high school classmate—were inseparable, thick as thieves.

Rehvana tends the shop. She models the ridiculous outfits—products of Enryck's wildest whims—which she only wears for a few days, until he gets bored with them or sells them when he urgently needs cash. Their fabrics are so heavy and prone to tearing that they don't bother to clean the clothes before putting them up for sale; they hang them on racks, as is, unwashed and reeking of sweat, or hand them over to the occasional customers.

Rehvana spends hours on end in the ghost shop buried in the heart of Terres-Sainville, where no one ever visits; she feels sickly, idle and alone. Yet of all the Fort-de-France neighbourhoods, it's the one with the most soul—neither commercial nor very lively—one of the city's most popular yet least populated parts of town, easy-going and peaceful, where, so they say, people relocated after fleeing the city of Saint-Pierre, under siege by the awakened volcano, and moved to the quaint, quiet, grid-like labyrinthine streets, lined with half-crumbling, one-storey wooden houses—dwellings whose dim, weakly framed and termite-infested underbellies were open to the frenzied matings of hierarchical packs of pariah hounds—coquettishly made up in tropical, candied pastel paints faded by the torrential rains of hurricanes: green quénette, sour purple icaque, bright yellow of marakoudja, or ochre carambola, more delicate still, or the tart pink of guava flesh or mauve lychee, all of them 'colonial' cottages—but so modest, so poor—'colonial' in style, not in spirit—a few of them sophisticated and self-consciously luxurious, with balustrades and balconies, scalloped mouldings and pillars, multicoloured, lopsided like childhood berlingot hard candies. From an inner-courtyard garden wafts the spicy aroma of ripe mangoes and peppers while the oddly pontificating fingers of the breadfruit tree's leaves—wild and green—bless, here and there, with a smooth caress and breeze-swept solemnity, the huddled sheet-metal roofs; squeezed at the bottom of steep foothills, Terres-Sainville looks for shade, kneeling in heat and hazy devotion, blessedly sun-scorched, not far from Morne Abéla, sweating and sensible, and above, the shantytowns in the heights of Trénelle; but its pavements come alive when night falls, with joyous exhalation—at last!—of an infinite variety of fauna and of insects delivered from daylight terrors, crushings and burnings; life is teeming there, concealed and patiently mortal; there's land in Terres-Sainville, minuscule plots for unassuming homes and humble, most humble gardens where it feels good to knead the loose, saintly, silky, warmish soil and where the succulent smell of cooking sings in the midday heat, and the dented aluminium, rattling away, screams of life. The mâle-femme under the shade of the porch tosses the scales of fish she's gutting into the gleaming sun, so much so that the pungent, marine stench of roe blends with the odour of sweat beading her scruffy and frizzy mess of armpit hair, which you see each time the femme-l'estrade raises her massive, round arm to deliver a glancing blow to the pesky mosquito—a real gourmand—flitting about: '*Ba mwen lè, chè!*' ('Get out of my face, go away!')

Roaring and fiercely rolling her shoulders, her two meaty thighs spread out on either side of the stool, she's grabbing at the fabric of her skirt with the thumb and forefinger of each hand to lift it up and air out her overheated intimate parts, and demands to be left alone, but she also could be addressing the man lolling around in the shack, up to no good, and whom Rehvana cannot see.

'Give me some peace, I tell you! Stop bugging me!' the virago yelps.

Rehvana observes and imbibes this world; it's her only distraction.

If someone were looking to inquire about the shop's location, they'd be told it's in Terres-Sainville, rue Amédée-Knight, right across from the hair salon, whose wooden sign at the street corner reads:

SALOᴎ

ROSY

FOLLOW

HERE⇨

with its backwards N, and its arrow awkwardly drawn in Rastafarian colours.

One day, Enryck rushed into the quiet, benign and phlegmatic little street, as if pursued by infernal flames and a thousand devils wielding pitchforks. Without a word, he yanked all the hangers and grabbed, on the fly, the clothes on display. He'd had a fight with the store's third co-owner, though Rehvana doesn't know the details. Together with Chabin, they've knocked down the counter, shattered the display cabinets and smashed the fan, slashed the dressing-room curtains, twisted the plastic curtain rods, trampled the English brocades and dismembered the wax mannequins before hastily heaving Rehvana and the dresses into the BMW, curse words thundering in her ears.

BY THE TIME JÉRÉMIE HAD BEGUN TO WONDER about the Cartier watches and Vuitton handbags being showered upon Rehvana by a mysterious rival, as well as her unexplained disappearances and her renewed nervous gaiety, Rehvana was already gone.

By way of Matildana, he eventually learnt, though much too late, what had become of her. She had flown to Fort-de-France with another man.

IT'S SIX O'CLOCK, AND NIGHT HAS SUDDENLY FALLEN. Locusts and frogs have burst into strident song, taking turns to signal night-time; all around, thousands of crickets and giant leprous toads sing at the top of their lungs—clickety-clacking calls—and already the day has ended, in a haze of orange-tinged, deep red perfumes.

Rehvana has run out of the house to hurriedly gather the laundry she'd left on the grass to dry—true follower of that tra-dition of Antillean laundrywomen of old—although she got somewhat annoyed at having to shoo away, with a disgusted hand, the multitude of insects embedded in the fabric folds.

It's not because she's afraid of rain. No, Rehvana knows that laundry, especially underwear, is in great danger if left alone at night, at the mercy of quimboiseurs, wizards, she-devils with billy-goat feet and other troublemakers. A witches' Sabbath of ancient superstitions, half-understood and reclaimed with reso-lute fervour, has found asylum in the wild imagination of this Martiniquan from Paris, dictating each of her moves, ruling her life and filling her nights with dread. She's deliberately bought into the most irrational fears—the most comical and the most constraining—just like she makes a point of respecting the most preposterous taboos and the most extreme prohibitions. She's convinced herself that it's impossible to gut fish right after ironing without experiencing mysterious pains due to the 'hot-cold', and she makes a deferential detour to steer clear of the koui brimming with bizarre herbs that a witch doctor has placed at the cross-roads of Chère-Épice.

Docile disciple of local precepts, Rehvana is very careful never to leave even her panties out to dry at night. Fired up and filled with a pious excitement, she fiercely gives in to practices from the past, never failing to burn tampons and sanitary nap-kins drenched in her monthly blood, for fear that a malevolent being might seize them for a demonic rite, cast a spell on her or subjugate her.

From the time she'd been living with Enryck in the large house in Café, Rehvana had willingly welcomed a whole pack of savagely silent zombies to terrify and haunt her and indoctrinate her into the mysteries of her race.

And now that she'd decided to believe in them, her distress was all the more relentless.

She'd invented an entirely personal set of terrors she thought were salutary; with fervent frenzy, trembling with fear, she's bowed before the yoke of ancient beliefs. Since her return to Martinique, Rehvana had consciously cultivated this forced credulity and blind faith, for she saw these as the occult essence of the Antillean soul; she believed in their power to reclaim her ties to her atrophied roots—a way to renew the fractured unity.

On those nights when Enryck hadn't yet returned, and when dreadful darkness descended upon Chère-Épice, teeming with the fiendish bestiary born out of a soul bent on becoming a true Antillean, Rehvana, delirious and dazed, sank into a self-inflicted, nightmarish vigil.

She lets dusk surround her; she waits, humble and dutiful companion, despondent in demure resignation, for the man who doesn't come home.

Alone on the huge porch, she tries hard to extract exhilarating, ancestral terrors from the slightest creak, minute shadow or vague sigh. Transfixed by fear in night's dark breath, she suddenly flinches and shivers, rises and looks through all the rooms of the house, only to sit back down, dishevelled and fulfilled.

The veranda is now completely packed with scowling demons, pasty and gaunt, but no snickering soucougnan will fly above her tonight, for Rehvana has taken great pains to secure all brooms in the kitchen, standing each one religiously on its head, and has left no personal object outside, which a sorceress might steal to take on a sordid ride. The woman next door, who runs around stooped over, foul-smelling and unkempt in daylight, has already shed her human skin in the darkness of her room. With care, she's hung it on a hook on the back of the door, and waits patiently, for just a short while, to ensure that the household is sound asleep, before morphing into a winged creature and secretly flying off into the night.

But at the first glimmer of dawn, if the euphoria from her unholy delights has kept her up until sunrise, she'll have to return home as fast as possible, to stash away feathers and wings and quickly don her human flesh before anyone sees her—quick, quick—so that no one witnesses her appalling metamorphosis. For those who involuntarily see what no mortal should see will have to do all in their power to destroy the cursed apparition, or try to chase the evil spell as far away as possible. And when, at the end of the night, the exhausted sorceress, returned from her murky dealings, furtively slips into her woman's skin, the agonizing pain will cause her to emit an indescribable howl—a sound beyond words—for the one who unwillingly stumbled upon the terrible secret will have taken advantage of her absence to steal the skin abandoned in her room, and coat the inside with a horribly stinging substance.

So all living creatures in the surrounding area will be struck with terror when they hear what no person should hear. And Rehvana already knows what she'll have to prepare on a full-moon night—what herbal teas to drink on an empty stomach on Good Friday, and into what brew made from bitter plants she'll need to plunge her head to erase from her ears the scream no human should hear. Yet she'd rather not have to perform these exorcisms whose outcome can be so uncertain, for the very idea of being driven to the edge of evil fills her with unbearable fear.

That's why the anxious young woman, forsaken and scorned by the man who still hasn't returned, implores all the spirits of the earth—all those from her island and all those from Africa—whoever will have her . . .

Soon, night will end and threadlike dawn will unfurl its golden filaments of mauve on her trembling form.

And the man will find her there, curled up in a shaky chaise longue, amid mouldy, old cushions, pitiful, easy prey for any lingering wild beasts.

The sickening smell of rotting, old fabric coalesces with the marine scent of a mysterious orgasm; little by little, Rehvana becomes aware of an unknown woman's scent that penetrates the air, brought back by the man, and which emanates from his entire body as he leans over Rehvana. Surely as destructive, as pitilessly depraved as the once-dreaded scream of the soucougnan, the bitter effluvia of a woman's sex envelops Rehvana and assaults her against her will, even though she wants to know nothing about it.

She struggles, already defeated. She tries to ignore the insidious and persistent lingering odour, as the foreign scent spreads over her without mercy or shame. Explicitly cruel, since each caress from the man is arrogantly stamped with it, the acrid perfume of the other envelops her, crucifying and mocking, as the man pins her down and pushes apart her thighs, about to satisfy his last desire of the night.

And Rehvana, wounded and numb from these fading odours, gives in to the dark-purple, animal turgescence that still reeks of pleasure from an unnamed rival.

Rehvana of my life,

Since you refuse to call me on the phone, I'm forced to write to you, although I'm dying to hear the sound of your voice. I, for one, have things to tell you. Even if you don't want to speak to me, I still feel we've got a lot to discuss, so don't be angry with me, my faraway beauty. You're wrong, I tell you, to decide that you want to be cut off from the world, cut off from us and from me! There's no good reason why you should keep news from us. Are you going through such horrible things that you don't want to share them with anyone, not even me?

What you did is quite shocking, I'm not denying it, and the fact that you did it so quickly has left us terribly distressed. But even our disapproval shouldn't justify your silence.

Not only do I miss you a lot, so much more than you think (I even miss our squabbles, and I'm longing to hear your inimitable 'tchip', you know, your trademark tchip, beautiful and very loud, when your pretty, sassy mouth twitches in irritated contempt, when you can't stand me telling it like it is . . . Yes, that's it, I can hear one now . . . that remarkable, little dry noise you just made with your lips, air blowing through your teeth, I just got one out of you—ah! So nice! Do it again, ah! She's so cute when she tchips—the more I get on her nerves and kid her, the more she tchips, ah, what a pleasure), and not only do I miss you both, you and your bad little temper, but I'm also worried to death about the two of you.

Now that you're finally smiling (don't shrug, stop shaking your head, it's enough now, I'm not playing any more), I'd like to speak to you about serious things.

You know, Rehvana dear, our parents would love for you to write real letters to them once in a while; even though Papa perfunctorily pretended to disown you, he's been suffering awful migraines since you left; he never talks about you, out of pride, but I do feel his harshness is only for appearance's sake, dictated by his unbelievably hopeless fear of gossip (I wonder if there's anything in the world more ridiculous than such an unhealthy worry!) and I'm sure he rushed like a madman to interrogate Maman as soon as I'd shared news from you, 'way back when', when you still were talking to me . . .

As for Maminette, she only deferred to the dictates from the all-powerful father, but you know her: no need to tell you how happy she'd be if she received something else from you besides three hasty words on a postcard, once in a blue moon. (As far as I know, you've only sent them two postcards since you arrived in Martinique, which makes six words in all—is this really reasonable?)

Bad development: Papa doesn't seem to want to reconsider his decision to 'cut your allowance' [sic], as long as you're not 'back on the straight and narrow', back to being a 'prim and proper young woman', until you start behaving like a 'well-brought-up daughter', when you stop 'going to pot', swear off your 'Negro gang' [sic] . . . and 'resume your studies'. He's convinced his method will work and he hopes it will force you to come back; as for me, I'm very sceptical and I'm trying to talk him out of it. In the meantime, I'll keep sending you half of what he gives me; don't thank me, it's a natural thing to do, since you are also entitled to half the studio apartment where I lounge about, all alone since you deserted, bad girl! It's ten times too big for me, now that I'm alone; I'd love for you to come back . . . You know, naughty girl, in rue de la Montagne-Sainte-Geneviève and even, in a pinch . . . rue Monsieur-le-Prince, there are people who love you and who are waiting for you. I somehow managed to comfort myself when you left me to go live with Jérémie, and, if you go back there, you know you have my blessing. But I can't stand the thought that you'd abandon me for a scandalous marriage to that Pithecanthropus, Enryck. I really wonder what you two talk about . . . I know you're not the intellectual type, but still, I'm having a hard time imagining how you can stay with this illiterate guy who can't carry on an intelligent discussion. Oh, well, I suppose Mr Muscles has all sorts of hidden charms . . .

I'm giving you news about Jérémie on purpose, although I certainly know you don't want me to: the dark, handsome guy is becoming increasingly morose; although he's losing hope that you'll return, his virtue, intellect and studiousness shine through with each day's passing. He's become increasingly handsome, heavenly handsome, I'm telling you, with his striking green eyes that contrast magnificently with the deep black of his skin . . . By the way, there's something I'm still unclear about: since Jérémie is ten times more handsome, a hundred times kinder, a thousand times smarter than the moron from Mount Pelée, and as much a 'son of Africa' as he, why on earth would you choose the worse one of the two? Would you be—as I've always feared— just a tad masochistic? Or must I regretfully tolerate nonsense like 'the heart has its reasons . . . ' or babble like 'one can live on love alone'? Fine, but nowhere is it said that it could be, that it should be, on 'one-way love'. Where do you see love in your story? Where could I, cured by Racine from passion ages ago, where could I see in your 'screwing' something that resembles love? They dare call this 'making' love! Such a corny phrase when, most often, it's about a thing where nothing is created— *least of all, love—and which is about everything* but *love!*

Getting back to your case—and you're quite a case, my sweet angel—I'll spare you what others have said . . . Whatever they say, whatever they think and whatever their opinions on the sub-ject might be, they can't stop talking about you since your mys-terious and romantic disappearance. You can be proud: you've unintentionally (but perhaps you wanted this . . .) made going back to one's roots a fashionable choice. The issues and questions raised by your life, your path, your choices and weird commit-ments are the talk of the town, my dear!

Jérémie, whom I see quite often, whether it pleases you or not (bis), refuses to analyse your case. But Marie-Aude, Jude and Anne-Sophie are convinced of your semi-madness; Luc and Bénédicte, preparing their little love nest for next spring, think 'you'll get over it' . . . Only Guillaume, Marion and Stéphanie find you quirky and 'fabulous' (where on earth did they get that from?) and they don't even know all the facts: they've only vaguely heard about your Ébonis and their colourful folklore! They've never met either Enryck or that jackass Abdoulaye!

As for me, I'll confess that although I'm the one who knows you the best out of everyone, or at least who's closest to you, I don't dare—you hear me, Rehvana, I don't dare—reveal my conclusions, and it's not that I'm confused by the outcome of your 'case' or that I refuse to take a side. If I don't have the heart to follow the logic of my reasoning, if I impose on myself this aporia that trips up my reason, it's because what I glimpse in there fills me with dread. You hear me, little sister! If I dared misquote Pascal, I'd tell you: 'When I contemplate your universe, I walk in fear.'

Yes, your departure has hurt me a lot and I'm afraid for you, Rehvana. Go then! Bill and coo with your Neanderthal but know, however, that I find it hard to forgive you for creating this turmoil in me, in Jérémie's heart and, most of all, in your own life.

You could at least answer me, write me a few lines to explain yourself—it would only be to me!

Me, who deep down, and despite all the love I have for you, can't find anything to say in your defence!

And especially not against your own self . . .

After all, you're nothing but a thoughtless, careless, reckless brat, someone who lets others down, a pain in the neck who doesn't even deserve a postcard!

Stop being such a show-off!

In fact, you see, I'm acting on my threats and I'm done with what I hear you calling—even from here—my sermons.

But I still send you hugs and kisses, you little rascal! And besides, I love you. I beg you to write me or call me.

Matildana

PS: As far as my own life is concerned, there's not much going on. Nothing to report. Nothing in plain sight. Nothing on the horizon—I mean nothing new, nothing to make headlines.

In any case, what I'm going through is not all that interesting. I'm interested in what you're going through, and I worry about what you're hiding inside yourself.

IN THE IMMENSE, MOULDY BATHROOM with damp, flaking walls leprous with saltpetre and black-speckled marble tiles that make each step and splash resonate, as in Roman thermal baths, Rehvana climbed into the tall, dark-green serpentine bathtub, and sank into the colossal lion's claw-footed tub. Suppressing her shivering she could barely control, face to face with huge mares frozen in a furious gallop, nostrils flared, forelegs raised, urged on by a verdigris Neptune, marred by marine salts, brandishing a truncated trident, Rehvana luxuriated in a long bath, thoroughly enjoying the pleasantly tepid water that flows from the cistern at day's end, in the company of tiny, transparent frogs with large, globulous eyes.

She doesn't dislike them and actually finds them rather beautiful: some are no bigger than her smallest fingernail. Rehvana has got used to these friendly creatures, straight out of a cartoon, but at times they still make her jump when they catch her off guard and leap between her legs.

She could not accept, however, the day after her arrival in the house, to share the bathroom with a humongous, inky toad, as big as a man's head, puffing out its warty jowls and sitting enthroned in the doorway, majestically corpulent like a grotesque creature sovereign in its perfect horror, blocking her way.

Enryck, alerted by her terrified scream, had been forced to wage an unlikely battle against the hulking, phlegmatic mass. Almost as frightened as the woman but making sure not to appear as such, he had pushed her aside with a wide, chivalrous gesture, to launch an attack on the monster and execute quixotic manoeuvres, armed with a broom handle. Foolhardy, not knowing where and how to disturb the imperturbable batrachian, he was hovering around it. Increasingly sweaty and exasperated, he was determined to find the enemy's Achilles heel. Seemingly deaf and blind, the giant remained impassive and placid, squatting in the dank hideousness of its sticky, quivering pustules.

Fascinated with this absolute yet lively quintessence of ugliness, this splendid and complete antithesis of beauty, Rehvana had to plea with Enryck, clinging to his arm in protest, to chase the beast away without killing it.

She'd felt something deep and disturbing for the toad, a kind of stifling attraction—in fact, almost admiring or even amorous. Stirred by an unknown yet familiar urge made of tender surges restrained by reverential fear, she longed to touch its cold skin, but when the animal started to move, and the fat, sticky legs unfolded for a leaden leap, she could do nothing but withdraw.

The memory of this encounter remained on her mind as she bathed each day and she'd scrutinize the dark marble tiles before entering the large room with its time-worn splendour, searching for the divinely ugly creature, without daring to admit to herself if she dreaded or desired to see it.

She's finished washing herself and is slowly drying her legs. Turning her back on the pitted bronze Neptune, she's now languorously anointing her thighs with an avocado-and-ginger cream she's just prepared in the groove of a banana leaf—right in the middle of that groove, near the vein where a milky sap flows. Each of her movements is infused with infinite grace. She twists around, a supple climbing vine, to oil her lower back, and this action makes the impudent, brown tips of her breasts poke out.

Rehvana examines her changing body: her breasts have grown heavy. She discovers an opulent cleavage, swollen breasts, and she bursts out laughing right under the beard of the old, impotent bronze statue, because her hands can no longer contain these two luscious fruits with brown, expanded areolas. Amused and seductive, she taunts the Greek god, reducing him to the rank of a Peeping Tom.

The frogs quietly titter with delight; their tiny hearts' frantic beating, visible to her naked eye, accelerates in fright as she approaches.

Similarly, in the tall black-spotted mirror, she focuses on a network of blue veins she's never seen before, quite visible under the fine, pale skin of her shrinking torso—its long, bluish sinuosities joining the heavy, pert breasts.

From the kitchen comes the hissing sound of the pressure cooker, where the shark stew is simmering, and the stew pot is steaming with yam.

Everything is ready. She's adorned herself for the man; she's waiting for him.

She's got dark-bluish shadows under her tired, almond eyes, just like an odalisque or a slave in high demand, or a sex slave.

Unaware of the passing hours, Rehvana—languid, with a smile on her lips—had lost herself in the contemplation of a hummingbird who had haughtily built its nest in the macramé hanging beneath the veranda's overhang. Dazed, as if hypnotized by the dizzyingly fast beating of its near-invisible wings, wildly whirling like aeroplane propellers, she could follow its dutiful merry-go-round routine for hours on end, and amuse herself by watching it fly in reverse, tirelessly flitting back and forth, as it carts around twigs or wisps of wool stolen from the living-room carpet, then hovers, without landing, curiously suspended in air, to line its borrowed nest with adorable loot. However, she prefers the bananaquit, native to the West Indies—a less common, carefree bandit with an impish yellow belly, who pecks in a charmingly mischievous manner at the bananas left to ripen in the basket on the table. Rehvana is not angry at either of them for their cute little acts of theft. They get on well with her and with the superb green lizards hanging from the curtains, who inflate their golden vocal sacs like balloons, in a strange pantomime—preliminary to love or war—when facing a female or an intruder. Rehvana spends her time with them, or she plays with the stretched-out body of a stick bug to test if it's truly alive, enthralled by this bizarre, frail insect that imitates twigs and stems, to the point of fooling itself. Green lizards, frogs and birds are now her only companions in the large house abandoned by Enryck.

Rehvana has scrubbed, scoured, soaked, rinsed ten times, dusted, disinfected; she's polished the faded splendour of the venerable house, waxed, on all fours, the rotting, imposing staircase carved from Guiana wood, sanded the rusty columns and burnished the dull rotunda.

She's trimmed the hedges, spruced up all the plants and fertilized the flowers. She's planted, sowed and grown hibiscus, allamandas and crotons. She's even aerated the soil at the foot of the ageing trees and repaired the old mower to restore the lawn to its former glory. She's repainted the gate, the doorway, the dilapidated arbour, and pulled frolicking weeds from the portly stone urns, polished all the stately silverware and restored the lustre of massive furniture: mahogany, rosewood and the imposing four-poster bed made from a wood she doesn't recognize. She's somehow reinforced the wooden floor, where holes could prove to be unsafe, and carefully replaced cracked tiles in well-worn passages.

She's cleaned and arranged the bedroom as best she could; it's the spacious master bedroom, square and austere, upstairs, well oriented towards the west, but she doesn't like to be there alone; when Enryck is away, she much prefers to wait for him downstairs, under the veranda, outside-inside, not fully exposed to the mysteries of the world but not shut inside this house, believed to be haunted, which Enryck had an exorcist deliver from evil spirits, soon after they'd arrived.

While waiting for the souls in torment to vacate the place, the couple had stayed with one of Enryck's aunts, and Rehvana still remembered, with great dislike, this unexpected exile with the shrewish old woman—suspicious and mean—and that ghastly exorcism from which she had been banned.

She usually believes everything Enryck tells her, but this time, the story of the haunted house had left her doubtful.

She doesn't believe in exorcisms. She's convinced that evil forces are still there, that this human mumbo jumbo hasn't harmed them one bit and that nothing can be done to drive them out. Or perhaps she takes some anxious pleasure in thinking this way. No matter what, it would be unthinkable not to live here: it's Enryck's house, the house of his forefathers, where they must live. It's how they do things: Enryck's father told his wife that the house would be passed on to his son, and to his son alone, as if he didn't have a daughter, or as if 'that' didn't count; and yet, there was a daughter who'd never set foot outside Martinique but had married and settled down soon after her father's death, and went on to rent a cramped and stuffy flat next to the highway in the Dillon housing projects, taking her old mother with her and leaving the vast, sacred, colonial villa empty for Enryck, who'd moved to Paris.

Rehvana now hides her hair, too straight for her taste; she's abandoned her regular sunbathing sessions—too shocking to those around her—because a well-bred Martiniquan woman wants to look Creole, not Negro, and takes great pains to avoid exposure to the sun. Anyway, the sunbathing had only managed to turn her peach-like skin more golden, without darkening it, making her look like a tanned tourist.

She hates the sight of her pasty arms and only wears long sleeves. She's tucked away her flowing mane—too close to that of a white woman—under a crude, white cotton square, the way Haitian women used to do.

You have to specify 'used to', since these days, newly arrived emigrant women from Haiti are quick to follow in the footsteps of stylish Fort-de-France ladies, as soon as they've found work and halfway decent wages which allow them to go to some hairdresser in Sainte-Thérèse or Trénelle to carry out the sacrifice of their small savings and their negritude. They promptly sport tresses ruthlessly straightened with a hot iron or acrid-smelling, greyish ointments, running the risk of cruelly burning the scalp or even losing the entire head of hair, lopped off to within two centimetres of the roots, as if by an invisible blade (that of an error in judgement, no doubt! Or of not feeling comfortable in one's own skin) or it might gradually fall out in stiff patches, dead clumps emptied of their lifeblood, irreversibly damaged, like frostbitten fingers in a murderous deep freeze.

There, where nature was burnt alive and violated with a vengeance, subjected to the accursed Gehenna of the daughters of Ham, and where undesirable, frizzy, Negro hair was martyred and pitilessly left to the hellish heat of the straightening iron, no hair will ever grow back again.

There, where the thick, proud vigour of Negro hair is denigrated and immolated on the damnable altar of psychological complexes, nothing survives but derisory, soulless, straight strands of hair. And those who refuse to let the world see the age-old nobility of a coconut-shaped head, the perfect roundness of a Fula skull or the untamed jungle of black hair of an Ewe from Togo are in great danger of being forced, sooner or later, to hide the inevitable scars of a diabolical folly under some wig. Combative, excessively strict, filled with militant, Antillean pride, Rehvana rebelled, a loner, against anything that in her eyes wasn't unquestionably authentic. Why prefer halberd-straight hair, ridiculously undone by the slightest breeze, and quite incapable, in its straightness gained by cosmetic tricks, to resume its position after the alarm is lifted—why not choose unpretentious, peaceful zeroes, serenely compressed in mutual respect, able to brave, with firm dignity, any trade wind from here and khamsin from somewhere else?

It's been a long time since Rehvana has bothered with cosmetic concerns; the only thing that really matters is the restitution of her being and she feels she's almost there. It seems as if she's reached the end of her quest.

Everything would be wonderful if only Enryck took any notice of her efforts, if he bestowed upon her words of support, if the beloved man didn't return home so late at night—when he came home at all!—to sit at the table and swallow, without a word, the fish stew she'd carefully simmered, after scaling and cleaning it with her delicate, city-dweller hands and letting it marinate in a koui for several hours, slathered in lime juice, amid the salt, green lemon, crushed garlic and a large kako pepper with its misleading cacao colour and promise of sweetness, concealing a formidable, spicy kick that voluptuously burns the tongue, dilates the nostrils and lights a fire in a man's eyes. None of these harsh chores deter her; without complaint, she lets the thorns on the lime-tree branches shred the skin of her obliging hands. With unspeakable joy, she splits the breadfruit into four parts and delights in the sticky milk trickling onto her palms. She draws immense pride from the large piece of tazar marinating on the potager, for she has reclaimed the names as well as the joys of native things.

Stoic, without any help, Rehvana armed herself with the old, rusty kitchen knife lying by the cistern and decapitated the coconuts, discovering in herself an unknown strength to accomplish these actions. And in case Enryck doesn't care for coconut water, she's also chilled some tamarind juice; early this morning, upon awakening, she'd soaked the brown pods in a warm water bath before turning them into a delectably sweet nectar.

The more difficult, complicated and time-consuming a dish, the more tedious and numerous the various steps of peeling, chopping and scraping, the more enthusiastically Rehvana tackles it all. Her fingernails did not flee from the bite of the grater when she brought back the green cythera plums from the bottom of the ravine, then proceeded to grind them into a fine powder, which, after adding water, makes a splendid beverage. The delicate skin of her hands won't cringe at the meat cleaver, her thin arms won't have to fend off fatigue when she severs the pig's tail, the bacon's stubborn rind that will serve to flavour the big kannari of red beans that were carefully soaked the night before, or when she savagely beats the lambi, due to a lack of experience largely offset by her newfound zeal. Without the slightest revulsion or disgust, Rehvana pummels the bloody and slimy entrails of the shark she'll turn into stew tomorrow.

She pays no attention to her nails—abraded, pitiful, gnawed—and when her nicked fingers, raw from harsh palm-oil soap, start to bleed from a cut while she's scaling fish for the red snapper blaff, she scarcely interrupts her work and, in pure delight, hurriedly sucks the acerbic droplets that taste like her newly recovered truth.

She's begun to raise hens, and with her own hands she's built a chicken coop of wire and scrap wooden planks at the back of the house, near the water tank.

She's got no use for food processors nor for any of the lazy, modern woman's appliances; anyway, what would she do with them in this house without electricity? During one of her rare trips to Fort-de-France, if she should sometimes end up in the supermarket, it's not to buy beets, endive or cheeses from France but to memorize, while standing in the book aisle, some Creole recipes from the cookbooks she can't afford. She's got no money of her own and refuses to ask Enryck for some. She survives on the allowance money sent by her sister and whatever her lover parsimoniously doles out every so often; she takes pride in her ability to have them live in an almost self-sufficient way, since the only things she buys—though infrequently—are fish or meat, sugar, flour and oil, and for the rest, she makes do with vegetables and fruits from the garden. So well that when the branches of the guava, jujube and mombin-plum trees begin to be weighed down with more fruit than she would be able to handle for juice, Rehvana rushes to make preserves—quick, quick—before it all spoils; then the house is infused with the delicious, warm smell of caramelized sugar and jams gurgling with tiny bubbles on the wobbly stove. Day after day, fine brown sugar crystals boil into syrup and coat papaya sticks and segments of star fruit. Burnt sugar fills the air and caramel will soon cover round slices of overripe apple banana, enhancing their unique pippin taste, halfway between cinnamon and vanilla, and she won't forget, of course, the sour orange zest for an additional boost of flavour.

She does all this for Enryck, and because it's Antillean.

She eats next to nothing. If Enryck doesn't come home, she waits for him, then falls asleep without supper, or stays awake, watching the night.

Sometimes she makes herself a toloman, returns to sit in the shadows of the veranda, then forgets about the barely touched, lukewarm bowl at her feet, where a spoon, set in motion by day-dreams, has fancifully meandered back and forth across the fluffy, chalky starch that congeals by dawn.

She doesn't complain about the worn-out state of the utensils—sieves riddled with holes, unstable saucepans—and the venerable furniture carved out of wood—a precarious china cab-inet weighed down by piles of rusted aluminium dinnerware she found scattered here and there, including in the middle of the kitchen—nor does she worry about the uncomfortable, old-fashioned, colonial-style pantry—a cramped hut covered with a patched, corrugated-iron roof, adjoining the main house, where all kinds of wildlife had taken refuge: rats, roaches and centipedes all had to be evicted *manu militari*. Of this population of crea-tures, the only ones she'd had pleasure finding again were the doodlebugs, the golden 'doo-doo bugs' of her childhood, smaller than those from Île-de-France but still similar to those they used to catch every four years at school in Sceaux (or perhaps it was every three years), and which had disappeared ever since. Once in Paris, talking about doodlebugs, a strange thought popped into her head—so long ago, she can't recall why—'Funny, I haven't seen any in a long time—perhaps there are no more.'

Or perhaps, quite simply, she'd stopped seeing them or paying attention to them?

The high-school yard was always buzzing during the 'doodlebug years'. The school kids lived only for them, and were compelled to grab them alive to claim them. They would catch them, give them names, keep them in boxes punched with holes, feed them, pet them, even dream they could be tamed.

It was always a contest to see who would have the most good-looking, plump, golden, vivacious, voracious and prolific doodle-bugs, and who owned the most. They would hold speed races, beauty competitions and even longevity contests. They would try to outdo one another in skill, know-how and patience in the treat-ment of these bugs. She would pick them up from under the trees and acclimate them to the house, into the mess and undefined odour of her teenage bedroom, among her sacrosanct treasures, intimate secrets, beheaded dolls and the dried flowers from her last vacation in Brittany, waiting for someone to admire them inside the yellowing pages of the Nelson collection or the Librairie Gründ.

The poor soul who had foolishly let her charges die, long before the others, and hadn't been able to repopulate (for bartering wasn't so easy), was almost suicidal, and even the death of a fellow classmate suffering from leukaemia, who would never earn her national diploma, drove fewer to tears than the inevitable decimation of the doodlebug population at the end of the season.

For days on end, these young ladies would live to the beat of the doodlebugs. Even so, Rehvana can't remember if they were especially fond of the bugs.

In any case, today in Vert-Pré, they're entitled to the full extent of her goodwill, except when the short, crooked legs of the poor, short-sighted critters grab hold of her hair and find themselves trapped while trying to make their escape.

All the same, they had nothing in common with the other insects! Hardly arrived in Café, armed with a raised stick and a lit candle, Rehvana wasted no time in mounting an attack on the filth, droppings, nests and hordes of pests infesting this house left uninhabited for such a long time. Now she hopes to be rewarded, even in the smallest way, for her tenacious struggle, her unwavering devotion. A word here or there or a smile from her laconic lover, who shares her life without really taking part in it and leaves her by herself all day in this empty house. He's home less and less, and returning later more and more.

She's trying hard and she's wearing herself out. Everything her once-inexperienced hands touch is a treat, but it's all in vain.

From the man who's the beneficiary of these delights, she receives, at most, a few dubious grunts, a satisfied glint in his eye. If he isn't firing off some snide wisecrack, comparing her cooking to his mother's and grandmothers', who can, of course, do anything ten times better than she can, he'll toss out a brief compliment on his best days, but most often he merely mutters under his breath, which could, in a pinch, be construed as contentment. Elated, she embraces him, but he shakes himself loose with a shrug to finish his meal.

She doesn't take time to sit and eat—she's so busy waiting on him and watching him stuffing himself with food. In a back-and-forth frenzy, she runs between kitchen and dining room, under night rain showers, to fetch each course, which she brings piping hot, without regard for her hands. Standing, she serves him, and lovingly hovers over her beloved's lips, now smudged with grease. She's overwhelmed by the bygone pleasure—still new to her and reinvented—of feeding her man.

Rehvana doesn't even have time to sit; she stays on her feet, hands clasped, and blissfully stares at him, relishing the sight of her man eating.

On the edges of her gashed, ragged, mangled nails, her flesh swells and cracks. The palms of her hands are now covered with brownish-red calluses and her fingers, swollen and slashed, look like stumps.

This is how she is now. Yes, that's how they see her: skin studded with bluish bruises, arms and legs ulcerated with ignored or badly-cared-for wounds, left to uncertain—indeed, foolish— cure-all remedies picked up at open-air markets, mostly inappropriate and against all common sense, and, in any case, powerless to defeat the forces of humidity and heat—fertile ground for unfriendly fermentation and unhealthy, microbial fauna or flora—more likely to spread infection than promote healing— and, for a fact, why her wounds' gaping lips were never allowed to close.

Ma Cidalise had told her a hundred times to always beware of the snake. In Café, Rehvana herself had seen a huge trigocephalus with her own eyes—white-bellied, splendid, demonic— its glazed, gleaming scales ringed with alternating colours, captured not too far from her house . . . With a kind of mystical and singular rapture, she sinks her bare feet into the garden, exposing her delicate ankles to the fierce and twisted network, to the biting jungle and its inextricable and lush depths. Shivering, pupils dilated, and haunted by the fleeting and feverish vision of a long, lethal beast snaking through the weeds—the deadly, elusive and fascinating image persisting in overwhelming her rhapsodic, almost hypnotized retinas, as the coolness of the damp humus gently greets and caresses her frenzied fever— Rehvana, disoriented, the only disciple of a ghoulish and orgiastic cult, often pushes far—very far—into the bottomless depths, through the slippery and teeming dégras, penetrated by blind presences and tangled with threats.

Whenever she shakes the leaves to make fruits tumble down—rose apples, grapefruit for glazing, or tamarind—her entire body is showered with a thick cloud of red ants and ticks; invisible, they eat her alive, this squad of stinging insects that bite her everywhere—even in the eyes—since she's forced to keep her head lifted and tilted towards the assassin leaves that seem to defend their fruits by firing bursts of biting bugs in her direction. Once or twice her foot remained swollen for more than a week— a painful inflammation around a minuscule insect bite she'd ignored.

She's made herself comfortable in this life and this universe is hers.

She's said it loud and clear.

She's sold off her return ticket at a rock-bottom price. Just like that, with no hesitation, but maybe a bit of showing-off on the day after Enryck had lost so much money at a cockfight. He'd been complaining, bemoaning the fact that he didn't even have a sou left to buy fabric and was up to his ears in debt . . . When she'd spread the wad of bills on the table, Enryck had pocketed the whole thing with a wide smile . . .

Rehvana makes it back from the garden without having crossed paths with the snake; on the other hand, the flying ants and ticks swooping down on her from the branches have viciously attacked her back, butt, legs . . . all the way down to her feet. But the bites spur her on, galvanize her, help her feel alive. From each descent into the garden—this luxuriant paradise, fertile and perfidious—she brings back pitiful suffering from strange cuts and marks up and down her body, which she bandages with herbal salves when she takes the time or which she takes pleasure in aggravating on the grater that gashes and abrades her hands because she insists on crushing her cythera-plum harvest into greenish dust.

She delays the moment for soothing her burns, and will only give in much later to the shower's liquid embrace, tearing her up like a memory, wistful and guilty, if she shuts her eyes and remembers . . .

And although she increases the water pressure so that the spray lashes her back, these long streams of warm liquidity awaken in her the long-gone echo of a forgotten sweetness. The warmth of another body.

HE'S HERE, OR, RATHER, THEY'RE HERE.

Enryck kisses her and pulls her to him, but what she sees behind his shoulder brings up the taste of bile to her throat.

Excited, the fat and lecherous Chabin, blocking the flood of outside light, stands in the door frame; he brandishes in her face the carcasses of two opossums—not roadkill but caught 'game', a hunter's trophy, so he says—two bodies that he triumphantly tosses on the table, still warm.

Rehvana, moved by this sight, can hardly bear to look at the miserable, pale shapes, feeling nothing for them but pity and disgust. They're so repulsively ugly and one of them is so small!

Laughing at the woman's sickened expression, the two friends have conspicuously dismembered one carcass. When it comes to upsetting the young woman and doing something dramatic and off-the-wall, the two macho men stop at nothing: tonight they proudly boast about their hidden culinary talents, unsuspected by Rehvana, and they successfully prove it by cooking an excellent opossum stew. With a knowing smile, they say it tastes like rabbit, but more subtle—rather like cat, they clarify . . .

Amid the sickening odour of dead flesh, they poke one another and guffaw, slobbering over and over, 'I'm telling you!' and, in unison, 'ou ké wé!' ('you'll see!') and 'a wi nèg!' ('ah, yes, Negro!'). Enryck asks her to pour them some rum punch and the fat Chabin bellows, 'My friends, it's five to rum o'clock!' while pretending to look at his watch, then points his pudgy finger towards the small carafe of straw-coloured rum and the bottle of La Mauny.

But Rehvana has already left the room. She felt another bout of nausea coming on and, without waiting for them to carve the second opossum, she rushed upstairs, palms plastered against her mouth, almost breaking her neck on the rickety staircase.

She dashed to the bathroom and was still there—precariously balanced on the side of the tub, all her energy concentrated in her gaunt hands, her endlessly long, slender fingers hooked on the hard, wet, cold marble, watching the water flow in the foul-smelling sink—when Enryck called her name.

And now, docked to this man's cruelty, bound without a mooring line to insentient splendours, she sees her life pouring down the drain, into the mud, without understanding why.

She should have answered him right away and immediately gone back downstairs.

But she's unable to speak or move. How many times has he called?

He storms into the room, grabs her by the arm, shakes her and throws her into a panic. All she sees is the leather with its big buckle. He's speaking too loudly for her; he doesn't know how badly her ears are buzzing; he's making fun of her because she threw up; he's furious she went upstairs and is complaining about her poor manners . . .

She really should have returned downstairs right away. But she has no sense of time. Had she slipped away for so long? He pretends she's been up here for ages, lays into her education, her character and the nature of her love, her type and her race (. . . if she has a race at all).

He dragged her into the living room.

In a cloud, she saw the unfriendly bulk of the large Chabin; she quickly noticed the bloody remains had been removed from the table, though the two young men hadn't deigned to clean off the rivulets of fresh blood.

They'd made their own rum-punch drinks.

She barely understood what they wanted; she didn't comprehend what they were saying, nor why Enryck suddenly became so enraged.

At the very least, it seemed he shouldn't have done this in front of the other one; yet she was so passive, so slack, she felt neither Enryck's slaps nor what followed, nor the violent gust of air when they'd thrown open the door.

They left without turning the stove off, leaving the useless opossum stew to burn. Enryck buckled his belt again and Chabin noisily belched up a mouthful of rum.

Someone Else

'LET ME TELL YOU, DARLIN', it's been mighty long since I took up my ros'ry, and men's problems are no longer my problems. Now I'm prayin', I pray to God, and then I'm done with it! See, I have my Bible here somewhere . . .

'Hush now, enough cryin', girl, you're a pretty young thing, leave that bugger to 'is business! You think you can stay here snivellin' for an hour! Think you got nuthin' else to do?'

Concentrating on hauling a huge basin of water by balancing it on her head, Ma Cidalise had shown neither surprise nor outrage at the sight of the defeated young woman.

'Enough wailin' I tell you—you ain't got no need to shed mo' tears! A big girl like you, don't tell me you take two, three of 'em slaps and be down for the count! You got to harden your body!

'Lord a-mercy, but your li'l body is burnin' up, like you got some fever. Let's go drink a cure-all potion or a li'l lemongrass tisane. I'll fix you a cup.'

While she's moving her plump, bouncing bonda—so maternal and still firm—around the old stove, Ma Cidalise continues her litany.

'Woman fallen but not hopeless: leave this man to 'is business! Though 'e be comin' and goin', he'll come home in the end . . . '

Rehvana's mind hardly registers the nagging hum buzzing around her brain; she vacantly stares ahead, now collapsed into a chair.

'My God-Lord-Virgin Mary! Don't tell me you're always like this, a-cryin', not movin', like a molocoye, since the day you seen your man run off!'

She couldn't say how long she's been like this—shrivelled and limp.

She felt neither the healing, herb-infused cloths Ma Cidalise tenderly applied to her bruised face, nor the warm toloman parting her puffy lips.

The broom made from latanier-palm fronds restlessly rustles on the damaged tiles.

'Look! I took some thrashings, my dear, all sorts of beatings that would put yours to shame—'e barely laid his fingers on you! I took some blows, girl, you can say that, since I was li'l, not slaps, no! I been beaten by leather, cut with a large kitchen knife, bashed with a calabash, bashed with a shoe, bashed with a mad-joumbé, bashed with a rigoise, bashed with a rod, bashed with a roquille, bashed with a lélé, bashed with a boutou, bashed with a fifth of rum, bashed with a bottle of wine, bashed with a boulder, bashed with a chain, bashed with damp linen, bashed with dry wood, bashed in the front, bashed in the back, bashed on the right hand, bashed on the left, bashed from the top, bashed from the bott'm, all sorts of blows! Money's the only thing that's never bashed into me.

'Afterwards, I couldn't even lift my head.

'Mother of God! I took so many beatings, girl! To tell the truth, I got used to it. Beatings mornin' to night, for a piece of bread I took without askin'—that was my mother—and my step-father, yes suh!—damn how that man liked to beat me! And with Boniface, fights and mo' fights! I didn't even know why, most of the time.

'Who knows with all this here beatin' if my head is still screwed on . . . Jesus, Mary, Joseph! I been pushed 'round mo' times than I can say by Peter, Paul . . . and the list goes on!

'Well, I'm still here! Now I'm a woman who's still standin'! No mo' men in my house, not even my boys, I'm done with all that, *Deo gratias*, centuries ago!'

Time spins around Rehvana without her being aware—without her making the slightest move.

'Nuthin' but blows is what I've received since I was li'l . . . You can say that! They never gave me nuthin' else but blows here, blows there, it looked like they wanted to break my back! Those gentlemen!

'But, still, I knew how to resist, make my body stiff, not soft . . . You got to take what's yours, li'l one, take what's yours . . .

'And 'e who does bad things, 'e won't get the chance to do 'em in heaven. There's justice, sweet li'il miss! Look at Boniface, well 'e is so bad that even 'is sons never go see 'im, they come to kiss me sometimes, but they don't want nuthin' to do with their father! Must say 'e never gave 'em no money since before the time of the Marquis d'Antin . . . '

She slices open the fish and forcefully sticks her fingers into its belly; her ochre hand emerges, dripping with fresh blood, as she yanks out a fistful of guts. Covered in sweat, she brusquely wipes her face with the corner of a kitchen towel, then bends over Rehvana to delicately dab her forehead.

'Go! Move! Don't tell me you gonna stay here, twiddlin' your thumbs the whole blessed day.'

Rehvana hears nothing; the old woman's words scatter around her in a hopeless farandole.

How long has she been here? When did she run to the neighbour's place to hide, and from what?

'Enough I say! You must be goin' back home now. If you want to stay here in my house, that's fine with me, but if you don't wanna get another beatin', better go back and make 'is dinner for whenever 'e gets home.'

Rehvana still doesn't move. She hasn't noticed the darkness gradually invading the room while the old woman goes about her business and lights a kerosene lamp that hisses as it illuminates the room.

'Atta girl, time to get up! No mo' lettin' you'self go. Look at you!

'I'm not goin' to let you go with nuthin', poor li'l devil! Take this bunch of bananas, this here fish and this home-made veg-'table soup. (I cleaned the fish for you; you jus' need to warm up the soup.)

'Go make you'self pretty, and prepare dinner for your man!'

Before leaving, Rehvana delves into Ma Cidalise's incredible stock of pills. Randomly, she grabs something to help her sleep, analgesics and some antipyretics (most well past their expiration dates). She's ignoring Ma Cidalise, who is muttering through the few teeth she's got left: 'Pity, pretty girl like you, what got into you, why hang out with those Negroes from the sticks and get you'self all banged up! Ah, you really fixed you'self good!'

It's Saturday. A clear Saturday in late winter, dazzling after a fine drizzle.

A warm alertness permeates the air; the clouds over Vert-Pré have dispersed into the night, into a stealthy flock of hawks.

As soon as they are unleashed, the two gamecocks furiously hurl themselves at each other and begin the sort of circle dance that boxers do; they try to stare each other down, prance and parade about, then awkwardly try to take flight at the same time with a brief flapping of atrophied wings. Rehvana is vaguely aware of a collision of beaks, a rapid rustling of feathers, perhaps a kind of distress.

Everything went so fast; the action lasted a few seconds; the fight was over in a heartbeat. Despite the elaborate staging and the deep concentration of the cock owners, there was something slipshod about the whole thing.

Sometimes, in the middle of a fight, a particularly cowardly cock will start the preliminary dance again, alone this time, and will try to flee by going round and round in circles—pelted with Creole jeers—a good distance from the adversary, in hot pursuit—until its owner nabs it, readjusts its spurs, splashes it with water, urges it on and returns it to the middle of the pitt to face the future victor. The instinct of these bellicose birds appears to be faultless, since each time Rehvana saw one of them turn tail, the poor thing was put back in place, only to escape once more, bringing even more disgrace onto itself, until ultimately defeated and booed.

Rehvana had welcomed this outing as a godsend. Inseparable Chabin still at his side, Enryck had still deigned to invite Rehvana to join them and she was overjoyed. Sitting proudly on the hard bench, the white embroidery of her fancy gole caught on the rough wood, she was sweating heavily in this heat thick with musk and blood. She was on display and she felt like his wife— one of the few women at the start, in the rugged rows of seats at this rural pitt only frequented by locals—and she was beaming by his side. Pretending to be afraid, she nestled into his arms, feeling so good inside, despite the rum-fuelled squawking all around them.

Novice that she is to this game, duel after duel, Rehvana discovers she's got a sixth sense for this kind of combat, with an unexpected prescience, and though it's her first time, she's able to pick the winner right from the start, when the contenders— calagouaille or straw-coloured, ash-coloured or gros-sirop— stand erect on their armed spurs to spar and challenge each other.

Enryck bets every time on the one she doesn't pick. He's gambling more and more, and keeps losing. Feverishly, he pulls out wads of suspicious-looking bills from his pockets. What's the source of all this money? She doesn't know. Greasy Chabin wins once in a while and takes advantage of it to flirt with Rehvana, seated between the two men. His obscene bragging overwhelms her in the oppressive air, deepening the dusty dimness in an aggressive way. Rehvana, increasingly dumbfounded, understands practically nothing of this half-witted chitchat amid the dizzying tumult of the pitt.

'REHVANA, LI'L MISS, HOW COME YOU'RE NOT COMIN' to see me anymo', huh? You'd think I was givin' you raw chicken guts to eat last week.'

'. . .'

'Lordy, lordy, if I knew you were all cagou like that since yesterday night, I would've come visited you bright and early! Why didn't you call me? You already know I get up with the pipiris. (Don't think I'm lettin' myself go!)

'I wanted to visit two, three times already, I peeked through your window, and I think you saw me; why don't you have nuthin' to say to me? I'm tir'd of goin' on and on like this, repeatin' myself: you can always call on Ma Cidalise to lend you a hand.'

'. . .'

'So . . . in case of emergency—if couri-vini somethin' bad happens to you all of a sudden—I can't even be sure you'd be callin' on Ma Cidalise to help . . . No! we can't keep goin' on like this!'

She leans over the sprawled young woman and frowns as she examines her, then pulls herself up, stirring the air around her.

'What's this again? . . . Jesus, Mary, Joseph and all the saints! You can't jus' stay there with your hands chained, and all the while see such misery! Lord have mercy, since the day . . . '

The old neighbour, a bit nutty, who has developed a strange friendship with Rehvana, plunged deep into thought, before proceeding, in a solemn and learned tone: 'But I saw you the other day, when Enryck came by to take you to the pitt, and now, jus' look at you, such a mess, despite all that, poor li'l one! *Sa ki rivé'w*? (What happened?)'

'What you need, girl, is a nice, bewitched coin—a "totor". I'm not Mother Nature but I can do a li'l somethin' for you.'

The congress of dogs from last night, the oppressive heat, and Enryck's absence in the bed's depression had kept Rehvana awake. She'd tossed and turned in the large four-poster bed, suffocating under the mosquito net, unable to sleep. Outside, an unrelentingly loud pack of stray dogs had outrageously gathered beneath her window, their endless howling and persistent, high-pitched yelping drilling into her ears.

She stretches, sluggishly sits up and opens her eyes wide.

'A magical totor?'

Although intrigued, she resumes her lounging in the hammock, leisurely extending her legs while sighing and softly lowering her eyelids. With half-closed eyes ready to dream, she languidly waits, and yawns.

Two zigzagging ribbons of busy ants carry off zachari crumbs while a team of other workers zealously hauls a colossal, dead cockroach. She knows too well that Ma Cidalise won't need coaxing to answer her question, because she's only too happy to have found in Rehvana a captive audience, always willing to be lulled by her boundless babbling. But you have to let the answer come on its own . . . all in good time; you can't rush these things. Rehvana understands and docilely makes the best of it. In fact, the old woman takes pleasure in keeping her waiting, pretending to be occupied with something else. For now, she half-heartedly rails against the dreadful critters and sets her gigantic backside in motion to scatter the roach's funeral procession with a hefty slap of the broom.

'A magical totor—yes, that's exactly right!'

She grumbles a bit more about God-knows-what imaginary vermin, shuffles around, then finally takes a seat. Unable to contain herself, she abruptly bursts out:

'You'd have to be born yesterday not to know what to do with a magical totor!'

' . . . '

'Good God, girl, enough already with starin' at me like that, you look like a dimwit.'

Rehvana had casually straightened up, leaning on her elbow, but she quickly returns to the hammock's rocking.

'Looks like I have to waste my time teachin' you the important stuff . . . *sa sa yé sa*? (What's this?) What do they teach you at school then? They never told you 'bout totors?

'Let me tell you,' she continues. 'As I live and breathe, I never studied no history or geography, never learnt science or 'rhitmetic, but girl, I know a totor is a coin worth two sous, and I've seen, like I see you, many nice totors, big totors, stamped with the head of Victor-Emmanuel. Victor-Emmanuel was a Belgian king or maybe Italian, beats me . . . ' and she makes a big circle with her index finger and thumb to describe the unlikely size of the mythical coin.

'And also I seen a pile of them during General Robert's time and the Second World War. Two sous, that was really a heap of money in those days, but there were devilish women with expensive tastes. These la-di-da women, they always wanted to be better dressed than the rest. They didn't want to walk in michelins, oh lordy, no, they wanted high-heeled boots on their feet! And others, they probably gave all their spare change to vagrants . . . So they clutched tight their totor 'til when they could find some wizard to cast a spell on the totor for 'em. I don't know how much the sorc'rer got: maybe two or three sous for the totor, but it's the price, take it or leave it!

'Some of these greedy women made a good business with the magical totors: they went to market, bought a pile of bagailles, then paid with their totors. The shopkeeper gave 'em change and secured the totor in the register—they had no idea. But this totor was hexed: on its own, it went right smack back into the woman's purse!

'There was a beautiful woman, a real lady, who loved a short, poor man, the kind that goes where the wind blows, you know? Nobody knew 'is name: nobody knew where 'e came from. I even think that this here guy was a sorc'rer. In my opinion, I think 'e had to be one sure smart wizard-type to hold onto a good-lookin' woman like this (and not no stumpa wood, mind you, she was high class!), since he hisself was hunched over, ugly and black as mortal sin! I can tell you one thing, girl, you don't need to rack your brains to know who did the devil's work for the lady! Ah, that man knew what he was doin', you hear me? To satisfy the woman, 'e was takin' all sorts of love potions, and 'e could ride her, and ride her, and ride her . . .

'He's the guy who found that "afroparadisiac" spring on La Trace Road, and another one, near Bassignac, between Gros-Morne and La Trinité. If your belov'd drinks from it, my dear, 'e's goin' to keep on lovin' you 'til the cottage roof falls in! And 'e was the jealous type, so 'e made some sort of concoction for the woman. When that woman was feelin' hot and bothered, she'd go off with other men, but 'e always let her go 'cause 'e smeared that stuff deep inside her coucoune. So when those other men penetrated her—yessiree, they could go in—but they come a-crawlin' and a-screamin' out. They could be doin' all sorts of sweet things to her and comin' from behind, but as soon as they got stuck in her patate-l'ombrage, bam!—that remedy ripped off the head of their cal, all torn off, jus' like that! and then it falls, kerplop! Like grabbin' a banana from a tree and throwin' it on the ground. Those guys went runnin' like the devil and she never seen them again. And the best part—that damn hot-to-trot woman, she felt nuthin', not a drop of pain, fancy that! She remained a good girl for her old man—this guy took 'is revenge only against men. The old sorc'rer was so taken by that capistrelle woman! Believe you me: he was happy with her, she was 'is honey pot! And with 'is secret weapon, he knew she'd always come back to 'im, since she couldn't go twice with the same guy. And she could still be left in peace, goin' 'bout her business, 'cause those guys runnin' 'round with the lopped-off cal, they were too 'shamed to tell anyone. And they were too cowardly to seek revenge: those lover boys, nuthin' but a bunch of yellow-bellied chickens and double-crossers, I tell you! The old man gave her ev'ry li'l thing she wanted, and since Madame wanted and wanted and wanted, this here massibol, crazy in love, used all 'is pow'r to put a hex on a big, shiny totor jus' for her. Ladies and gentlemen, you can say that this here man was clever, mo' clever than Satan and all hell's devils!

'But you'll see how the old guy was eventu'lly outsmarted . . . There was a pile of people with magical totors, but they took precautions. Only that matador woman—since she'd been doin' this for a long time—she became mo' darin'. She kept handin' out her totor left and right, never worryin' that it wouldn't come back to her . . . But there was a sly, old fox of a shopkeeper in rue Saint-Louis . . . The woman was showin' up in all those shops the whole bless'd day long; she was doin' her food shoppin', she was buyin' oil, manioc and sugar, and a heap of stuff for makin' sweets, and then an armful of those fabrics for makin' herself look good: damask and lisle, and also khaki for her man. Then, real quiet-like, she placed her totor in that shopkeeper's hand. The merchant put it in 'is cash drawer, and when she was turnin' the street corner, she gently called out for the totor to come back into her hand. At the end of the day, she had her purchases, plus the change from the shopkeeper, and that beaut'ful, fat, golden totor, right there, in the palm of her hand. But this really smart shopkeeper starts noticin' stuff missin' from 'is cash drawer and starts scratchin' 'is head: "But how? Where's that totor? Where did I put the totor Ma Rodrigue gave me jus' now?" So he ended up goin' to see a wizard to find out where the totor had disappeared to. But the guy gave 'im this warnin': "You best be careful, if I do this for you, that totor won't vanish no mo', but its owner gonna have a heap of troubles on her head fo' sure, not jus' maybe!"

'The woman, she comes back to 'is shop like she's done before, and she goes 'bout her business. He leaves her alone— she pays, and the shopkeeper makes like 'e knows nuthin'. That woman simply leaves the shop, struttin' 'bout, practisin' her scales, a l'il off-key, so proud of herself! *I ka fè djèz, fout I prélè!* (No one can bother her, she's like a queen!) And then, boom! She runs into an old male acquaintance of hers (they were both, what d'you call that, when they're holdin' that baby girl on the baptismal thingamajig . . .) . . . and I forget the baby's name!

'Hey! You're not sleepin', are you? I still don't even know who it . . . '

Of course she's not asleep! She hangs on Ma Cidalise's every word, assiduous and studious as a good schoolgirl. She wholeheartedly believes—wants to believe—everything the old woman recounts, and powerful shudders run through her body at the high points.

She breaks out in a cold sweat when the story enters the supernatural realm, intensified by the old woman's credulous animation. As soon as Ma Cidalise takes on her old-wives'-tale voice—part mythical, part ridiculous—Rehvana literally feels exquisite goose bumps spontaneously erupt on her own arms— the physical manifestation of her people's irrational beliefs, gullible to any so-called dark arts. She can read on her skin the corporeal emotion—violent and physical—offered to her by the memory of her race—its 'unreal' embedded in everyday life— where 'history' and 'story' merge, steeped in the inconceivable and the occult.

'So you don't know who I'm talkin' 'bout. I didn't get to hold that ti-manmaille on the day she was baptized . . . Anyways, forget about her! I'm not wastin' my time tryin' to name this baby for you. You're cartin' around so much nonsense in you already, you're goin' to forget it too, and anyways, you don't know these people from Adam, wretched people who lived near the Caca River, which they now call "Levassor Canal" or perhaps "Madame River", or somethin' like this . . . These folks had weird, uncivilized customs, they emptied their chamber pots in there, yes, in the river! And when the caca-guard came by, the father would make 'is alarm clock go off—dringg, dringg—and pretend 'e was on the phone with the governor: "Hello-o? Yes, please connect me with the governorr? Verry well, thank you . . . Hello? Is it you, Louis-Geôrrges? How are you my dearr? How nice of you to call your friend Arrrnolphe . . . I'm doing well, busy with the congrress . . . Yes . . . yes . . . I'll see to it at my office on Monday, as an emerrgency, all rright! To the extent that . . . the rreferendum? But surre! . . . Yes that's rright! To the extent that I give praise to the public prosecutorr . . . But of courrrse, I can do this for you my dearrr! Howeverr, this little caca-guard herre is botherring me! You want to talk to him? Ah, but no, it's not worrth it, you arre not really going to have him . . . " The rascal was talkin' loud and clear and supposedly with the governor, rolling the *r*'s in the best French from France! But there was no need, 'e kept it up jus' to please hisself: the poor devil had already taken to runnin' away, like 'e was stung in the butt. The caca-guard was hittin' the road so fast, like runnin' is never out of season!

'Anyways, enough with these people's dirty caca business . . . So the godmother is chattin' with the godfather ('e hisself told me the whole story, so that's why I'm tellin' you it's all true). They start walkin' together, gossipin'—first godfather, then godmother—and 'e walks with her for a while; 'e knows her and 'e knows the hot-blooded lady likes to strut 'round town in mixed company . . . She tells 'im she's goin' to rue Ernest-Renan, and when they get there, oh good God, my Lord!' Ma Cidalise whispers while quickly crossing herself, as if she needs God's immediate protection to proceed with the story and keep herself safe from the evil spell. 'He told me 'e seen her twistin' and turnin' somethin' awful-like, and she's softly callin' out. At first, 'e doesn't understand what she's sayin'. They're still walkin', and then the lady stops to tie her bootlace, only it wasn't even untied. As she's bent over like this, the guy tries to listen to what she's sayin'—'e hears her call in a soft voice: "Totor! Totor! My Totor, come back!" And she's payin' no mind to 'im, as if 'e was a hairless dog from hell.

'They keep goin' and the woman begins to lose her temper: "Come back, I tell you!" Usually she liked paradin' 'bout town, especially arm in arm with a handsome mulatto guy, but on that day she was actin' real crazy-like, and not allurin' at all. She walked up and down the street, like a lost soul, waitin' for her totor to come back. Girl, this is what her male acquaintance told me, that as soon as they got near the colonial boarding school, the woman, she started to shake and move about. She was squeakin' like a mouse caught in the straw of a broom. She looked like a real bag of fleas, and she was runnin' left and right like an insane ant, until she wore herself out, so tir'd she began cryin' her eyes out. She never said a word 'bout what happened . . . She looked like she was havin' one of those Grand Mal seizures.

'Meanwhile, in the shop, you could hear a big fight goin' on among the coins in the cash drawer, tokoto tokoto: that totor was fightin' the others to get out. What a mess it was makin' in the drawer! It was somethin', girl! But it couldn't get out, it was stuck. Stuck, 'cause the wizard hired by the shopkeeper had done 'is job: that totor was exorcized! *Rôye papa!* Oh-la-la! . . .

'They say the massoucrelle lady went mad, and that all kinds of awful things happened to her since the day the totor couldn't come back to her. She vanished into thin air, and my guess? never to be heard from again.

'Is the li'l miss sleepin'? Look ev'rybody, I'm here talkin' nonsense for an hour and this li'l cattechiopine goes to sleep on me like that! Hey, answer me, I'm no pile of dog poop, after all!'

But no, Rehvana is not asleep, and if she keeps her eyes closed, it's to better soak up the tale, for she knows the old woman is just beginning and she's not going to stop there. Neither of them has quite had her fill, and Rehvana patiently lets the old woman's excitement build to reach the highest levels of fantasy and frenzy.

'After this, bewitched twenty-five-franc notes appeared: huge notes, big as bed sheets,' and she widens her arms to demonstrate. 'You never seen these—they were marked "Banque de la Martinique", with coconut trees and a picture of Empress Joséphine . . . But the shopkeepers began to get wind of 'em: ev'ry time they were given one, they had to leave the shop, pretendin' to look for somethin' out back. For example, they might go to the courtyard, then bite into a corner of the bill—two, three li'l teeth marks—to exorcise it. Sometimes it worked, but not always . . .

'So, some of the people got really rich with this hexed money business. 'Cause the totors not only came back to their masters, but some of 'em also took all the money in the drawer with 'em! (What I'm tellin' you, missy, is all true—so true that if you plant it, it'll root for sure!) And they got away with murder: no way to send the police to track 'em down.'

' . . . '

'But you see, what's annoyin' with all this, it's this business with the exorcized totor! It would be great for you, if it worked, but if I find a clever sorc'rer who can do it for you, we won't have a totor to give him; what we need is a five-hundred-franc note . . .

'When I get my pension, I can loan you the money . . . I used to know a whole bunch of wizards in my time, but I'm not sure where I'm goin' to be able to find one now for you, poor li'l devil!'

' . . . '

'And you heard me, it's dangerous! But you, my sweet doe, you're shrewd: you're not gonna go back to the same shop twice, thinkin' the shopkeeper won't know what's goin' on!'

Ma Cidalise feigns a face deep in thought, seemingly struggling with a serious matter. She takes on the appearance of a high-ranking dignitary, charged with a high-stakes mission, and it's with the most sincere sense of urgency that she tries to control Rehvana's precarious fate—with nothing but a bunch of tales. Her entire voluminous being, focused and reflective, attests to the gravity of the hour. Holding herself very upright, hands flat on vast, full hips, she considers the scope and scale of her responsibilities. It's true these last few days have taken an alarming turn: for all she knows (for Rehvana doesn't tell her much: she makes do with what she sees) this good-for-nothing Enryck has taken to drinking more and more absinthe when he's home, and at all hours of the day. He hardly ever works: it seems like ages since he's made a new dress; otherwise, Rehvana would've proudly shown it off, like she usually does . . . Those two kids don't have a sou between them, and the poor girl can't even go home to France, since she sold her only prized possession, her return ticket, via a classified ad . . . No way for her to cross the water again!

'Ah, if only I could find someone who'd know how to protect you, like in the olden days. 'Cause there's somethin' better than a totor: what you need is a li'l monster (some folks call it "Antikri", but I think they mean "Antichrist") but after the dirty work is done, it's a tall order to get rid of it!

'Let me tell you: it's not that hard, you need to take the egg of a black, curly-feathered hen, laid at three o'clock in the afternoon on Good Friday, and then you let it hatch under your arm—*sa yo ka kriyé l'aisselle* (what one calls the armpit)—for twenty-one days. Among the eggs laid on Good Friday, one or two, no mo', are good to make the Antikri. At the end of the twenty-one days, if you have a good egg, you'll see that li'l monster comin' out and then it's goin' to grow and grow, but not for long, it's goin' to stop in its tracks when it gets like this,' she knowledgeably demonstrates by placing her right index finger onto her extended left forearm.

'They say the monster is always dressed up real nice, in clothes for goin' out at night, with a tailcoat, my dear! Or it'll wear a frock coat, but always wearin' a tie, and then, most important of all, it'll be wearin' a top hat, not one of those bowlers, mind you, no, but a shiny top hat for "gentilmin". It'll be slippin' into the house, comin' and goin' without nobody ever seein' it . . . With your li'l monster, you can do all sorts of stuff: you can send it to play nasty tricks on somebody, do some dirty business 'cause it's so small it can shimmy under shutters, no place'll be off limits: it's mighty powerful . . . Only, on the whole, it'll be doin' a lot of bad things; I'm tellin' you all this to pass the time, to make conversation, but enough dreamin', this is not for you: I've been told it would beat up its own mother!

' . . . Look here, these folks with Antikris, they used them to be makin' their neighbours' lives miserable, turnin' a house upside down, smashin' plates to bits, openin' and closin' doors, turnin' lights on, blowin' out lamps, bangin' on the ceilin' at night jus' to keep folks awake. And worse, in the dark, things started happenin': that Antikri stole all their jewels, dug up all their money, it stole ev'ry last thing! No one could see it, but they sure could hear it, only they were too 'fraid to get out of bed!

'Other times, the li'l monster went listenin' to what folks were sayin' in their houses, and reported back to its master. Later, the Antikri master would know all 'bout their business and folks would be wonderin' how it could be!

' . . . But careful, I tell you! This beast is evil, it eats meat: when it's feelin' hungry, nuthin' but meat will do. (Some folks go 'round sayin' it likes human flesh—most of all, children's flesh—and some even say newborn baby flesh, but I hear they're fib-bin'.) Anyways, this here li'l beast is very polite when you see it, 'cause it's so two-faced . . . And when you got you'self one, you can't never get rid of it! I don't know how it is now, but in those olden days, when the Antikri's master had died, he had to pay . . . You ever wonder why there are wakes for the dead? Well, my God! You can't never leave the dead man alone, child, you need to have folks 'round 'im all the time. 'Cause who knows, 'e could disappear, jus' like that! No one knows what the dead man did during 'is time on earth, so when's 'e's dead, anything can happen to 'im! You've got to keep watch until the time 'e goes under! That's why we form a tight circle 'round 'im. Whoever owned an Antikri, even if 'e looked like a run-of-the-mill sort of guy, when 'e's dead, you've got to watch out. The li'l monster doesn't want to let 'im go, so it does all it can to make off with the body, and if you let 'im, you'll find in the coffin—instead of a body—a banana tree trunk . . . I can't tell you why the Antikri needs to be grabbin' the dead man, but I can tell you, 'e must have a really good reason to! So when the time comes for the men to be liftin' the coffin, when they carry 'im from the hills down to the church in the village, that's when the trouble begins: the pall bearers stop for no reason, or they start runnin' away like a pack of devils, or they jus' stand there, no one knows why, and watch the coffin start shakin' like a bag of fleas; next, the people in the procession get kicked in the behind: they look all over the place but are seein' no one around. When they start walkin' again, somethin' stings them in the calf, the Antikri goes from one to the other, and each time there's one who jumps up and then drops down again, plop! it's pinchin', it's whippin', it's doin' all sorts of silly stuff to bother people. In the olden days, men on horses led the coffin with the shrouded corpse inside. Well, the Antikri also was attackin' the horses, if you can imagine that! So the only thing they could do was call a sorc'rer who'd know what to do. When he gets there, he tap-tap-taps on the coffin with an acacia stick to calm the Antikri, and this poor guy has to keep on tappin', tappin', tappin', tappin' ... until they arrive at the church, where they light the votive candles and the Virgin Mary and Jesus Christ are now all there, and the Antikri, he be gettin' scared ... '

'With an acacia stick?'

'Of course! The acacia wand is what you are needin' to ward off evil. When the dead don't want to be movin' on, or when someone is engagé, you know, they've sold their soul to the devil, and it's plain as day they've got powers, only you can't do nuthin' against 'em, well, that's when you use it to chase 'em away. Why d'you not know this already? Supposin' you have a tree that doesn't bear fruit: you jus' need to give it a good beatin'. You take an acacia branch, and then you beat the hell out of the trunk, 'bout one meter twenty centimetres from the ground, and the tree gets goin' again. You see my star apple tree, and that other one over there, custard apple? That's exac'ly what I did to 'em last year, and now I dunno what I'm goin' to do with all the fruit, since you told me you didn't like 'em, you find them too gooey. Who knows, I may jus' chop 'em down one of these days.'

' ... '

'I'd like to do all these things for you, but I'm afraid. That's why, the other day, when I was goin' to see the psychic for you, I didn't ask for real strong remedies for keepin' your Enryck calm, because these kinds of schemes are too risky. They don't always work, and they can come back to haunt you! Later on, you could be havin' aches and pains all over, and a heap of trouble, until one fine mornin' you find you'self dead!

'Ah! you're smilin'? Well, let me tell you what happened to Ma Samson, who was not 'fraid to trade with the devil. Ma Samson lived in the large village of Marigot (on the ravine side, they called it "The Outlet" 'cause that's where the neighbours came to fetch water). She was known for bein' engagée; anyways, she was workin' some magnetism on a certain Rigobert, a guy who lived alone, and she was keepin' 'im from gettin' any women. The mo' evil charms she forced on 'im, the mo' failures 'e got from 'is fishin', so to speak ... So one evenin', 'bout ten o'clock, 'e stripped naked ('cause you have to be stark naked for this, without a stitch of clothes on your body), grabbed 'is acacia stick and marched into Ma Samson's house where 'e gave her a good thrashin'.

'Folks could hear the commotion, 'cause 'e didn't jus' hit her once, believe you me! Ev'ryone came out to see what was happenin': when Ma ran away shriekin', "Help! Kouililik, kouililik!" many folks told me they saw the devil's horns on her head (though I know this woman wore braids on both sides of her head, so they could've been mistakin' 'em for devil's horns, 'cause as she was bein' chased and Rigobert was beatin' her, those braids ended up lookin' like they were stickin' straight out of the top of her head!).'

Ma Cidalise bursts out laughing out of her large, toothless mouth and heartily shakes her sagging bosom while repeating in a high-pitched voice: '*Man wè kòn djab-la, man di'w!*' ('I saw the devil's horns, I tell you!') She merrily mimes Ma Samson's alleged and ridiculous metamorphosis, fingers hooked like horns in her frizzy hair, which she manages to shape into a spike at each temple. Then she drops into a chair, hair unkempt, all tuckered out from her antics.

'You know, Ma Samson didn't have pretty, straight hair like yours! She had wool on her head, like me!' she adds while unceremoniously and speedily trying to flatten her 'pretend horns', returning her hairstyle to something a bit less diabolical.

Her aggressive fingernails disagreeably grate the tough, thick and dense foliage of her rebel hair, inextricable jungle of black vines entwined with grey vines, which she fiercely but unsuccessfully attempts to smooth.

'I'm goin' to look like a mad woman after all this clownin' around; only good for Colson's madhouse!' she concludes, just a bit annoyed.

Still out of breath, she casts a critical glance at the veranda floor and bluntly exclaims, 'What's this! My dear! you haven't mopped the floor yet! . . . Well, well, well . . . '

With a determined stride, she was heading towards the kitchen for mop and pail when Rehvana called her back, plaintive and pleading, like a sick child who's terrified of being left alone.

'No! Leave it! I'll do it later. You exhaust me, moving about like that. Relax, and come sit near me again. We have plenty of time . . .'

Rehvana wipes her burning forehead with the back of her weary hand. She feels a bit wobbly, and her eyelids droop; the rising sun's brightness compels her to shut her eyes. The slanted rays have gradually created opalescent and blurred geometric figures on the shadowy, old tile floor. Despite a vague and vacillating breeze, the air has grown heavy with heat; you see it more than you feel it, in the shade of the veranda, in the patient and progressive oppression of all in its path, in the hazy iridescence of expectation, borne by waves of light softly penetrating the clouds—those perpetual clouds!—perpetually above Vert-Pré.

'Such a pity to be seein' you like this! And where is 'e, that wretch! Must be in prison by now, if there's any justice in the world . . . ,' suggests Ma Cidalise, daydreaming, as if relishing the thought. You'd swear these simple words are enough to make her mouth water.

'Poor thing, to be so mistreated! There was a time when a lowlife like 'im didn't get 'way with it!'

But since her suggestion of prosecution and punishment produced no outward sign of support or assent from Rehvana, she pensively lowers her voice and stares off into the distance.

' . . . Ah, yes, there were also the evil spells they cast on dead people! And not only on dead people! . . . Do you know the story of Jeanne?'

' . . . '

'It's a true story. I wasn't around then, but the folks who told me 'bout it, you can trust 'em, they were family. Jules was promised to Esther, and they were engaged, pretty much like people do today. Esther's mother (Jeanne was her name) was 'fraid

that Jules would abandon Esther. She must've gone and got somethin' to make Jules stay. Jules was the captain of my uncle's
pirogue, and 'e woke up tir'd ev'ry single, blessed day, 'e was
sleepin' poorly, 'e was havin' tons of nightmares and dreams, 'e
got up in the mornin' 'cause 'e had to, but 'e jus' didn't feel good.
So 'e goes to see someone to make things right. When the psychic
had finished listenin' to 'im, 'e looked 'im straight in the eye and
said, "Well then, my dear Monsieur, this is serious business,
'cause all this trouble you now have, it's comin' from somebody
real close to you." Jules said, "But how?" "You came to me to
learn the truth, so here it is, your future mother-in-law is puttin'
a spell on you!"

'So Jules told 'im, "Listen, if she cast a spell on me, perhaps
it's possible to break it?" And that's exac'ly what they decided.
But the wizard warned 'im: "She'll have to be careful, 'cause I can
protect you, but for your mother-in-law, I can't guarantee . . ."
Jules said, "Well, too bad, 'cause I ain't gonna stay like this." So
the psychic did 'is job. Each night, in 'is sleep, Jules began to see
how 'is mother-in-law would lead 'im to the river behind the
house, and would baptize 'im, night after night, again and again,
and of course, that's what was makin' 'im so tir'd. But when the
sorc'rer's work was done, Jules began to feel well again. Then
one night, after the evenin' meal, Jeanne was sittin' in a corner,
doin' some sewin' with a needle in her hand . . . Esther was there,
and Jules too, and there was maybe another two or three folks,
I don't know. They saw the oil lamp start smokin', and then
blowin' out, and the whole room was fillin' with thick smoke.
They were all surprised, since the door had been tightly shut.
They quickly lit the lamp again. When light came back, they all
noticed right 'way a big, white duck where Jeanne had been
sittin'. Then the duck took off and left through the keyhole. From
that night on, Jeanne couldn't be found . . . A week went by, and
Jules told Esther the whole story and she cried her eyes out, and
after she was done with cryin' all the tears in her body, Esther
said, "Well, you can't disrespect my mother like that, even so, so
go back to your sorc'rer and ask if 'e can do somethin' for her."

'Jules went back to 'im and told 'im 'bout ev'rythin'—the big duck, the smoke, ev'rythin' that took place. The wizard replied, "Yes, I already know all this, but it'll be difficult, I've already warned you. I can try again . . . Come back in two days time." So Jules came back two days later and the wizard said, "Listen, go to this place at the crossroads after Fonds-Saint-Jacques, and you'll find your mother-in-law there—she'll have a letter in her right hand and a five hundred franc bill in her left. You mustn't take the letter or the money from her hands. She'll try to give 'em to you, but you mustn't take anything from her hands! Jus' the opp'site, you've got to be gettin' her to put the money and letter into her own pocket. And then you tell her it's all been fixed and she can come home with you." Jules did as he'd been told and Jeanne followed 'im home.

'Jeanne stayed put in the house two or three days, and then was never seen again. Madame Destournelles, who owned the pastry shop on rue Blondel at the time, was a relative of theirs ('cause like I said, it's a family story). She hears somethin' unusual happened: the body of a woman was discovered on the bank of the Levassor Canal. The body had been stoned, and was "disfigured" and covered with scratches and wounds . . . A crowd rushed to go see the woman: it was a pretty sickenin' sight. So she shows up, snakes her way to the front row, jus' like that, takes a look and recognizes Jeanne . . . No one ever claimed the body of the poor woman, and it was Madame Destournelles who told ev'ryone at Fonds-Saint-Jacques that the body found in Fort-de-France was Jeanne . . .

'Neighbourhood folks said that durin' the whole night before, they heard screams (no, it wasn't a duck, it was a human voice that was screamin', screamin', as if someone was bein' chased and beaten). They thought it was a husband givin' 'is wife a good beatin' and they didn't pay no attention.'

Ma Cidalise savours the moment, relishing the effect of these atrocities on her audience. A pair of slender anoles hang upside down on the crest of a wall and focus their eyes—fine protrusions of small orbs, kindly and artfully black, outlined, as if with an eyeliner of the most intense fluorescent blue—on the storyteller. Their minuscule ears—imperceptible lateral slits—are open and attentive, but their quick, pink tongues coyly lap up ants, with rapid flicks of the neck, affected and graceful. The top of each one's narrow head is all glittery and gold with a perfect and peaceful allure. Rehvana quietly leans on the railing and seems to be on the lookout for something, through lowered eyelids. After a slight shrug, Ma Cidalise plants her feet, stands up straight with hands on hips, facing the sun already high in the sky.

'My God! It's so late! Gotta go fix a li'l somethin' to eat . . . And here I'm tellin' you tales when the sun's shinin' bright! Bad luck's gonna come bite me!'

But no force in the world could remove her, at least as long as Rehvana needs her—she, herself, and the strange kind of intoxication Ma Cidalise instills in her, dizzying her with tales as if she were nourishing her with oblivion. For now, it's all she can do for Rehvana. Despite the feeble protests of the young woman, Ma Cidalise has almost finished doing the housework, nonchalantly gliding across the tile floor, fast as a fairy, from tap to closet, modulating her delivery and tone to the rhythm of her back-and-forth movements—raising her voice in a declamatory way when she moves away, and softly lowering it in a tender decrescendo each time she approaches the hammock, without a pause in lulling Rehvana's lethargy, so that the young woman notices nothing. Soon she'll bring her a portion of her own meal; otherwise she's sure the young one will indefinitely remain there, not bothering to eat.

Back from one of her trips to the kitchen, Ma Cidalise finishes firmly twisting the mop and, since Rehvana is still not moving, she segues into another story: 'Well, I'm not proud or anythin', but I can't believe how dirty the floor was! A real pigsty! . . . Since you love magic so much, it's too bad you never got to know the cobbler from Marigot. He had the *Petit Albert*, the big book of magic and sorc'ry. My cousin Jude told me this cobbler had taken to 'im 'cause 'e looked sharp as a tack when 'e was li'l, and was a good student at school. He showed Jude things! *Kouté sa* (Listen to this): one fine day 'e told 'im, "Can you see li'l Chimène, *qui ka pasé* (who's walking) down the street over there? Well, let me show you what I can do." He closed 'is eyes, puckered up 'is face like a monkey, and *mi ti manzèl-la ki ka rété tout soudain en mitan lari-a* (and the young girl stopped kind of sudden-like in the middle of the street) to look left, right, all around. And then she resumed her walkin'. She was 'bout two hundred yards from them, and then she came up to the cobbler, and said, "*Ou kriyé mwen, mèt Pilate?*" ("You called me, Master Pilate?") He replied, "*Han-han, manzèl, ay fè zafè'w!*" ("No, young lady, go back to your business!")

'My father had a real sharp mind and 'e read all kinds of polit'cal books ('e was a "rationaliss-marxiss"), and he didn't want to believe in these sorc'rer stories. But 'e couldn't sleep, poor guy, and each night he'd lay back in 'is rockin' chair on the porch and stay there enjoyin' his Cuban cigar. (In any case, 'e couldn't smoke inside, 'cause my mother couldn't stand it. She hated the smell.)

'There was a large stone staircase leading up to the church, and then to the cem'tery. My father built a house at the top of these stairs. From there 'e could see the sea, and most of the entire town. Well, one night, it was 'bout one o'clock in the mornin', my father started hearin' some noise that kept gettin' closer: boom bang! boom bang! He looked in the direction where it came from—in the middle of the stairs, a bit past the cobbler's shop, there was this orb of light, tall as a standin' man. It was slowly movin' up the stairs, luminous like a li'l sun. Yes, that ball was climbin' those stairs by i'self! . . . Ev'ry once in a while, it would stop—you might say it appeared to be strugglin'. My father raised the brim of his panama hat, which was coverin' his face. He opened 'is eyes wide, then 'e closed 'em, open again, closed, open again. He thought 'e was havin' a bad dream. But the ball kept on goin', slowly, unrushed, boom bang, boom bang, and my father squeezed 'is eyes shut, 'cause he ended up thinkin' 'e was sleepin' for good. After two or three l'il minutes though, 'e opened them again anyways—the orb was now facin' 'is house, on the other side of the street, leavin' only that street between 'im and that orb.

'He thought to hisself: "Time to go inside, now." So, no sooner said than done, 'e jumped from 'is seat and ran back into the house, bam! And at that very same second 'e was double lockin' the door, baroom! 'e heard a great commotion on the porch, as if somethin' was explodin', which made light pour in under the door, and all over the place, and my father 'eard a loud voice sayin': "*Orès, ou ni chans!*" ("Orestes, you are lucky!") Ah, my dear! I was so mis'rable the day Master Orestes really did die! That day marked the beginnin' of my sufferin', me bein' so li'l and all!'

'...'

'If you're not feelin' so good, *pov ti bolonm!* (poor li'l thing!) go get some rest. You don't wanna go lay down upstairs in your bedroom for a li'l nap? Must be a bit less hot up there ...'

'No, not in the bedroom! Please, keep going ... What happened after that?'

The thought of the bedroom and the canopy bed with its twisted posts gave her the shivers.

'Well, then, Master Pilate tried to teach 'is craft to Jude, the slacker ... For e'sample, I told you a while back 'bout the magical totors, but I can tell you, 'e also knew how to be conjurin' up magical kicks. There were these danmié dancers who'd have their feet bewitched. With their magical foot, guys would be fightin' the champion, or their mentor, or another one of the best dancers around. You don't know what "danmié" is? There was a field planted with sea grape and almond trees and, on the other side, there was a li'l s'vannah. Ev'ry year on Holy Satu'day there was a feast day, and a crowd of folks came from all over to go see the danmié. It was a kind of martial arts fightin' 'tween two men. There was a drum with the drummer sittin' on top of it. Usually, 'e banged and 'e sang at the same time. The drum was a big vat built 'specially for the occasion, with sheepskin on top, maybe a meter across, 'cause the drummer—they call 'im a "percussionist" now, but I ain't never heard that name before—was sittin' astride the drum, with one leg on either side, and with 'is heel, 'e was able to change the sound of the drum—it was so nice! And behind 'im, there was the other part of the drum, and another guy was holdin' the li'l sticks, rat-a-tat-tat, rat-a-tat-tat! The drum controlled the rhythm of the match. Those who came to dance the danmié were young 'uns, but you had to be real good to make it inside the circle. It was a battle of the best—the ones bein' at the top of their class: the best from Dominante, the best from Saint-Guinaud, the best from Fond-Papin, the best from all around! The danmié started 'round two, three o'clock in the afternoon and didn't last all day, no! jus' maybe one or two hours max. Folks would be comin' down from Dominante, Morne-des-Esses, Fonds-Saint-Jacques and Plateforme to see a nice danmié in Marigot.

'The story goes that one of 'em—a champion named Fernand Joséphine—had gone undefeated for three, four, maybe even five years, until a young upstart had a spell cast on 'is leg to be bringin' down the champion with jus' one kick. On that fine day, the champion had been warned, and he'd caref'lly managed to stay clear of that foot in order to beat that cheat. But the poor wretch, 'e wasn't supposed to keep his foot under a spell for too long ('cause if someone bewitched your foot, you had to kick with it to break the spell)! So there was only one thing 'e could do. There was an enormous tree there, a large sea grape tree, right in the middle of the s'vannah where they did the danmié, and 'e gave it a big kick! That tree shrivelled and died, like it had been struck by lightnin'. It stood there for years 'cause no one would chop it down for fear of supe'tissions.

'Yeah, you don't know what people do when they're 'fraid of devils and she-devils! When I was all li'l, I went to the funeral of a li'l cousin named Zozor. We took the bus, Marcelle, me and the others, and 'bout six kilometres from Vauclin, we see an old woman selling coal who wants to buy a ticket to get onboard. So the driver says, "What ticket? There's no room for you, not even a li'l one, and all these people are dressed in white, all white, so don't be gettin' 'em all dirty!" Me and all my cousins, we were wearin' our best mournin' clothes, spotless and starched, whiter than the whites of your eye. "You really don't have a li'l corner for me?"

'"Do you see any room? *Loto-a plen!*" (The bus is jam-packed!)

'"Well, then, you're not goin' to make it past that li'l mango tree over there!"

'And the bus goes drivin' on and stops right at the foot of the mango tree . . . So my cousin says to the driver: "Joseph, look, enough foolin' around! Don't go stoppin' here, my dear, let's go!"

'"Well, Monsieur, the bus can't go no further."

'And it was true, the bus couldn't get goin' again. The old woman caught up with the bus: "*Pa zot, han? Mi zot!* (If it isn't you again!) *Man té di zot ki zot* . . . (I already told you . . .)" She kept on walkin' and the bus stayed all broke down. My dear, we got to Vauclin on a bull-drawn cart!'

'Really?'

'A few of us . . . and by then the funeral was over. It was well past nine o'clock at night, and we were still in Vauclin. We were gettin' a li'l worried, but 'round ten o'clock, we saw the mail truck that was supposed to take us back to Fort-de-France. But we arrived there 'round the same time as the body—Zozor's body bein' brought back. So we saw somethin' we never seen before: when you carry a body all day, those who are carryin' it, they chuck their tir'dness onto the corpse by makin' all kinds of gestures at the coffin.

'I couldn't help smilin': I wasn't very used to seein' this sort of thing 'cause I was so li'l, too li'l to see all this. And later you say to you'self, "OK now, what should you be doin'? You should be mournin'; let's be mournin'!" And then you go stand next to your parents . . . When you're young, dear! *Man pa sav kisa sé boug-la bwè avan yo rantré adan légliz-la!* (I don't know what those guys were drinkin' before goin' to church!), but they played the funeral march like it was a beguine! So my friend and I who'd been mournin' so far, we were so embarr'ssed (in fact, we thought we'd die laughin'), that I bent down to be tyin' my shoelaces . . . but the entire funeral procession walked all over me! After I get up, I'm at the back of the cortege, and I see Joseph Maurice standin' next to me. *I té kité lantèman!* *Tèlman i té ka mò ri* (He'd left the cortege! He was laughin' hard), jus' like me. We began to feel 'shamed 'cause Zozor was a good li'l friend, and they sent 'im to the river and 'e drowned. (Back then, folks died! They died of typhus, appendicitis, malnutrition . . . I saw mounds of schoolmates die. Many didn't make it outta element'ry school . . .) So, let me tell you, I was feelin' lots of guilt, oh, yes, guilt! I was 'shamed, you hear me? I was cryin' my eyes out 'cause of this, and so we arrive at the church, and then, right in the middle of church, who do I see? Gabrielle Phanor! Fat Gaby, with four big coiled mounds of hair on her head and a stink bug suckin' her blood on the back of her neck. This Zozor day had turned into such an unlucky day. Gabrielle began to itch like the dickens . . . And guess what happened next . . .

'*Rôye papa!* Oh-la-la! All hands on deck! Looks like the men have arrived! There they are! There's Enryck and the other one, the one with the mongoose hair. Wouldcha look at that! He's back, and with that con-artist-with-claws, at that! From what dive have they been bounced? They must've been traipsin' around . . . Why do they need to be bringin' all that stuff in here? *Sa sa yé sa?* (What's this?) Man, that looks heavy! And who's comin' now? Who's this one? I don't know this car . . . '

Ma Cidalise twists her neck as she leans over the railing, painfully torn between her insatiable curiosity and her refusal to confront the two men.

'So what's this, huh? What are they cartin' 'round like this now? Where did they get all this stuff from? Can you tell me what all this movin' business is about?'

' . . . '

'No-good Chabin! Damned money-or-your-life thief! I can't stand seein' this dirty bum . . . Let me go, dear, otherwise the Mista is gonna say Ma Cidalise filled your head with crazy stories, and you do nuthin' but stay and listen to gossip! I'm outta here 'cause I don't wanna put up with 'is insults and threats. So, see you later, God willin'!'

With a sweeping of skirts—halfway between laughter and alarm—Ma Cidalise leaps towards the hammock, light as a kayali on long legs, though one with twisting veins and bulbous knees, above which a majestic caboose swings through the air— intoxicating and female, fragrant, bouncing, tamed. Then she affectionately kisses Rehvana goodbye. Hands on hips, she plants herself in front of the young woman—authoritarian as a head- wind—briefly scrutinizes the thin, wan face, begins to say some- thing, gives up and abruptly spins around in a tense swish of skirts, pretending once more to be panicked.

'So long, Mam'selle Rehvana, I'll be goin' now! I'll bring you shredded-cod salad, in a bit. I won't be able to be bringin' you turkey—but beggars can't be choosers!' shouts the old woman without looking back as she walks down the uneven front steps.

She bypasses the grass, in order to leave unseen, unrecog- nized, through the side of the house, avoiding the garage and a possibly bad run-in. She abandons her story, the corpse and her young friend, still half-asleep in the torpid late morning air, but only after stealthily placing an old, couch grass broom behind the door, so as to shorten the visit of the unwelcome guest. She's run out of time to slip into the kitchen to grab a pinch of salt, which she'd gladly have spread on the threshold after Chabin walked in.

This would have ensured his never coming back.

She walks away as fast as she can, her buoyant rear end swinging left and right, up and down, swivelling around with each of her fast steps.

'No point in me stickin' 'round, waitin' for this li'l nitwit with no father or mother to curse me out and throw mud at my face!' she loudly proclaims, to no one in particular.

THIS TIME, ENRYCK DECIDED TO BRING HER ALONG in the evening. She knows too well what unfounded suspicion has prompted this surprising honour, and she still feels its cruel sting on her cheeks, but she's happy all the same: she'll be with him—and that's the only thing that counts. As luck would have it, chubby Chabin had suddenly faked a mysterious illness and had turned down Enryck's offer to join him on their usual nightly escapades.

Rehvana had hit the jackpot: a falling-out between them and a chance to go crabbing.

She could care less about the big scene, which never reached the level of violence—far from it!—of the fights caused by her own jealousy, because she was so excited by the unexpected joy of being included (O miracle!) in this exclusive pleasure for men, and by the chance to experience it with Enryck—this Antillean ritual, which keeps half of the island busy preparing for the Easter matoutou. She would have loved for him to take her fishing far from the coast—just the two of them in the frail gum-tree boat—instead of dragging along that big, no-good lug. A few lucky times she'd settled for helping him throw the fishing net, side by side, on the beach at Grand-Anse. She'd flex her muscles, soft and small, in the shadow of his tall body of living ebony, in those early days when the man's munificence rewarded her with a seaside vacation.

That night, however, she would have to make do with crabbing. Rehvana was greatly looking forward to it, even though it only involved spending the night in the car in the middle of nowhere, to slog, hour by hour, into the dark sludge of the mangroves, and grab the poor land crabs who'd been lured into a rat trap with a piece of sugar cane—even though she knew that the car's interior would still hold the perfume of other nights, other fishing expeditions, other hunts that didn't include her.

Chabin had overstayed his welcome—bawdy-eyed, with all his pale rolls of fat and his obscene potbelly spread on the couch—while Enryck finished working on his traps. Rehvana busied herself beside him. Full of goodwill and novice zeal, she was devoutly soaking up Enryck's deep explanations and did her best to make herself useful without asking too many questions. Guided by Enryck—completely confident with his 'science'—she handed him bits of string and wire, wood scraps and springs, always conscious of inebriated Chabin's menacing eyes fixed on the small of her back. Seemingly lost in the enjoyment of his umpteenth ti-sec—a generous glass of white rhum agricole, without sugar syrup or lemon, which he christened his 'non-virgin sugar-cane juice' and noisily slurped—he was contentedly keeping a close watch on the couple as they checked the rat traps, as if he wanted to make sure, before he left the place, that Enryck would really go crabbing this evening and, as a result, Rehvana would be home alone that night.

She no longer could stand his satisfied tongue-clacking, his sinister silence, but Chabin could do no wrong and she knew that all too well! After all, he was Enryck's childhood friend, his partner in crime for all his escapades; it was turning out to be impossible to fault any of sacrosanct Chabin's actions. The red-headed Negro was worth a thousand times more than she, and anyway, her greatest fault, no matter what she said, was that she was only a woman. Rehvana had quickly learnt to refrain from making any comment, complaint or critical remark. She had even come to regret and view as blasphemous the few reflections she'd bashfully dared to express at the start. Nothing seemed to be able to drive a wedge between Enryck and his seedy and depraved sidekick. In fact, he had such a high opinion of Chabin that Rehvana had begun to blame herself for her instinctive antipathy for the one she couldn't help herself from regarding as a harmful intruder, a useless slug, venomous and vile. She had gone so far as to feel guilty, accusing herself of being jealous and possessive. She forced herself to make an effort to be pleasant with Chabin, persuading herself that her possessiveness was the only reason for her detesting the fair-headed, chubby macho guy.

When he kissed her hello, Rehvana inhaled his acrid sweat without shrinking back. As he squashed his thick, leech-like lips to her cheeks, drooling with desire and rum, she fought the urge to sponge down her face and wash away the sour slime torment-ing her skin. She was trying so hard that when Chabin faked being extremely tired and pretended to go home to bed, Enryck barely waited for him to cross the threshold before laying into the dumbstruck young woman, pestering her with offensive ques-tions, accusing her of being provocative and giving the other guy reason to believe that she, Rehvana, wanted nothing more than to see him, once she was alone, as soon as her live-in lover turned his back. She had certainly seduced him—that much was clear. Otherwise his friend would never have had the thought himself!

'I'm not up for crabbing,' he'd mumbled, with a burning look in his eyes. 'It's not crabs I want to hunt tonight . . . '

Even though Enryck had belatedly grasped the meaning of the salacious insinuations whispered by his friend in Rehvana's ear as he left, he had held her solely responsible. When Rehvana had dared to mention Chabin's lecherous looks, when she had taken a risk, shaking from her own boldness, to report the sug-gestive winks and, finally, when she'd rashly blurted out the truth about the prolonged kisses, so obvious, which she'd had to endure, without protest, ad nauseam, for fear she'd displease Enryck, she only succeeded in unleashing his blind rage.

And there, where the lascivious lips had left their stain, where Rehvana had just put up with their repulsive suction just to keep the peace—there, Enryck had, once more, one time too many, slapped his large hand—the hand of a furious man.

Nevertheless, against all odds, he'd immediately turned this unde-served roughness into great happiness. Since there was no other way to dodge the risk of disgrace because of the woman and still partake of a profitable, as well as pleasant, pursuit, he'd decided to bring her along. With his strong, powerful arm holding her so tight he almost hurt her, he'd led her to the damp mangrove swamp.

From behind the shutters, Ma Cidalise, misty-eyed, had blessed the couple as they left arm in arm.

SITTING ON A CHAIR IN THE SHADE, in front of her door, Ma Cidalise is fashioning hair curlers from scraps of newspaper she briskly rips, to tightly coil her strands of hair—detangled with difficulty and attacked with a rasping, wide-toothed comb. Her hair is sectioned into eight, then sixteen, then thirty-two thick tufts, where Rehvana gets the chance to read the daily news, here and there—'tourist safety', 'jobs wanted', 'key problems that obstruct', 'a number of people', 'we're saying a number of people', 'social issues', 'they can afford to indulge in'—before they are twisted like corkscrews by the large, bony hands. The morning hairstyling ritual is fierce, furious and long. Head lowered, relentlessly raking, with energy and grit, a tangle of shorter strands on the nape of her neck, Ma Cidalise hadn't seen her approaching.

'Is it you, dear? What a nightmare gettin' this mop of hair combed out! Damn, what a pain! I'd love to trade your hair for the blackberry bush on my head, God, my Saviour!'

Aggressive and intense, comb or newspaper scrap clasped between her lips, seated on the body part where her generous womanliness has long been hiding, but in such a way that she looks somehow deformed, with the remnants of her cleavage rising with the effort, hair all wrapped up or standing on end, Ma Cidalise is a scary sight. Rehvana uneasily dances around her, attempts a few vague, disjointed words that make little sense, wrings her hands, unconsciously clenching them so tight they cause her knuckles to ache. As if hypnotized, she repeatedly digs her right thumbnail so deeply into the palm of her left hand that it leaves crescent-shaped marks, and then, for the time being, giving up hope for any help from this shaggy-haired gorgon—a kind of stone-statue-come-to-life straight from a horror film, with grotesque, heartless, robotic movements—Rehvana beats a silent retreat towards home, as once more she's overcome with a strange feeling of guilt. She leaves without a word, bleeding from the palm of her hand—like an unheeded official seal of distress— stigmata she doesn't even feel and which she inflicted upon herself.

'Hush, it's time!' Ma Cidalise had abruptly whispered, as one of her fingers emerged from swishing in her dishevelled hair and landed on her mouth, vertically, as though Rehvana's feeble attempts to speak from half-closed lips could possibly run the risk of drowning out the throbbing brass of Louis Armstrong's 'New Orleans Function' whose roaring brass horns suddenly filled the room.

Under no circumstances does Ma Cidalise miss the daily obituaries broadcast morning, noon and night on the radio. Every day, dropping everything—a loyal audience—she never fails to glue her ear to the transistor radio to find out who has died—it's vital to her life.

Ma Cidalise's hand was waving frenetically in the direction of the radio to signal Rehvana to increase the volume, since the old lady was stubbornly keeping her head lowered and hadn't noticed the young woman leaving on tiptoes, with a heavy heart, not daring to interrupt to confess her secret.

In the humidity of the morning drizzle, thick with heavy vapours, the voice of a tired mulatto woman rattled off a host of deaths, announcing, with a jaded tone: 'We regret to inform you of the death of Mr Misanthrope Modestin Arcade, in his eighty-second year, decorated with the Order of Agricultural Merit; the death of Mrs Milidate Amante Apolline Edouarlise, known as Siméone, in her ninety-fourth year, a member of all the sororities of the Church; the death of Mr Bochote Pélardie Agésilas, in his seventy-sixth year . . . ,' her voice droning on and on as Rehvana was slowly moving away: ' . . . This notice is shared on behalf of her family, her partner Théotiste Omer Philippe, known as Pipo, her daughters, Erepmoc Tertulie, Hannibale, George and Rolantine, her grandchildren and great-grandchildren, her daughter Yoyote Félixine, known as Mother-Godmother, her nephews and nieces, other blood relatives, in-laws, friends, and by the Brothers and Sisters of Macouba Eucharistic Awakening; bus service will be available . . . ' Ma Cidalise's radio wailed so loudly in the early morning hours that Rehvana heard it all the way home, though she had put her fingers in her ears, and didn't bother to wipe the tears quietly rolling down her cheeks.

THE MAN IS IN PAIN.

Despite the fasting and the trance, the man's body is twisted in agony. At the end of a strange dance—plodding, bouncy, simple and grandly formal, clumsy and sublime, his face both contorted and inspired, he presents the tortured sole of his foot to the sky, to the goddess. In a single motion mid-air, he spins and slices the top of a row of lemons placed on a leaf canopy. Leaning on the two officiants, their linen-wrapped hands holding the long, horizontal sword, he leaps onto the sharp-edged blade with a dreadful *ooouf*! He holds this pose for a good long while, shifting most of his body weight onto the sabre's edge, despite the negligible support of his hands on his bearers' shoulders. The great coolie—breathtaking with his body chiselled against the sky—deeply inhales to control the suffering, and with each inspiration draws pleasure from pain. He apportions his torment into brief, muted cries which aren't moans but at times speed up towards a paroxysm of pain. To attenuate the torture of the blade, he stands first on one foot, then on the other, focused, and draws staccato sighs from the depths of his half-naked chest drenched in sweat—a fanatical panting where ecstasy and agony blend in a vibrant evocation.

Caught up in the suffering of the man who puffs and pants, lifted, solemn, on the edge of the sword, and in his smouldering Indian eyes, dark as soot in his trance, with burning embers meandering and drifting somewhere else, Rehvana is enthralled. A finger landed on her forehead and dabbed a sticky grey paste between her brows. She barely reacted when the honed blade severed the two bent heads. The beheaded bodies writhed for a while, and then the sacrificed sheep were dragged aside, leaving a spatter of bright blood on the trampled grass.

From the unfettered spirit of the 'Coolie Good Lord', did she draw the courage to admit to Enryck the long-held secret she hadn't dared confess to Ma Cidalise the other morning? The old woman had to flush out the truth herself and deploy a thousand irrefutable arguments to convince Rehvana to tell Enryck, pointing out that each passing day only made her situation worse and concluding, after many words of advice and old wives' tales on how best to break the news: 'Anyways, even if the guy is violent, 'e won't split your head open 'cause you're knocked up! But what a story, eh? As far as I'm concerned, men who father children when they're not married, well . . . I can tell you're comin' from France . . . But if the Mista is happy with you . . . Even if that child isn't his . . . '

WITH INTERMINABLE SLOWNESS, Enryck inspects Rehvana's full curves.

She'd waited until her belly's swelling was unmistakable and was living proof of her pregnant state. At first, he stormed, gave her a first smack, and then exploded, in the throes of a murderous rage, when the undeniable evidence hit him, despite the confusion of his mind—insolent evidence of dates and quick calculations staring him in the face. Then, little by little, the respite came, his remorse, replete with all his tenderness, because Rehvana lets herself be pushed around, since Rehvana offers him, once more, the gold and amber of her malleable patience. Babbling loving and vacuous words, Enryck caresses the soft skin of her thigh where his belt buckle had left its blue imprint. Finally, as Rehvana capsizes, without regard to her condition or pain, he penetrates her, as if to erase the shame. Still shaken by the Indian ceremony's singular and disturbing splendour, both stunning and raw, where Ma Cidalise took her this morning to distract her and make the most of the lucky charm—the third eye—which a smiling young girl draws on your forehead while your ears are subjected to an unintelligible Tamil blessing, and you're standing in full sun on a banana-tree plantation in the northern part of the island near a small temple lavishly decorated with statues, pennants and lit candles, where the oil destined for grilling mutton chops after the sacrifice awaits at the foot of the altar in yellow plastic cans, next to a large, blackened frying pan and colourful figurines, among the candles' incandescent, cascading wax, Rehvana submits to Enryck, as if the Indian's trance had spread throughout her body with the purity of the fast—a catharsis—in a miraculous and brief yet enduring union.

When she woke and talked to him about an abortion, Enryck treated her like a criminal. She only succeeded in provoking a new, unexpected bout of fury, much worse than the night before, after which Enryck—magnanimous, pacified again—triumphantly assured her that he loved her enough, cared for her enough and was strong enough to live with her shame and accept her child.

The One and the Other

Dear Stranger,

*Since I don't know how I should be addressing You, Dearest
Sister . . .*

*You seem to be living it up: fashion shows, et cetera, et
cetera . . . (I saw a photo of you in* Antilla; *I found the magazine
at a kiosk on boulevard Saint-Michel, and it helped me feel a little
bit closer to you.)*

*So Enryck's business appears to be doing well; I'm so pleased
for you. But that's no reason for remaining silent.*

*How's your pregnancy going? In any case, I'll be there for
my godson's birth. I say 'my godson' because I have a hunch it
would be good for you to have a son. But enough sexist talk since
these things are silly. (Speaking of which, is it true, what I've
heard, that in Martinique, the first birth bonus is seven hundred
francs for a girl and twelve hundred francs for a boy?) Make a
girl, if you want; no one would accuse me of being part of that
vile herd of male chauvinist pigs, just because of an innocent
wish—and by the way, it's not only a male crowd—our own sisters are well represented among them, to boot! So, do what you
want, but do it well.*

And, for God's sake, write to me.

*You still don't have a phone; you don't send a single
letter . . . Have you counted the number of phone calls you've
made to me since my return to Paris? A few minutes, at most, in*

constant fear that you'll run out of coins! What a nuisance that no one can call collect from Martinique!

Honestly, I think you're taking things too far! I'd like a letter, a real letter!

I can easily see why you don't want to write to Jérémie (who, however, would jump for joy, poor guy, to read even one word from you). But I, your 'favourite-older-sister', what have I done to you? Now what have you made up in that head of yours?

Anyway, I'll be in Fort-de-France soon, you'll tell me all your little nonsense, and we'll go dance the zouk like there's no tomorrow. Cross my heart and hope to die, I promise I'll end my rant!

It was much too short at Christmas; this time, I think I can stay longer.

I haven't got much news to tell: nihil novi sub sole—*nothing new under the sun—I'm studying for my midterms, and the Sorbonne is the same as ever, except that the statue was moved . . .*

It's hard for me to joke around; your silence worries me.

I'll stop here: I can't tell you about my life when I don't know anything about yours, or so little . . . You seem to distrust me and that hurts. But even if I no longer have the honour of being your confidante (and to this day I still don't know what I've done to deserve the blame), please know you can always rely on me.

No matter what happens, know in your heart that I am and will always be your 'older-sister-who-loves-you'.

(But do you still love me with your 'l'il SweeTART heart'?)

Yours,

Mat

PS: I realize that I mentioned Jérémie without specifying that he's doing well, thank you very much! I guess you couldn't care less but I'll tell you anyway.

Beware of Marie-Aude, she's on the prowl . . . Oh, yes! Your departure has transfigured her and I'm afraid she's pulling out all the stops to comfort your handsome Desdichado.

Matildana's letters all went unanswered.

Not only has Rehvana always loathed writing—and especially writing to Matildana, who was her class' best student in dictation and who would condescendingly wrinkle her Cleopatraesque nose at her sister's whimsical, one-of-a-kind spelling—but she doesn't know where to begin to unravel the tangled tale of these tumultuous crises, these reconciliations followed by new upheavals. She can't even bring herself to admit that she doesn't dare confess to her sister the failure of her 'triumphant return'.

What should she tell her of her rocky Calvary of wasted works and barren attempts?

One day Enryck will find the letters and, without even reading them, will slap Rehvana, forbidding her to reply to her 'bitch of a sister'.

Rays of afternoon sun creep in and pierce the shade of the vast veranda. The two young women, motionless and silent, lie side by side on two rickety, old beach chairs. The thick wooden frames and canvas cushion their heads in such a way they can't quite see each other. Rehvana's chair squeals when she throws a leg over one side and leaps up.

She takes her time stretching, feline, head raised towards the sky, lost in thought.

With hands clasped behind her neck, she stands, drawing out the silence, the thin slits of her eyes lost on the horizon. Suddenly, without looking at Matildana, she whispers, breaking the silence: 'Let's go inside! This sun is driving me nuts! I hate this slanted light. *We go back.*'

She sings these last words to a Creole tune, crooning away on a high note. Matildana shoots her a strange look—playful, perhaps—then complies without a word, following her into the living room where cloudier patches of sky cast a diffused brightness through delicate shards of light. Nevertheless, her sister, smiling, retreats further into the darkest nooks. She appears to be tottering a bit, like a blind child, or a child engaged in some kind of game she doesn't quite understand.

The long fingers lovingly clutch the small, precious, rolled-up cylinder of thin cardboard covered with occult writing and stained with brownish streaks—signs of prior smoking sessions.

Matildana's eyes follow Rehvana, crouched next to her on the rug, preparing her favourite blend—just as she'd learnt from the Ébonis in Paris—as she expertly rolls a twisted joint from the lucky Métro ticket she keeps on her at all times.

'You're not really going to smoke this? You're forgetting you're pregnant?'

'Pregnant? Oh! barely . . . It's hardly begun . . . I still have plenty of time before I'll have to stop . . . In the meantime, I need to smoke myself a good little joint—don't start being a killjoy, you just got here!'

Matildana ignores the provocation but the look in her eye speaks volumes.

'OK, OK! I tell you I'll stop . . . But quit staring at me like that—I haven't killed anyone yet!'

Engrossed in her careful work of thinning and twisting the crude paper cone at one end, face glacial and withdrawn, Rehvana looks up for only a brief second and raises an eyebrow at her sister.

'Here, why don't you have some? It'll do you good—you too—and keep you from blowing things out of proportion!

'If only you could see how grouchy you look . . . What's the point of travelling all this distance to come see me if you're going to sulk around!

'Come on, the evening is so sweet . . . Look, it's the exquisite hour . . . Don't you worry. Anyway, it's the only thing I have left!

' . . . The only thing I have left!' she adds, lowering her voice, her tone so opaque and painfully vague that Matildana purses her lips and finds nothing to say.

For a second, she bites her lips as if to hold something back, some words she doesn't want to say, no, not now! She was so happy to be here, to have come and seen Rehvana and get the chance to be alone with her tonight, together at last, after so much time apart—and then, when she'd finished talking about Paris, there had been a heavy silence filling the veranda.

Matildana's focus shifts away from the room for a moment, although her eyes remain fixed on Rehvana. Her thoughts are taking her back to the 'Other Side'—over there in Paris—to a former time, and to him—the one who had charged her, before her departure, with a mission doomed to fail from the start.

Matildana keeps quiet and resigns herself to observing a nervous and increasingly worked-up Rehvana, rummaging through the room, oblivious to her sister and the poor lizard she crushes under her foot. The mabouya flees, half-dead, guts spread on the tile floor, but her sister's face is the only image that haunts Matildana's mind.

'There are never any matches in this house! And I can't find that damn lighter! I wonder where it went; I've been looking for it for ever! It's beyond comprehension—I know I had it the other night, and Chabin was even admiring it and was making fun of us, saying we had gold everywhere in the family . . . '

'And then Enryck declared it a man's lighter, so what are you complaining about? It was a warning—one of the two must have taken it.'

'Of course . . . Always overflowing with faith and loving kindness for the people I love. In any case, I don't care. And instead of insinuating foul play, why not just lend me your share?!'

'My share? What share?' an irritated Matildana replies, midway between irony and rage, pretending to be confused. 'Ah, excuse me, I'm forgetting, you must mean "mine",' she adds after a few seconds and a furious shrug from Rehvana.

All her goodwill and strained patience seem to have evaporated at once, and she continues, feigning surprise but with deliberate indignation:

'I hadn't noticed how gifted you are at linguistic imitation! You've become a real "local" . . . How many expressions do you know like this? "We go back." "Lend me your share." You're truly soaking it up! And you're enjoying it, my God, you're enjoying it! Ooh la la! But she's teaching me lessons, the sneaky little one! It's true, I'm guilty of forgetting who I am. I speak the way they do in France, I dress like a wanton zorèy, without a petticoat under my skirt, I don't find it normal to be submissive to a bully and to forgive men for everything they do, simply because I'm a woman, and I know how to use possessive pronouns like the good French woman I am! In so doing, I suppose I'm betraying our slave ancestors . . . them again, always them!' she mutters through her teeth, subtly lowering her voice with aggravation that's barely contained.

'Oh yes, Rehvana, thank you very much! You catch me red-handed, renouncing my roots. I'm grateful you discreetly pry open my eyes, you let me see my treason, my despicable deception. It's true that by not saying "my share, your share", I'm insulting our forefathers' memory, I'm turning my back on my past, and I'm committing the crime of hiding my servile origins by forgetting that my great-great-great-grandfather was considered the property of a master and therefore could not say "my this, my that", for the good reason that he owned nothing, since he himself was owned by someone and didn't own himself. Yes, you must be right: the Negro slave would say "my share", because the only possession known to him was his portion of food—the sack of dried beans and the famous piece of cod distributed every now and then; so he took "his share", as handed out by the housekeeper, but, besides that, he couldn't imagine any other property . . . And how do you say that in Creole? "*Ta'w*, *ta mwen* . . . " Yes, that's it, a type of dative case to evoke the distribution: "It's yours, it's mine . . . " This theory appeals to me. Ah, well, it probably merits more study,' Matildana continues, frowning, in a deliberately pontificating, half-amused manner.

'I'll refer this matter to my professors at the Sorbonne with the utmost urgency as soon as I get back,' she goes on, in a pompous tone which barely conceals her growing irritation.

'As for me, I've lost my mind, I'm a traitor, I'm a renegade, I've gone astray, I'm guilty of shamelessly crossing the line in every sense, because what you call "return" seems to me no more than a carnivalesque regression, and because I don't practise systematic regression and I don't espouse the extremism of a fanatic fundamentalist.

'Woe is me, a pox on me, shame on me! I am denegrified. You can't stoop any lower than that . . . Yes, I forgot the catechism of that dear Abdoulaye—what a saint! Article one, *identity*: since I'm not wholly white at the start, if I don't negrify myself, then I'm nothing. I've got no colour or race, no identity or culture, I'm nothing. I'm a nothing, a nobody. I'm less than nothing. Because it's so important, so primordial, to be an authentic something! Even if you've got to force yourself to do it, and use tricks to cultivate the authentic. There are whites, Indo-Aryans, blacks, real Negros, "people of colour", Chinese people, Asians, Native Americans, Arabs, Jews and so forth. You absolutely must classify people, otherwise it creates havoc and folks lose their bearings. There are pure races—that's how the world stays balanced—blessed are those who are ethnically pure! Outside of race, there's no salvation! You can't just be a man, you have to choose a race—no mixing, no breaking ranks! Watch out for those who don't stay with their own, or who wander about . . . My goodness, you've got to know what you are and be proud of it!

'You're so kind, Rehvana, for leading your poor, lost sister back to original purity!' she continues, with an affected tone. 'How nice of you to use all possible means and, especially, by teaching from example, help restore her integrity! But please, you have to forgive me—I'm having a hard time with this. Grandmother used to recommend whitening the race as much as possible, and you, you say, "Blacken the race!" Don't hold it against me—I don't know what I should think any more . . . '

'When you're finished, Matildana, would you mind giving me your lighter? You can write all the essays you want on the topic, you can laugh at me if it makes you feel better—to each his own! But I'd like you to give me a light. It's useless to provoke me—I have no desire to discuss these things with you. I've already told you so.

'You can let off steam however you want but, first, be nice and go get me your lighter . . .

'Once I've lit this little marvel of a firecracker, you can soliloquize as much as you like.

'We've got all the time we need.

'The men are out on the town—the night is ours.'

'AGANILA? WHAT A STRANGE NAME! Do you really want to saddle all the girls in the family with unpronounceable names? Where did you find this one? Because when you add Matildana as a middle name, since I'm her godmother—thank you very much for asking, dearest—her ID card is going to look ridiculous! We at least have good old first names of saints, straight from prestigious hagiographies, to make up for our esteemed mother's romantic leanings: Rehvana Thérèse Blandine and Matildana Eulalie Scholastique Euphrosyne, amen! (Luckily she showed a bit more restraint for you . . .) Anyway, your names have a good Christian ring to them, and give a gal class! You've got great patron saints watching over you: Saint Thérèse of Avila, Jesus' fiancée, or, better yet, less mystical, Saint Thérèse of Lisieux. And Blandine, the sweet, virgin martyr who stood with her hands clasped in prayer in the lions' pit—exactly what you need, don't you agree? . . . Eulalie, the sweet talker, Scholastique, the scholar, and Euphrosyne, the righteous one—they set expectations, don't they? But Aganila Matildana Enricka—what a mess! What's she supposed to do with all this? Poor little munchkin! Your mother took no pity on you! Not only did she give you a string of impossible names but, to top it off, and against my better judgement, she added the caveman's name—granted, in a feminized form— but even that won't be enough to make it more civilized—you'd need a lot more to make it easier to swallow! Why is he involved in all this, anyway? . . . And where did you unearth the sweet Christian name of "Aganila"?'

The proud young mother brandishes the baby like a banner.

'Why, my dear, you don't know Agar? Who doesn't know Agar? My daughter is Agar's Daughter.'

'I may not know Agar, but sadly I know Aganila's father very well, and I'd like to know why you persist in hiding everything from him! You're completely nuts and, in any case, you've got no right. I, too, was completely out of my mind to agree to take part in this disastrous charade, but today I'm again asking you to release me from my promise. This makes no sense: Jérémie is a nice guy, one of a kind, he loves you, and you leave him moping and wandering around Paris like a lost soul while you've just had a beautiful baby and he's the father! I've had more than enough of your irrational whims. Do me a favour and call Jérémie on the phone right away. I'll drive you to town after you feed the baby. And how does your Enryck fit into all this? You tell me he's going to give his name to the baby? I'd like to see that!'

'You won't be seeing anything because it's none of your business. You're Aganila's godmother, period! I appreciate your coming for the christening and helping me out with the baby, thank you for everything, but for the rest—could you please just stay out of my life?'

'You're living your dream, my poor Rehvana—is this what you call your life?'

Matildana is trembling, her face inflamed, but her last words are hopelessly lost, since Rehvana suddenly exits the room, leaving behind the baby, who is delighted to be discovering the world, and Matildana, dismayed at being ignored.

'My daughter has no father, so what?' Rehvana proclaims, coming back with a baby bottle filled with toloman. 'She'll never be like the majority of our countrymen! Why are you so attached to this antiquated family structure—daddy, mummy, marriage—do you really think it's helped the two of us? For centuries, they stopped us from getting married, forbade us from starting a family, because a slave's child can't belong to a slave, since the slave doesn't belong to himself, as you yourself said so well, not long ago, and now you tell me that my daughter needs a "real" father, that Aganila can only be Jérémie's and therefore he must be told about her at all costs! I don't want to give you orders but I'd love for you to mind your own business. You told me you'd keep my secret! Matildana, remember: "A princess must always keep her promises . . . " So now, just give it a rest, OK?'

Matildana has long since given up trying to convince Rehvana; she knew she was wasting her time, just now, even though she kept attempting to persuade her. She knows she's powerless, almost useless.

In a few days, she'll be back in Paris, all the more powerless and useless.

Enryck lavishes extravagant gifts on the baby, paid for with God-only-knows-from-where-he-got-it money. It's almost as if he's acting an unfamiliar part with a surprising sense of duty. His schedule has been more consistent since the child's birth, and perhaps Matildana's presence in the house prompts him to spend most nights there and eat at regular hours with the two sisters— in short, to flaunt the settled lifestyle of a good father, good spouse and good brother-in-law, on the whole. All smiles, he goes through the motions of being part of a well-ordered, married existence, ostensibly submitting to the pseudo-routines of a household that's well maintained, which had never been the case in the past—not that he would have respected them, anyway. For a good ten days, he even spared them the sight of his friend Chabin, mysteriously excluded from these friendly family gatherings around the newborn child. But the two women have to endure his own presence—perverse and contemptuous—during these touching dinners by the oil lamp, where one woman's icy eyes go right through his athletic build, without acknowledging him, seated straight across from her at the monstrous wooden table, while the other, lost in silent prayer, keeps a plaintive eye on the baby, soothed at last. They have to sit through these evenings in which the bleak echoes of his inept jokes reverberate in the large room, because no one feels like laughing. Rehvana was responsible for the seating arrangements and had laid out the place settings with what she'd salvaged from the incredible mess in the kitchen and the rickety old silverware cabinet, which had survived an earthquake a long time ago: a set of unmatched but exquisitely engraved crystal glasses, a few porcelain plates with chipped gold trim, three pairs of tarnished silver forks she'd revived with lemon and a sand rub, and harmless knives with blades blunted by time. Rehvana, spectral and expressionless, constantly gets up to watch over Aganila or serve the next dish. She only finds a semblance of strength to imperiously protest and clutch Matildana's shoulder when the sister attempts to leave her seat to clear the table. To her fingers' pressure, she adds the unbearable weight of her weary gaze, immoderately despotic and pleading, so much so that Matildana complies and remains seated across from Enryck, wondering why Rehvana is so insistent.

Ferociously eating, with forced cheer, the master of the house, between two hoarse swigs, continues to soliloquize in his Cyclops voice, coarse from booze and his salacious thoughts, which the high walls coldly echo back to him as if from beyond the grave—the only response other than the clinking of plates.

One day, Chabin reappears; another, Matildana leaves and returns to Paris. Enryck has apparently succeeded in legitimizing his unusual paternity, without much trouble or shame.

Matildana, however, has achieved nothing. The day before she left, she managed to alienate her sister even more. Though she knew better, seizing upon the topic of breastfeeding for want of being able to talk about something else, someone else or someone else's crimes, she suddenly exclaimed, out of the blue:

'But why do you insist on breastfeeding this poor, tiny one, since you don't have enough milk, and whatever little you have isn't even rich enough? What do you think is in your milk? You're making yourself weaker, that's all, and your child doesn't get enough nourishment—that's why she cries all the time. You're going to wind up with a scrawny kid full of "gas", like Mum says—her belly will be full of air from sucking for nothing. And your beloved toloman won't give her the nutrients she needs—it's not a panacea! People are making a big deal about it but, at the end of the day, it's nothing but a poor vegetable gruel for those who can't afford anything more. Stop listening to these old wives' tales . . . We may have eaten toloman ourselves when we were little but we also had a nanny with two good tits that gave us good sweet milk!'

'. . .'

'What's this about keeping your child at the breast for hours on end? Is this the latest fad? Honestly, you'd be better off buying her a pacifier!'

'. . .'

'Listen, Rehvana, for once, why don't you do like everyone else and stop your nonsense? Tradition is great, but if you don't have enough milk, it's not the end of the world. You go buy some formula at the pharmacy—easy as pie. Does your baby care that you're breastfeeding her as befits "Agar's Daughter"? All she wants is enough to eat! You're ridiculous and criminal in your fanatical selfishness. OK, you have such beautiful, full breasts you look like you could be feeding quintuplets, but what comes out is tchololo! Be reasonable.'

Without paying the least bit of attention to her sister, eyes lowered towards the child, Rehvana had continued to slowly remove her bra and gently, nobly, presented the baby with a gloriously taut nipple, as if stiffened by anger and affirmation of self.

After a few long minutes, she deigned to answer in a hushed tone, her index briefly applied to her lips, as if her hand shouldn't be removed from the baby for more than a moment:

'Shhh! If you get on my nerves, it'll be you who makes my milk sour. I don't see what the problem is. You find it necessary to always insult me and make mountains out of molehills. Here women have always had enough milk to nurse our children. You should know that! I'm an Antillean woman, I have milk and I'll breastfeed my baby. Nothing more natural than that! I don't see why I shouldn't, unless someone tries hard enough to spoil my milk, by angering me, for example . . . You always ruin everything.'

Astounded by such an inaccurate accusation, the older sister felt she was, once more, hearing the recitation of some lunatic catechism.

The next morning, when Matildana kissed her goodbye on her way to catch her plane, Rehvana hadn't moved, pretending instead to have to remain immobile for the baby's sake; she grudgingly whispered a terse goodbye. Matildana could have sworn her sister had purposely begun one of her much-vaunted 'on-demand' breastfeeding sessions right at the time of her departure. The matter of how they would say their goodbyes had been settled in advance. Matildana would drive herself to the airport and return the car she'd rented, as always. It was, of course, out of the question that Rehvana should accompany her to Lamentin to wave goodbye from the terrace overlooking the runway; she'd always hated the scarf ceremony and the 'Adieu Madras'. And anyway, how would she have driven back to Vert-Pré, after all the hugging and kissing, with Enryck, naturally, not there?

Walking out of the door, suitcase in hand, Matildana still turned around to glance at Rehvana, who had remained silent and didn't even get up, as if she were completely enthralled by her noble task. Aganila continued to suck in vain on a breast that was almost dried up.

As early as Fat Saturday, and perhaps even before that, the masks overrun the town. Everyone's disguised, girded with golden sashes and sprinkled with sequins, even at post office counters. Spindly skeletons jingle and impatiently hop up and down, and a pretend policeman whistles loudly at a spirited, plump panther who's crossing the street while smoothing her whiskers and waving her shaggy tail at a titillated, greenish extra-terrestrial—probably a Martian—with a cardboard nasal appendage, escorted by a hideous Venusian with tangled antennae.

Despite one disparaging remark ('What's the point of taking the pill now, you should have thought about it before!'), Enryck has been loveable lately, almost worthy of Rehvana's unconditional idol worship, and he's been hyped up by Carnival's approach.

'I'm going to meet Chabin on rue Lamartine, and then I'll come back and pick you up. You'll be ready? Bring things to stay over in Fort-de-France, don't forget your pill, and give Ma Cidalise all she needs for the little one. We won't be back in Vert-Pré for a while, you'll see! You'll have to be in shape: four days of the vidé and non-stop zouks before we bury Vaval, the Carnival king!'

They brought all the baby's things to the neighbour's, packed all the costumes and thought about every detail. They drew Carnival arabesques on their faces, applied make-up to Chabin's fat cheeks in a futile attempt to turn him into a butterfly, coated his lips—limp and slimy, like an overfed slug—with garish lipstick. It took all that, and a few of Enryck's impatient slaps, for Rehvana to find herself right in the middle of boulevard Général-de-Gaulle among the thundering crowd, the competing screams of dozens of loudspeakers perched on trucks, broadcasting popular tunes, amid revellers shrieking songs in Creole at the top of their lungs: '*Eh, Damizo, eh ya*! . . . *Pa lévé lanmen asou krapo*! . . . *Papillon, volez*! *C'est volé nou ka volé*!' ('Hey, squire, hidey-ho! Hands off the toad! Fly butterfly! Let's fly for good!') Suddenly separated from Enryck, Rehvana is swept away by the wave of monsters and masks, into an alley adjacent to boulevard de la Levée, nostrils irritated by tear gas, gift of a prankster who was instantly and furiously besieged by a mob of grimacing freaks. Eyes burning with flour, she's lost Enryck in the dancing hydra; she'll find him again, hours later, on the banged-up hood of an antediluvian jalopy covered in vulgar, cabalistic graffiti, collapsing under the weight of a swarm of raving young people, all jeers and screams. And yet, on Fat Monday, she'd appreciated the invitation of an unknown elderly man who'd sweetly led her into a dance step, performed without ceremony, right in the middle of the street, under the misty eye of a violinist from a different epoch; filled with deep emotion, she'd heeded the call of the drummers, knocking themselves out on the big drum, the noble ka of slaves. But at the sound of drumming, Enryck rubs against an outrageously effeminate, self-styled dandy with ruffles, necktie and hat, and moves to the beat, hands feeling the curves of a brownish creature with chubby hips, next to a tall Negro of the most beautiful black, with endless, fluttering false eyelashes—a Mandingo Negro wearing a dress, who totters and twists his feet on stilettos, and whose hand keeps hiking up his dress, exposing a garter belt, in order to stroke his nine-month-pregnant belly in an obscene pantomime, or lifting up, with a provocative wink, one huge, drooping, lopsided, home-made breast of rags. Not to be outdone, Chabin pulls out a sanitary napkin heavily stained with pig's blood from under his petticoat and waves it in the faces of spectators gathered on the pavements.

Rehvana had enjoyed taking part in the burlesque weddings, though despite being thin, she had to squeeze into the small-sized First Communion suit—slightly moth-eaten and reeking of naphthalene—that had belonged to Enryck's father. She and Enryck, clad in a frilly, violet dress, had made such a lovely couple . . . such a perfect Carnival wedding . . . She'd graciously welcomed the fake threats of the red devils, their small bells jingling, the good-natured pitchfork thrusts, and the hands—sticky with molasses—of the magnificent nègres-gros-sirop coming out of nowhere, in squads of ten or twelve: you should see the stampede! Yes, you should see how this band of magnificent, muscular bodies, completely coated in black molasses and soot, scatters the crowd when, coming from God knows where, they suddenly charge into the throng with their towering, statuesque naked bodies—volcanic companions of an obsidian Spartacus— wearing only plain, worn-out, molasses-coloured shorts or an ancient African loincloth. Rehvana, smiling, embraces their shenanigans as they move closer with their hands outstretched as if reaching to smear with molasses the opulent ballroom gown she'd pulled out of a hundred-year-old steamer trunk, in exquisite condition, with its dainty, creased slip, under the lustrous, damask fabric. She readjusts her chaudière, precariously tilted on her coiled hair, and laughs again at having been afraid of the gros-sirop giants who haven't, in fact, laid a finger on her.

Well-built, strong and superb, their beautiful bodies glistening with black grease—all blackness, except for rows of dazzling teeth which show with each Olympian laugh—they've moved on to frighten a group of old-time street vendors, each balancing on her head a tray made from Caribbean wickerwork brimming with colourful fruit, ginger and vanilla beans . . . With utmost poise, they take a few steps back, without dropping a thing, forming a circle around Rehvana in the blinding sun where Enryck has evaporated.

She strains her eyes in vain, scrutinizing the crowd around her, as floats go by, blaring, '*Papillon, volez! C'est volé nou ka volé!*' ('Fly butterfly! Let's fly for good!') She's suddenly aware of her aching feet, due to the stiff leather of her narrow vintage shoes that dig into her flesh, and she's suffocating under the heavy damask; the unbalanced chaudière, reinforced with hard cardboard, presses into her forehead. As Fat Tuesday draws to an end, Rehvana returns alone to the house near the Savane Gardens, amid the crush of the crowd, the comforting grid of perpendicular streets, and the broken pavements of a Fort-de-France consumed by hysteria. She tries to hide behind the blinds, eyes closed, hands over ears, to get some sleep and forget about the frenzy outside, with its firecrackers and songs, and Carnival all around her, but the city's outlandish madness and laughter has seeped into her, submerged her and swallowed her whole.

On the last morning, intoxicated with release from his conquests, his sleepless night—face dusted with flour and eyes lined with kohl—a happy-go-lucky, relaxed, black-and-white Enryck, meticulously dressed from head to toe in a half-black, half-white livery—black shoe on one foot, white sneaker on the other—banged on the door and shook her awake to go bury Vaval. Rehvana didn't ask whose delicious little hand, expert and feminine, had spread flour all over her lover's face and deftly darkened the area around his eyelids with black pencil. Since she was taking too long—composing her face for burying the bwa-bwa, the Carnival king—Chabin, always with impeccable timing, suggested she could meet them later. She could sense that Enryck was relieved. She never put the finishing touches to her Ash Wednesday costume, and the Pierrot tears were only roughed out on her cheeks. Towards evening, high-pitched screams announced that somewhere in the city the wood-and-cloth puppet—the short-lived king of Carnival—had been set on fire, but neither Enryck nor Chabin made their way back to rue Lamartine before going to the great zouk, which brings the festivities to a close.

The next afternoon, Chabin, sent by Enryck, without word or explanation, drove her back to Vert-Pré. Probably exhausted from his carnivalesque excesses, the lecherous fat man showered her with unmitigated kindness.

Sitting on top of the hill, nose in the air, the child was smiling, but without joy. From all directions, deployed high and wide in the sky, the large, multicoloured squares—solid, striped or splotched—stamp the clouds with vibrant hues. Lazy and calm, they move slowly, yet proud as cranes. You can barely see what tethers them to the ground, nor their masters, releasing and tugging strings.

Rehvana chooses one and flies away on it.

There, on the ground at Morne-Rouge, on the slopes of Mount Pelée, a few enthusiasts are flying the colourful kites.

She'd taken Aganila for a stroll or, rather, Cidalise had dragged both of them along, keeping alive that centuries-old tradition to make lazy Easter Sundays seem less long. 'Come on, sweetheart,' the old woman had gently grumbled. 'You're not gonna let you'-self go, now that you're the mother of a child!'

Over the course of weeks and months, Ma Cidalise has tried hard to distract the lonely, young woman. The devout old woman, deeply superstitious, had made the rounds with her to a foot washing ceremony in Balata on Maundy Thursday, to the scorching Stations of the Cross on Fort-de-France's steep Calvary Hill, and to the anteroom of the great seer of Pérou, who gave her the once-over, gentle as a veil, and instantly recreated, down to the last detail, her entire life—her present and her past—though he knew nothing about her. He only asked her where she lived. When she gave him the address, without revealing her name or anything else, the old man marked the paper, drawing in fits and starts a series of obscure signs which to her looked cabalistic. Then he said, 'But it's not your house. You're in some-one else's house. You need to watch out for yourself: this house isn't a good house. It was worse in the past, and certainly, yes, some of its evil was purged, but it's still not quite right, despite all that.'

So he described the place—the entire house in Café—with disturbing accuracy and disconcerting precision, in a strange, hybrid language straddling French and Creole, while nervously writing his odd, hurried handwriting—jerky and robotic-like—with a frail, bony, ascetic hand, rattling Rehvana and sending shivers down her spine as he appeared to decipher, through the magical intervention of the yellowed parchment, the veranda with its jalousie windows, and the tall four-poster bed; then the location of the chaise longue and the shape of the cloudy mirrors, and the wobbly pergola and even the unusual stack of new card-board boxes under the great staircase. 'This tells me there are bulky cardboard boxes. I can't quite see what's inside—looks like very modern appliances. I'm not familiar with these machines—

I wouldn't know how to say their names. What are you keeping there?'

Rehvana listened, trembling and troubled, without a response; he wasn't expecting any answer—as if he knew she couldn't provide an explanation—and continued to deliver an accurate account of her life. But as for the future, he became sibylline, evasive, almost reticent. He offered her no clear prophecy. He invited her to return, if she wished, so he could do what was needed for her salvation, and gave her an appointment a long way off, as he was entering a period of mortification and anchorite fasting, in preparation for Lent and Easter.

Some evenings they'd go up together to *Le Miroir* of Vert-Pré, the quaint cinema, where the best part of the show takes place in the rows of seats. There's rustling underfoot, perfumes filling the room, audience participation and stamping of feet, as a foot crushes 'pistachio' shells (that's what Ma Cidalise calls peanuts) and another squashes the back of a roach, making shoes reek from the greenish ichor staining the soles.

Naughty love scenes make the room break out in a collective, hoarse wave of gasps, and fights unleash a crescendo of '*i salé!*'('serves you right!'), and when the bad guy, left for dead, doesn't succeed in taking the hero by surprise, one hundred voices have already warned him of danger. And the most tragic silence is abruptly broken when a shrill wisecrack bursts forth from the darkness, dissipating the tense mood.

Sometimes Rehvana nestles in Cidalise's warmth, against her soft bosom, as her own sorrow melts from watching others suffer and die on screen. Sometimes the audience's howls of laughter burst inside her, scattering her grief. For a few minutes—a few brief minutes—she can be part of this contagious joy. Greedily, she immerses herself in this wholesome glee, these short slivers of communion that distract her until they dissolve into the warm and hazy air as they start for home.

Together, at nightfall, the two women piously lit candles for All Saints' Day, having spent the Day of the Dead in the hilly cemetery filled with flowers, faultlessly clean at this time of year.

Together they'd lingered to watch a thousand lights flicker and fade on the graves.

At the cemetery's exit, young and old clumped around street vendors selling codfish fritters, ice cream and popsicles, cheerfully exchanging family news.

Rehvana has taken off on the vibrant wings of the largest kite.

Two days earlier, elated by the fasting and deep meditation of the Holy Triduum, while at Ma Cidalise's side, Rehvana had been readying herself for an intense religious experience— thrilling with the throng climbing up to Golgotha in communion with her people. Rehvana had gone to the foot of the hill where Fort-de-France's Calvary church stood, so white in the pure Lenten sunshine, that it looked like a Mozarabic or Mudéjar chapel. Soaked in sweat, leaning on Ma Cidalise's solid, rotund arm, she walked up the stony path.

'First station: Jesus is sentenced to death.'

'I walked in front of you . . . and you led me to Pilate's tribunal.'

The crystal-clear adolescent voice is the only thing to slice through the silence, under the beating sun.

'Seeing this was leading nowhere except to incite a riot, Pilate took some water, washed his hands in front of the crowd, and said, "I am innocent of the blood of this righteous man! You yourselves must see to it!"'

'Let his blood be on us and on our children!' the group repeated in unison.

Eyes were trying to decipher the tiny, low-relief carvings, partially faded, and guessed, more than actually read, the events of the trial.

'So he released Barabbas to the crowd. Jesus was scourged, then handed over to the soldiers to be crucified.'

Dust motes writhed in the intense light before Rehvana's eyes.

'Second station: Jesus carries his cross.'

At each station, the rows of the faithful made a half circle around the stone marker, eyes fixed on the diminutive bronze plaque, worn away by weather and time.

'The governor's soldiers took Jesus to the general's tent. They assembled the entire company around him. They stripped away his garments and draped a scarlet robe over his shoulders, then crowned him with thorns and placed a rod in his right hand. Kneeling before him, they mocked him, "Hail, King of the Jews!"'

At each station, the two women were surrounded by a half dozen unknown young people who were taking turns reading the Passion text from a bound booklet, which they were passing around.

'They spat on his face, took the rod from him, and hit him over the head.'

Without another word, the boys and girls had adopted Cidalise and Rehvana, who were both moved by this communion with such a brotherly and beautiful generation of Catholic youth.

'When they were done mocking him, they removed the robe and put his own garments back on him. Then they lead him away to be crucified.'

A sacred sweat streams down Rehvana's face; the slope is getting gradually steeper, with more and more stones that hurt her bare feet, clad only in Senegalese sandals, and Cidalise is weighing her down.

'Fifth station: Simon of Cyrene helps Jesus carry his cross.

'As they were leaving, they found a man from Cyrene named Simon, and they forced him to carry Jesus's cross.'

A line of sweat has appeared on her bodice, making the fabric stick to her chest, and the perspiration from Cidalise's fleshy arm adds to her own heat. Rehvana tries to pinch and pull away the heavy boubou fabric clinging to her skin like gangue, and fans herself with the prayer book Cidalise gave her. She isn't free to move about, because the old woman, still hanging onto her, is heavy, heated and weary.

'Sixth station: a pious woman wipes Jesus's face.'

Cidalise is exhausted; stoically, she continues, her old, twisted legs slowly climbing the path, painfully and sluggishly, while Rehvana must carry most of her body's weight.

The young woman's feet are bloody; the craggy path is strewn with brambles, broken glass and small sharp rocks; she can't avoid them as much as she'd like since she has to support Cidalise.

'Eighth station: Jesus consoles the women of Jerusalem.'

But now a young man is following her, and unavoidably steps next to her, then pursues her on the path, and Rehvana is distressed at having to step aside to avoid desecrating these sacred moments with an unholy, loud slap.

'Ninth station: Jesus falls for the third time.'

The young man acts casual. Now he's the one reading the text in the booklet, which he's grabbed from his sister's hands. (The young girl who read so well looks a lot like him.)

'Tenth station: Jesus is stripped of his garments.'

He reads with a deepish tone that occasionally reveals his recent change of voice, and he attentively articulates, with a focused look.

'And when they came to a place called Golgotha, which means the place of the skull or Calvary, they offered him wine mixed with gall; he tasted it, but didn't want to dull the pain.'

Everything seems back to normal; the boy concentrates on his reading without a glance towards Rehvana, who's careful anyway to stand at a distance.

'And having crucified him, they divided his garments between themselves, casting lots, then settled in to keep watch.'

Cidalise doesn't understand why Rehvana walks so slowly on the path. The old woman picks up her limping pace to catch up to the young ones, while Rehvana unsuccessfully tries to slow her down.

'Twelfth station: Jesus dies on the cross.'

Cidalise forces Rehvana to move closer to the reader: she can't hear anything! Why on earth is Rehvana so intent on standing apart?

'Above his head they'd inscribed the charge against him: "This is Jesus, King of the Jews." Then they crucified the two thieves with him—one on his right, the other one on his left.'

Cidalise's pig-headedness makes Rehvana uncomfortable; she hangs her head, flushed with heat and shame, victim of the old woman's insistence on remaining with the group, as she clings to Rehvana's arm with a steely hand, close to the reader.

'From the noon hour until the third hour, there was darkness all over the land.'

Rehvana keeps her eyelids lowered, her hands clasped, her torso inclined in fierce humility.

'And behold, the veil of the temple was torn in two from top to bottom, the earth shook, and the rocks were split. The tombs broke open, and the bodies of many saints came back to life. After Jesus arose from the dead, they came out of their tombs and entered the Holy City, appearing to family and friends.'

The candles' melting wax drips in the sun along the Stations of the Cross, and high above, at the end of the road to Calvary, after the fourteenth station, after kneeling in front of the enormous crucifix that blinded her with its silver reflections, Rehvana makes her way through crushed, empty candle boxes, twisted canteens, squashed cans of Caresse Antillaise and broken bottles of Royal Soda, with a deep feeling of relief and an astonished glance at the unavoidable women selling refreshments and codfish fritters, faithful to their post on this Good Friday, just like Saturday nights in front of the cinema, peddling pistachios and Sno Balls, or on All Saints' Day with their zacharis, or at Carnival with their kidney skewers. She doesn't consider them anything like those merchants driven out of the temple long ago . . . far from it: Rehvana madly embraces all of her island's traditions—offers her entire being to her island—and is head over heels in love with its disarming warmth, which so easily blends

Christianity and voodoo, sweets and Lent. Deep down, she hopes all of this will never prove to be mere hypocrisy.

Ma Cidalise's hand had been gently resting on her shoulder for quite some time, as the old woman whispered in her ear. The melodious purring gradually became more intelligible, turning out to be more pressing: they must leave now to make it back to Vert-Pré before dark. The last kites have landed on the ground, the air no longer swells their sails, and their colourful cloths repose on the grass, wrinkled and warped; their owners rewind their strings while bantering back and forth.

AGANILA'S SCREAMS HAVE AWAKENED ENRYCK, who sits bolt upright in bed between the tall posts, wondering aloud, to no one in particular, how to get this spoiled brat to shut up. He violently throws back the sheets; he's just come home and gone to bed, and already this intolerable racket has interfered with his falling into a deep sleep.

Rehvana is no longer beside him. He gets up, walks with long, furious steps to Aganila's bedroom, shoves aside the mother, and rips the damn kid from her arms, who begins to howl louder. At this point, rocking her no longer makes sense: the baby wails and writhes in pain and terror from these huge, powerful arms that pin her down. She feels the force of these strong fingers—their coarse pressure—which nervously grabbed hold of her. The man shakes her; the child is terrified. Eager to get back to bed, Enryck paces the room at breakneck speed, waving the baby like a puppet, then holds her up to the level of his eyes with his two hands and commands her to quit her bawling, spitting in her face that she's going to shut up, goddammit, won't she shut up for God's sake! The child doesn't comply, and her protests increase as she takes the full brunt of his foul breath; she recognizes the smell of booze—beastly breath so different from her mother's sweetened perfume. In the dim glow of the night-light, she can make out the brute's features, bloated from absinthe and lack of sleep, abruptly dragged from his stupor. Again she must endure the features and the fetid smell of this large, savage creature who snatches her from her mother's adoring arms to hold her in a painful embrace, and sometimes waves a small, gaudy toy that disagreeably screeches in her ears. The one who sometimes comes and hurts her all over when her belly aches. She's scared and screams her head off to drown out the gruff voice that keeps repeating things she doesn't understand, louder and louder, while she's being shaken harder and harder. She craves her mommy's arms. Mommy must stop the big monster from getting her. Mommy is a fairy: just like in the tales she reads to her, she can make her tormenter disappear with a wave of her magic wand. Mommy can't leave her in his arms!

Rehvana tries to intervene, in a meek protest. Her hands reach out to plead with him and to try to reclaim the baby, still scolded and shaken by the man.

Rehvana, dizzy from screams, dazed from terror, is afraid for her child, who's now seized by sobs, but won't calm down; a continuous lament pours forth from the small, now distorted mouth, almost square-shaped like a Gorgon or a tragic mask. Aganila has worn herself out. Already she's out of breath, her face mottled with alarming crimson blotches.

'You see, there's no point; you're making her crying worse. Give her to me, Enryck; I swear I can get her to hush, just stop shaking her like this!'

Enryck knocks her out of the way with an angry elbow shove, as she clings to his arm and implores him to give her Aganila. With a tongue slowed from inebriation and belching, he proclaims, he maintains, against all reason, he's going to calm the child. Rehvana is worthless; she can do nothing but chase after the man who takes out his wrath, with an obduracy beyond understanding, on the small, choking body; she's only good for crawling behind Enryck, like a wreck, and getting him more worked up with her pleas.

'What do you expect? Why put yourself in such a state? I'll take care of her, please, give her back to me ... '

How does she, this creeping worm, dare to tell him he's inept at getting a baby to sleep?

Enryck staggers but doesn't lose his grip on the child. Dishevelled, with bulging eyes, Rehvana whimpers like a mad woman. It's not real, it's not true, it's happened so fast, all at once: one moment she was there, caring for her baby girl, softly singing 'Adieu Madras' to her, when suddenly the nightmare broke out. Impossible: she doesn't have the right to have such ungodly bad dreams.

The man she loves is threatening Aganila. He swears he's going to give her a reason to cry, and he brings down his large hand on the child's contorted face.

The baby's crying stopped.

With a gasp, the mother clutches the massive arm raised to strike again, when the man savagely throws the baby at her. Rehvana barely has time to catch the child's belly, while the heavy hand continues to slap at random. Stupified, transfixed with terror, Rehvana is no longer able to articulate a single intelligible word. Her body doesn't respond to her. The young mother is nothing but sobs, spasms and gut-wrenching wails. Reeling, she uses her last ounce of strength to press the baby into her belly, in the space made by her hunched body, to try to shield her from the frenzied blows battering the two huddled forms, helpless against the man's insane rage.

When Enryck can no longer feel his hand, when his muscles begin to ache, when the unrestrained slaps give him more pain than euphoria and relief—that's when his own suffering sobers him up and orders him to stop at once.

Only then does Enryck leave, slamming the door, mumbling—although no one can hear him now—that it's impossible to get any sleep in this house.

ABOVE THE HOSPITAL BED OF THE BABY covered with purplish-blue bruises, Enryck and Matildana spitefully try to stare each other down.

Of course Rehvana has lied to her: how else could a baby so young fall from her cradle on her own, in the middle of the night, and almost break her skull?

Matildana is here. She's looking him up and down with scorn. She's boiling with horror, helplessness and shame.

He was the first one to blink and shrink from her unbearable gaze, but he only gave in to his illegitimate sister-in-law in order to get a good look at her. Pointedly and filled with lust, he leisurely surveyed her shoulders, her breasts and the arch of her back, while he swayed in place, acting nonchalant, hands in his pockets. He'd only lowered his eyes to take his lewd revenge by hungrily gauging his opponent's curves from the viewpoint of a real connoisseur, as if the reminder of his sex could conceal his defeat. That's undoubtedly all he'd found—a virile pretence of power—to give himself the illusion of having won. He almost whistled and complimented her on her dress . . . However, there's no longer anything Enryck could do that would increase her contempt. He'd crossed the line a long time ago.

Once again a hospital with Matildana at her side. The young mother paces up and down with a vacant stare, like a sleep-walker.

What malevolent and impossible force had condemned the three of them to this hellish room with no easy exit, this silent conclave, in such an oppressive mood, with the air filled with mute cries and the overpowering smell of ether?

The man had managed to look contrite, and to a naïve observer, could even look concerned. To a less-informed, less-biased audience—or at least one more favourably inclined than Matildana—he appeared to be the perfect and pleasant image of a vigorous and healthy young man. However, it was best not to look at the two tell-tale, dark-skinned battering rams poised on the bed rail.

Yet they were all the young woman could see. For a long while, she couldn't stop staring at these two living objects—as if animated by a life of their own—these fidgety, insufferable things.

After flawlessly playing the part of the kind, visiting step-dad—after expressing fake concern for the baby's health, and even attempting to whisper in her ear, as if the small, inert body lying between the bars of the metal bed could hear anything at all—Enryck left the room without saying where he was headed.

Rehvana sadly lets him kiss her goodbye.

Matildana has ostensibly turned towards the window's light, eyebrows furrowed, apparently very absorbed in decoding the skull X-rays the baby had required. She positions and tilts the stiff films—greyish and opaque—into the sunlight, and although she can't make sense of them, she can't help but try, though the mere sight of them makes her furious.

As soon as the door has closed, Matildana tears herself away from her tedious inspection and turns on her heel, her face crimson, flushed with repressed rage. In an intimidating manner, she walks towards her sister, the large manila envelope still in hand, and gravely waves it in the air, almost grazing Rehvana's chin.

'This time, I warn you, no more messing around. You've got to file a complaint against this dangerous madman; you've got to do whatever it takes to stop him. Your guy is completely deranged! I'm going to do all I can to prevent him from causing more harm.'

'Please, Matildana, don't get mixed up in this. You're wearing me out with your clichés. File a complaint, file a complaint, it's all you ever talk about. Try to understand, this is the norm: give him some credit for keeping us both, my daughter and me—don't forget that Aganila isn't his! He was entitled to throw me out, based on the way I behaved. For once, try to put yourself in other people's shoes, instead of passing judgement from the height of your so-called wisdom . . . '

The older sister sadly smiles. 'Really? I thought you said it was an accident . . . Now you're trying to absolve your precious love! You're betraying yourself, my poor Rehvana—you're out of your mind. Can't you see there's no way out?'

Matildana has calmly placed the envelope with the fairly reassuring reports on the metal night-stand above the immaculate wash basin, stupidly shaped like a white kidney bean. Her fingers mechanically graze the thermometer, docilely swimming in its water glass, while she smiles, head bowed, lost in thought. The child's condition is not too bad—at least, that's what the doctors have said.

Rehvana collects her things and seems impatient to leave. But the pensive older sister pretends to ignore these preparations.

'Don't think for a moment I could forget this idiotic promise you're making me keep! I swear, Rehvana, there's something's wrong with you: leave this guy, or lock him up, do something, anything, but I can no longer let you keep living like this. How am I supposed to calmly return to my life in Paris, knowing that you and your daughter are prisoners in this brute's house?'

'...'

'What do you plan to do now? You're going to take Aganila back to this maniac's house? I forbid it! If that's your intention, you may as well kill her right now! ...'

'...'

'To think I tried everything to convince you, but I could do nothing to prevent you from keeping the child ... Why on earth do you want to remain faithful to the precepts of your lamebrain sect, after all they did to you! "Abortion is forbidden, it's bad," yada yada ...

'And maybe *this* isn't bad?' she adds, pointing to the white bed where the little form, connected by tubing to an upside down bag, disappears between the metal bars. 'Your daughter hooked up to a drip, covered in bruises, and God knows what else is wrong—that's what you think is fine?'

Matildana moderates her tone and casually adds, 'I just wanted to mention that Jérémie is still waiting for you ...'

'Well, let him wait! I'm sick and tired of your jeremiads and your sermons! Who do you think you are, the two of you?'

Rehvana behaves like a spoiled child again, putting on her pig-headed pout and her offended princess look which no longer work with Enryck, but which she reverts to, almost instantaneously, in Matildana's presence.

'I've already told you we're not speaking the same language. I wish I hadn't asked you to come, since all you do is give me crappy advice! Not everyone is required to live by your standards! I love a man and I like living with him. What can you know about this, you, the Amazon warrior?'

'And what do you do—you, in your so-called life—what do you do for your child? You can't even defend yourself! . . . The one you love above all, revere, and worship as a God, is some guy who beats you and strikes your child . . . What do you want me to say about that?'

Rehvana has a quick laugh.

'Actually nothing. You've got nothing to say. It's my life, not yours.'

'And your child shares your life?'

Matildana hesitates a second before she continues, in a whisper, as if speaking to herself: 'No, Rehvana, I've already promised you a lot of things and I'm kicking myself for it, but I won't promise that I'll never try to take Aganila away from you, even though I'm still not sure how. It seems to be the wisest thing to do, until . . . '

'Until what? You're killing me with the "wisdom" you dispense. Listen to me: you're going to leave me alone now, and you know you're not going to do a thing . . . Come on, let's go—I've had enough of being in this room! It's pointless anyway.'

Matildana shrugs and grimly shakes her head; her voice is now reduced to a murmur, as if something, little by little, had just died within her.

'It's true, all this is useless . . . We should have taken her to a faith healer—who needs hospitals anyway? You're right, it's so meaningless, and Princess Rehvana knows what she's doing, she doesn't need my advice, she's so lucid, so strong . . . What am I doing? I'm an intruder in your happy trio. A strange sort of happiness nonetheless . . . It's true. What am I doing in all this?'

The young mother has already picked up her bag; she impatiently rummages through it, standing near the door, and pulls out a handkerchief to wipe her forehead. Matildana's mumbling has barely reached her consciousness. She nervously blots her neck and her full lips, and pats her temples where her hair is stuck.

Matildana is in no hurry; her fingers sink into the warmth of Rehvana's black whorls—flowing and full of life—that escape from under the madras scarf. For all eternity—for their eternity together—she gathers the evidence of so much shipwrecked beauty; she quietly soaks it all up. 'Pearls before swine,' she simply whispers, stroking Rehvana's hair. And that was all. She only spoke these three words repeated by so many others—these empty, borrowed words—and then Matildana fell silent. Nothing she could say would matter now.

Rehvana preempts her sister. She knows her so well.

'Matildana, you're such a bore. You've always been a pain with your preaching.' Rehvana abruptly pulls away, walks towards the door and speaks with a cold tone.

'You never change, you know. I love a man, you understand? I love a man, I love Enryck, what's not to understand? I can't listen to you any more, so just go back from where you came . . . '

She stammers and gets tripped up on her words, then steps into the hallway, babbling away.

The large woman in front of the lift, picking at the few teeth she has left, openly stares at each of the two young women—so different from when they'd been talking together earlier in the day—now so unmistakenly at loggerheads.

In silence, Matildana drives the rental car back to Vert-Pré. She slows to a crawl down the menacing, sloped road that leads to Café.

Neither sister speak.

Neither sister dare speak, for fear of giving voice to irrevocable words—words reserved for elders—possibly indelible words. She drops off the younger sister a few yards from the house.

Matildana will leave in a week. She refuses to sleep, if only for one night, under the same roof as Enryck, even though there's a strong chance he won't be back tonight, nor anytime soon; she can't stand this house.

Matildana has held onto the bitter, infuriating memory of that Christmas Eve when she'd put herself in the middle of a quarrel between Rehvana and Enryck, when her little sister was crying for help. With her cheek still red from the slap she'd received, lips trembling, eyes full of hate, Rehvana had rebelled against her to defend her lover and her life, or, at least whatever she calls her life.

Before flying home, she'll spend a few days in Grand-Anse—timeless fishing village and fluid vision of Africa from her youth—her sister's and hers—authentic illusion of childhood and unchanging mirage of the world. Each evening she'll walk along the beach: she'll look up at the stars, at a sky more perfectly vaulted, more filled with stars than anywhere else—all this against the backdrop of the sea. She'll hang her legs from the side of the garishly-painted fishing boats made from gum-tree wood, and will indulge in rereading—this time with no joy—the names that charmed her childhood. Matildana had learnt to read at a very young age, thanks to the good work of her schoolteacher grandmother, and was the pride of the prim and proper old aunties when she conscientiously deciphered everything placed before her eyes—names of shops, streets, and even, on the beach at Grand-Anse, the names of multicoloured skiffs: *Souvenire* [sic] *of the Colonial Army . . . The Dream . . . Social Debt . . . Hope . . . Patience and Fortitude . . . The Eldest Child . . . The Day Has Come* and *Long Live the Letter B . . .*

She understood none of it, and wasn't concerned by anything she'd sounded out—cryptic between the cynical ellipses of their fate.

With one hand, she'll hike up her raw silk skirt to her thigh, while she holds her ballet flats with the other hand, and she'll get her bare feet wet at the water's edge to avoid the swamp. Then she'll quicken her pace, ripping through the surf's frigid force until it hurts, and the sea spray will splash all over her face—yes!—bursts of little waves will reach her eyes, and the salt of the sea, like the salt of her tears, will sting, etching iridescent lines on the glowing amber of her skin.

She'll sit off to one side, sheltered from the wind, not too far from the muddy dump strewn with gaping fish guts, where young, black-grey sows slosh around.

She, the older sister, strong as a rock, will daydream about her arrogant sister who's all fire and brimstone. She feels strong enough to go back through their life histories from start to finish, and not be hurt, but she's unable to hold back Rehvana from the blinding, burning pit, and the searing and lethal lava flow bursting its banks, to which she exposes her life, like the proud martyr of a self-sacrifice, like the testy and haughty burnt offering—not consenting, but willing!—of some novel immolation, secret and never-before-seen.

An offering of the zealotry she'd mocked because it was so mysterious to her, back in the days of the squat and the Rule and the outrageous Ébonis, about whom Matildana bitterly wishes she could still laugh.

She'll be sitting there, in the Grand-Anse darkness, incredulous and perplexed, gazing at the lonely kapok tree—majestic and covered with spines—at the edge of the swamp next to the savannah—the marshy land bombastically baptized MARACANA STADIUM, as inscribed on a crude wooden sign, wobbly and almost illegible, in clumsy letters bleeding into one another, partially faded by rains or sea salt, where, between two football games, four or five Brahman bulls crossbred with zebus—humpbacked and bony, their pallid flesh miserably limp under their paunches—stoically graze on the sparse grass, among puddles and mud, from island to island of firm-but-miry earth, as if on a slippery archipelago with unproductive and perilous soil. She'll raise her head towards the formidable giant tree with its indigenous, prehistoric, melancholy robustness—a thousand round heads lacking eyes and mouths, topped with a mane of delirious branches, immeasurably covered in leaves—and its large trunk racked with spines extending like long, thin, brown, tormented tentacles into the mud. And she will not be certain of anything—neither of this tree's unreality, in which she so wants to believe—just like she hopes her own nightmare will turn out to be untrue—nor of its vegetal essence, nor even of the name she gives it—'ceiba'—removed, remote and obscure—as if to mitigate the pain of another name—to better supplant it and forget. She'll also close her eyes, as she lowers her gaze, so as not to have to see the troubled water, thick with murky silt where so much efflorescent magnificence plunges and cleaves and sinks and bonds and appears to thrive.

THE RATS ARE HIDING OUT, now that it's broad daylight. Too many humans have overrun their realm but rodents and bugs are still masters of the house, as evidenced by a thousand signs, a thousand little teeth marks, suspect damage, carcasses crawling with ants, and dozens of holes strategically placed in the squalid, stale-smelling building.

Remorville's foundations shelter rats, excrement and vermin-infested filth. Rehvana suppresses a shiver, for she's barely escaped falling into it: just in time, she was able to pull her foot from a gaping hole in the broken floorboards. The children swear they saw Madame Augustin-Lucile fall in last year and get buried to her waist.

A telegram arrived from the Board of Education, where she'd applied for a position, without much hope—following Matildana's advice and under heavy pressure from Ma Cidalise.

'Since neither heaven nor hell care 'bout you, do like your sister says—you're smart enough to do it, my girl.'

She quickly became attached to her howling, over-active little pack—calmed down in a flash and ready to work—bent over notebooks, chewing on their lips, under the agreeable thumb of the sweet and strange schoolteacher. Despite being in middle school, they still have a tendency to call her 'mistress', and even informally address her, but with affectionate respect. Their youthful humour helps Rehvana find a new purpose in life, and she adores them all: the little dear—birdbrain and brilliant at the same time—who can't stop jabbering away, delighting the class with her irresistible lisp, and the overweight, mollusc-like kid, eager to please—swimming champion and a fan of *Le Cid*, for whom French remains a glorious foreign language—who fights with giant fists for the right to wipe the blackboard clean, employing his imposing weight to scare away any contenders among the picturesque horde of students swarming her desk each morning who might challenge him for bucket or sponge. She loves big booty Rachel—sassy and busty—who looks like she's already reared an entire family with an iron fist, and also the one she's nicknamed 'Gendarmette', all rosy and red-haired—a short and shy white, daughter of a sergeant major in the gendarmerie— at first lost, but by October, had found true friendship with a cheery sacatra girl with soft, caramel skin.

The students are charmed by their offbeat schoolteacher with fiery eyes, in boubou and African sandals, so different from the old, hoary schoolmasters with long metal rulers, who whack the back of your hand. She's so unlike the pretentious pachyderms, maternal and uninformed, who treat them like 'little Negroes', and who despise, insult and crush them, comfortably spreading the arrogant jelly of their rumpled flesh behind the desk to better belch the fish stock from lunch—incensed at having to leave the affluent breeze from the hills of Clairière or Didier to come down and 'teach school' in the scorching heat of this poor suburb, roy- ally butchering English like a Spanish cow—or Spanish like a Holstein cow from Holland.

From essays and secrets revealed after class, she was privy to bits and pieces of information—shared in a half-trusting, half- reticent way—of all these budding microcosms: adolescent loves and childhoods filled with neglect, unknown fathers, drunken mothers, fly-by-night biological fathers, abusive stepdads, tyran- nical older brothers, Christmases without gifts, older sisters leaving the nest to earn suspect wages, pregnancies at age thir- teen, pigs to feed and young goats to lead to the field before leaving for school, adoptive and noble grandmothers who only speak Creole, simple joys, pristine ideals and murdered innocence.

Rehvana was hired as an assistant teacher without having received either guidelines or educational training. She makes do, more or less, armed with ancient annals of the National Diploma and some kind of curriculum unearthed from the cubbyhole that passes for a library—the pompously named 'Information and Documentation Centre', fiercely defended against adversity by a courageous female warrior, the chabine librarian, the only person in the building who appears to be endowed with the gift of speech, since she's the only one who speaks to Rehvana—but she adapts the curriculum to her taste, and tries, in vain, to convince one of her classes of the allure of *Masters of the Dew*, that classic of Caribbean literature, when almost all of them, with the exception of a light-skinned mulatto girl and the fair-haired Gendarmette, are dying to dive into Molière's *The Miser*, which she promised they'd read later in the school year.

She thinks of Matildana, smart and fulfilled, living in plush and timeless ease at her dear Sorbonne, sheltered by the sacrosanct and austere companionship of the Puvis de Chavannes murals that adorn its august galleries, redolent of wood and wax. But nothing frightens her, nothing unnerves her—neither the mosquito's attack, nor the venomous yen-yen, nor the acrid smell of rancid piss, nor the roaches, nor the rats that multiply under the piling, nor the condoms, still sticky with sperm, which she discovers each morning, at the foot of the blackboard, in this God-forsaken school, where all sorts of shifty individuals trespass at night to engage in shameful fights right in the middle of classrooms and steal or destroy school property. Nothing discourages her, not even the hellish heat, nor the heavy rains, suddenly beating on the old sheet metal roof, overpowering her reedy and shaky rookie schoolmistress voice with a thunderous roar.

She'd give anything to be sure she's truly making a difference in the lives of this flock of kids so eager to learn. She admires the patience of these students—so young—who've already had to endure injustice and misfortune, and are resolved to listen to lectures and get an education in this rowdy, run-down, ill-equipped place.

Such a curious fate—an unfair fate!—for these children who grow up speaking only Creole, and are reduced to supposedly learning French in unbearable bedlam where words and culture get swept away at the whim of trade winds.

Arriving well after the start of the school year, she rarely interacts with her colleagues—most of them unfriendly, somewhat distant, somewhat cold or, perhaps, simply shy and reserved. She listens to two or three vague ideas exchanged around her and brushes past a few pleasant-looking young women so absorbed in their own lives they're impervious to anything else; a venerable, straight-laced fellow who knew her family well and each morning furnishes her with a deliciously stiff nod, worthy of Versailles; a toad-like old man with a hideous but kindly face and a benevolently bent back—probably an old maths professor: she doesn't really know and doesn't speak to them. Timidity, apathy or complete vacuity? Rehvana can't really say . . . No one has made the slightest move towards her; no one has ventured to speak with her, so why should she? They're the kind of folks who've known each other for ages and who take eons to acknowledge you, and connect with only a chosen few in a type of false, verbal intimacy, hypocritically interwoven with a 'How are you, my dear?' without waiting for a response, and a 'See you later!' without a future.

She has no idea which worked-up roosters, which demented dogs—which anarchic dog choirs—welcome each dawn, as if howling at death, with endless ululations filled with despair and with painful protests laced with madness and hope that tear one another's cries apart, like great veils, and which slash through the still-dark house as if it were the first morning of the world.

Alone, huddled in the gloomy cave, devoid of even the human touch of fire, Rehvana hurriedly gets up and lights the oil lamp. Shivering and horrified by the clamours of dawn, she quickly gets ready, swaddles the sleeping baby in a blanket and races across the garden, where terrors and vain hopes of the world's creation linger.

She wakes up with the sun, often way before, and goes to whisper 'psst, psst, psst' at Ma Cidalise's door, who has already jumped out of bed and is at the stove, busy preparing Aganila's toloman. The enormous matron has given birth to a good fifteen children, most of whom have died, or left for the 'Other Side'— to Lyon and the Paris suburbs—and despite her age, she's so happy and proud to take care of Rehvana's child. When Rehvana told her she was looking for a nanny for her daughter, she stood up, hands on hips—grandiloquently and incensed—and declared, 'Enough with this nonsense! Jus' as you see me standin' right here, my dear, I'm still good enough to babysit a li'l tot without droppin' her on the floor, God help me! Who knows, I may still even have some milk left inside my tits! You're goin' to only make a mis'rably li'l salary—don't even think that for one minute I'm gonna let you pay for some nanny who's goin' to make this child sick, oh no!'

Days pass. At pipiri, with thousands of roosters crowing, Rehvana walks up to the crossroad of Chère-Épice to wait for the unreliable, shared taxi ride which won't drop her off in town before six o'clock if the driver, an affable coolie, overflowing with life, didn't pull himself fast enough from the warm bed of his paramour-of-the-day. He juggles several mistresses in tempestuous rotation—sometimes four, sometimes six—and depending on the day of the week and each woman's temperament, Rehvana can estimate Anastase's delay. She can tell when the golden-skinned chabine's morning fever makes way for the sleepier torpor of Thursday's mulatto, and when the bushy, pubic pompom of the the chappée-kouli has vanquished the strong temptation of the statuesque and musky Negress who alternates between Mondays and Wednesdays, though Rehvana doesn't know why but surmises it's because she's married—to a baker, she tells herself.

But the coolie with six sweeties doesn't play fair. He takes great pleasure in misleading Rehvana, throwing off her calculations by maliciously turning his amorous calendar upside down, and some days he's already waiting for her, like a true gentleman, at the top of the hill—his triumphant stature outlined against the sky, brazenly sucking on a stick of sugar cane—while she's strolling up the slope, betting he's still indulging in his warrior chabine's spicy, golden delights.

He's figured out she was obediently taking her post around five o'clock, give or take, depending on his lovers' dispositions and the day. He pokes fun at her dependency, and ingenuously enjoys proving her predictions wrong, just to be able to blurt out, when he sees her coming, 'So, Mam'selle Rehvana, I've taken root in this spot!' as if to make clear that she, too, could be part of his weekly schedule, if she so desired, that nothing in the world would make him want to be a slave to all these other women, and that she had the power to disrupt the whimsical order of his scattered and generous virility. Prodigious and bursting with exultant sexuality, he keeps leering at her, and takes advantage of these opportunities—those still nacreous dawns when he's decided to show up early—to drive very slowly on the road to Vert-Pré, to prolong the pleasure of having her there, in his car, if not in his arms, and, when he must reach the town (for he cannot make the trip last for ever), the sacrifice of his early morning friskiness offers him an even bigger reward—keeping company with Rehvana, alone with her in the pearly dawn and amid the retreating cool dew of the night, as she's forced to wait for the second bombe that will take her to Fort-de-France, while he's in no rush to go back down to Trinité.

At around five o'clock in the morning, they're all alone in the gleaming car, washed and scrubbed daily, pampered like a pin-up girl, dolled up in stickers and accessories from Vanity Auto.

And Anastase makes her head spin with his amorous tales which she pieces together day after day, from snippets and scraps, in the still-damp, pre-dawn light—in the immaculate car, freshly hosed down, barely dry in the rising sunlight—as he floods Rehvana with an exuberant flow of stories and true or false feats, perhaps with the secret hope to seduce the Elusive One through the narrative of his exploits—an account he censors himself as befits the decency required for a lady from France who teaches school in the city and speaks a pure French like they do in France, with rolling r's and no accent, to whom Anastase has fiercely devoted all the crude and boorish respect he can muster.

Rehvana wonders which of these women is the legitimate wife but soon learns that marriage is out of the question, that leading a woman to the altar is tantamount to becoming a slave, that men should be available and free and intend to remain so. Still, she would have loved to know who among these women was her sister in solitude, neglect and pain. She quickly figures out it was likely the whole lot of them, except, perhaps, the buxom black woman from La Plaisable, who, to Anastase's great dismay, appeared to be leading a double love life with her calling the shots—as despotic as if she were a man. Anastase badly hid his distaste at being summoned, as well as his fury at having to cancel evening plans already booked. Rehvana also understands, cruelly and confusedly, how Anastase's comments and theories about women and marriage were so like Enryck's, as if they'd both been cut from the same cloth.

However, Rehvana can't seem to elude the magic of the fiery, lingering gaze—the smouldering eyes—of the chappé-kouli, blazing with all the brilliance in the world.

Each morning, fresh out of bed, the handsome Indian with African blood appears before her, with his body's uniform blackness and the guileless obscenity of his simple gestures: the offhand, vulgar way he yanks up his pants—which are not even sliding down—rotating his belt with a pelvic thrust, legs innocently bent in the provocative impudence of his wide, bulging shoulders.

Enryck has become almost invisible, nothing more than the man-who-walks-through-walls, sometimes coming home after she—weary and completely drained once papers are graded, and the baby bathed and put to bed—has fallen asleep. When she leaves in the morning, he's still sleeping off god-only-knows what hangover, reeking of tafia and feminine scents.

From the black Indian wafts such a violent and devilish sexual charge that Rehvana kicks herself for being a one-man woman.

Every Friday, the motorized suitor—his presumptuous appetites frustrated—must tend to his sinful and unseemly heartache; he'd immediately be the laughing stock of every last person in Martinique if his secret were revealed. Driving at breakneck speed and mocked by Venus, the thwarted Don Juan barrels up the winding road to town, insults passengers and pedestrians, grudgingly stops when hailed and sadistically jolts his unlucky customers whenever the road curves, because Rehvana has the day off from work.

One Monday, during her lunch break, Rehvana attempted to walk up avenue Sainte-Thérèse but had to stop because of the heat. Standing in front of The Mariners' Marguerites, blinded by the sun, she was having a hard time deciphering the cursive words, written in chalk, on a gargantuan slate board:

BAR — RESTAURANT — DAILY SPECIAL — NO STOP SERVICE [sic] — MARINATED FISH WITH LOCAL VEGETABLES — OCTOPUS WITH RED BEANS — SMOKED CHICKEN — BLANCMANGE — HOMEMADE JUICES — TO TRY [sic] OUR TESTICLE KEBABS — PATÉ AND CHELLOU BY SPECIAL ORDER — TREMPAGE TUESDAY'S [sic].

In need of something to drink, she spoke to the toothless manager, whose age she couldn't guess, who fixed his inordinately inquisitive eyes on her. Caught off guard at seeing her walk through his door, and likely never to recover, all he could do was stand there, dumbstruck.

Feeling guilty for not having understood his inaudible response, Rehvana turns her head a bit and notices the bottles of

La Mauny—unequally full—given the place of honour at each table, next to thick glass bowls filled with coarse brown sugar clumped together in crystals by the humid air, as well as the perennial droplets of rum from prior customers' spoons. She self-consciously contemplates the tables for a good long while, then in a whisper, quickly orders a white rum punch. In a daze from the heat, she's standing with one hand gripping the sticky display case for balance, where a few gnats, gorged with marmalade and fattened with lard, listlessly buzz behind the cracked glass. Her other hand wipes her forehead with an awkward, robotic stiffness after her long and reckless walk in the glaring sun. She senses the insistent, almost tangible, glances of the seated men, glued to her slightest move—even when she's completely still—and pictures them plastered all over her skin, like a rigid film, prickly and paralysing—an intolerable poultice mixing with her sweat, which the blades of the fan cool and dry in an unpleasant way.

She's got no business being in this worthless place of leering hostility, with this onslaught of hateful desire. She doesn't belong here, with her manners from France. She's out of place with her woman's body and face, and her too-light skin tone—oh involuntary and nevertheless unforgivable provocation!—under the collective rancour of all these mute and hardened faces, reflecting only dislike and aggressive macho drives, but where, at the risk of being taken for some prostitute from the port, Rehvana lingers too long, looking in vain for something else.

However, after a while, even their curiosity subsides, and they slowly drown their sexual drives, like the sparks in their eyes—perhaps, deep down, more defensive than hostile—in the clear alcohol of their drinks, and Rehvana casually picks up her glass. There's no syrup, and she'll not dare to ask for some; the rum, barely diluted by the coarse sugar crystals that refuse to dissolve, burns her throat and her chest, but who cares? It's alive and kicking! And with the most impenetrable indifference, Rehvana sips, then swallows the rum in one gulp, asks for the price in a low voice, hastily pays and bolts towards the door to take refuge in the implacable light of day. She pauses a moment on the sunlit threshold, and, overwhelmed with regret, flees the incomprehensible darkness of this closed circle, where she sought communion and something fraternal but only found rejection.

Behind her back, conversations have resumed.

And booming behind her, the forbidden chant grows: the words they didn't want to speak, and this Creole language, oh God, this Creole! they'd shushed when she walked in, that cracks like the lash of a whip and pushes her into the merciless sun— towards the desert of the street from which everyone had fled for the siesta.

She pauses a second at the doorway while the withheld words scourge her back.

The words withheld from her.

They've kicked her out, under the cruel midday sun. She's got nowhere to go; everyone has withdrawn into the coolness of homes, into the shade offered by roofs, but her own home—her so-called home—is many kilometres away and the school is closed until two o'clock. Where else should she go in these circumstances, if not under the sun beating down on her head?

She'd forgotten to buy a tchébé-coeur, though she'd promised herself she would, and she aimlessly drifts in somewhat of a daze until school reopens, an outsider in Remorville's sleepy little streets, with their rows of small houses inhabited by unknown families, from which rises—muffled by the heat—a faint clinking of dishes or a few stifled voices.

The next day she walks in the opposite direction to explore a large, air-conditioned shopping mall and a postmodern cafeteria, where she absent-mindedly chews on a bent, baby-pink straw with curlicue designs, stuck into a blue paper cup with red and white stripes and a spray of stars, and nibbles on a stale slice of pizza while enjoying the chilled air, sitting between two pairs of office workers and their peaceful and amicable squeals.

'Why, my dear, it looks like you've put on a little weight?' Christelle blurts out to Marlène, interrupting her meal to kiss her high on the cheeks, while curvaceous Marlène graciously dodges the unsightly anointing from the oily lipstick's impressive suction as well as the syrupy innuendo.

Rehvana will never set foot in this place again.

In any event, she doesn't intend to eavesdrop on the rest of this pitiful reunion. Soon she hears nothing more than a dull drone, which fills her head with its irritating emptiness. Abandoning her shrivelled slice of pizza, Rehvana shoves aside table and chair with a sudden brusqueness that startles the gossipmongers, then throws out a random apology and steps out into the vast parking lot splashed with sunshine, desperately blinking under the excruciatingly harsh, blinding rays of sun that reverberate everywhere with their all-consuming presence—on trunks of cars and shopping carts—and surround her in a frenzy of light.

Exhausted from sleepless nights—all those nights consumed by awaiting Enryck's return, by enduring his prolonged assaults and interminable, nocturnal discussions based on his absurd suspicions, by looking after the sick child—all those nights when she finally manages to fall asleep cruelly cut short by the rude alarm at four o'clock in the morning, so she can be at the crossroads close to five o'clock and arrive on time for the start of the school day at seven o'clock—Rehvana is now a shadow of her former self.

When, more and more rarely, Enryck deigns to drop by, the young woman no longer tries to provoke him. She's now careful never to raise her voice, and never to reveal her jealousy, her pain or her worries about money. It's been a long time since she's asked the slightest question, or made the slightest innuendo or reproach. She weighs each word that comes out of her mouth, to the point of banning some. She's nothing but prudence and grace, and goes to great lengths to meekly offer Enryck her total submission. He's so quick to make up stories about playboys at her school! He accuses her of being unfaithful and a bad mother, since she's working outside the home .... On the rare occasions when she sees him, there's nothing in the little she tells him that can, in any way, resemble the insinuations of an overly suspicious partner or the recriminations of a housewife without two sous to buy food.

She valiantly makes do with her modest salary, and she's begun to support Enryck, who now generously helps himself to her cash. Far from protesting, she makes sure to leave him a few bills, prominently displayed. She never complains, as if it were the most natural thing in the world that the man who stingily doled out, whenever he was so moved, a ridiculous pittance insufficient to make ends meet, is now the one who blithely draws on her scant savings. She actually derives secret joy from this fact. She'd always made it a matter of pride to never request anything for herself, and would have rather died than unleash Enryck's anger by asking him for money for the child. She's even immensely grateful to him for having kept her when she was pregnant by another man, even though her confession had unleashed a cruel and violent scene of epic proportions. After having derided Matildana and her wise precepts, she'd found she'd had no choice but to follow her advice, upon realizing that the almost Spartan deprivation in which she lived was not fit for a child.

She's now proud of being able to buy Aganila her jars of baby food, vitamins and the many medications needed by the frail, premature infant; her mother was not so hardy herself, and perhaps the poor child had inherited this weak constitution and precarious state of health, despite the countless prayer scrolls the old woman has slipped, on her own authority, into the baby's crib— multiple prayers to cover all bases: to the Virgin Mary, Saint Matilda and to almost all the saints, since with Aganila's array of Christian names, the poor Cidalise doesn't really know whom to invoke—and which she inserts, whenever she gets the chance, into the folds, hems and tiniest pockets she can find in the baby's clothes, just as she herself carries in her own pockets a permanent collection of prayers—each scroll worn thin as a spider web— on blackened, lacy parchment paper covered in characters almost completely erased by constant handling, sweat and baby urine. The old woman often clenches them in her fist when life gets tough and she generously gives Aganila the scrolls she deems most expedient in easing the course of the day, and, in a secret exchange, takes back the ones that have proven to be ineffective, so they may be blessed again. In her naive faith, she believes that divine benediction can simply wear thin, like a blade becomes dull from too much use.

Either way, it appears that the thread that binds little Aganila to life is very thin, and Rehvana doesn't know what to do. Her African princess is only Aganila in name; she's a baby prone to violent attacks from worms which cause her to awaken each night with spasms and screams; neither Cidalise's garlic cloves nor drugs from the free clinic have succeeded in ridding her of these stubborn parasites, which Rehvana thought had long been eradicated from the Antilles. Despite being stuffed with deworming pills, the child convulses like an epileptic each night, can't catch her breath, foams at the mouth and wails, and Rehvana is unable to chase away the demons dwelling within.

That May night when Rehvana had thought the baby was about to breathe her last breath—her life slipping away with her heartbreaking cries—Ma Cidalise, alerted by the screams, had battled the small arms momentarily endowed with incredible strength, to strap the baby onto her bed and subdue her spasms and frightening convulsions, armed with her inseparable garlic head whose acrid odour had finally restored the peace. But each night, the baby was contorting herself like one possessed—her face grimacing horribly, and turning blue to the point where Ma Cidalise exhausted herself from repeating that someone had cast a spell on both of them—on Rehvana and her child.

Respectful of customs, the old Martiniquan woman only came running over to lend a hand with the sick child when she knew Enryck was away. She'd never have dared to intervene, at night, if the grey Mercedes parked in front of the door confirmed the presence of the master of the house.

It's not that she's afraid of Enryck, nor that she wouldn't be able to defend her two charges with her own large body. No, she carries enough strength in her massive girth to knock out two or three men like Enryck. However, there's something . . . something rising from time immemorial . . . something stupid and obscure that compels her to accept the situation and yield, without asking herself why, to this resignation known as reserve, respect, God knows what else! This criminal and culpable submissiveness unwittingly makes her the man's accomplice—Enryck's willing accomplice—just as she, herself, was the accomplice of all the men who'd ever beaten her—her father, stepfather, brothers, lovers—when despite her body's strength, it was baffling that she should bow under the blows without trying to fight back. Ma Cidalise's hesitation, stemming from backward and barbaric nonsense, is actually not so different from the one that prevents Rehvana from trying to overcome the so-called 'inferiority of her female condition' using any weapon at hand. If only Rehvana could lead the man—the enemy, since he'd declared himself as such, as soon as he'd imposed force and conditions of war on the relationship—she might hoist him, whether he liked it or not, onto a higher plane—pull him from the mindless mire in which he wallows and crawls—this animal who is allegedly blessed with reason but who's more to blame than any beast. And then she might try, with equal weapons—through language, which they say is his prerogative, and through the intervention of the rational, which supposedly distinguishes him from the beast—to elevate him to a higher degree of humanity.

Such a sad state of affairs that in order to speak—to simply have the right to speak—the most human thing in the world— you'd have to fight so hard! What a paradox—in truth, what a mockery!—to be compelled by violence to try and force a man, willingly or not, to be comfortable in a human's role.

Reason frightens and endlessly torments. Instinct is so nimble, so easy and provides such exquisite delights . . .

Ma Cidalise and Rehvana are among those beings driven by misdirected love—by unbridled, impassioned irrationality and, thus, of a torturous and fatal flaw.

Enryck took a very dim view of what he called 'this school busi-ness', because, among other things, it lent Rehvana a suspect independence, and she wasn't there on the rare occasions when he appeared at the house. Unfortunately, he actually used it as a pretext to come home less and less frequently, especially once Rehvana had unfortunately managed to arouse his suspicions. Desperate and pressured by Cidalise, the young woman had finally decided to get her runaway lover to drink some sort of bizarre love potion, unbeknown to him, of course. Rehvana had had a hard time getting him to swallow a few drops of this bitter witches' brew, prepared in secret and covertly mixed with his food or drink. Each time she served him, she couldn't control her shaking—standing stiff as a corpse, pale as a ghost, pupils dilated with fear. She didn't have complete confidence in Cidalise's magic, though she so wanted to believe in it!

Her old confidante had assured her that this brew, made from rare herbs and vaginal secretions from the forsaken lover, would bring any man back into the fold—even the worst wom-anizers of the lot. 'Yes, 'e's gonna stay in the house, 'e's gonna stay, yes! 'Cause where there's honey, that's where the fly is gonna stay' . . . and besides, the concoction had already begun to work, for the poor, bewitched guy had been stuck in bed for three days in a row with a vicious cacarelle. Unable to hold back his bowel movements and believing he was being poisoned despite Rehvana's pleas and denials, Enryck had used up the remainder of his failing strength to beat the incompetent sorceress, after which, completely drained by the thrashing he'd given her, as well as the umpteenth explosive episode at the toilet to find release from his guts—after having duly spat out his bile—he'd dis-patched Rehvana to the phone booth to call Chabin to his rescue. He was not likely to be back anytime soon to see this hysterical lunatic who was trying to poison him!

THERE ARE TWO OF THEM AT HER DOOR: same size, same toned calves squeezed into ribbed knee-high socks, same hairy, thick thighs—those of rustic men—sticking out of khaki shorts, same satisfied paunch piteously displaying the preposterous protuberance of the 'colonial egg', confirming beyond a shadow of doubt—by its outrageous oval—a pronounced taste for rum.

Suave and all smiles, Rehvana puts on her 'honest woman's face' while lying through her teeth. No, of course not, she knows nothing about this, she didn't know; ah, really, how awful, that chabin was wanted by the gendarmes; it's been a few days since she's last seen her boyfriend—Diony Nialiv, the chabin? It's the first time she's heard that name; she's always called him 'Chabin' . . . No, she doesn't know where he lives, she's only met him a few times, and, in any case, he hasn't been around much lately . . .

As they interrogate her, the two sidekicks quickly scan the ragtag living room: in the shade of the lowered louvred blinds, modern appliances stand alongside remnants from the past. The two men exchange glances in silence, consulting a paper the older one had produced from his pocket, then stoop to examine the videotape recorder more closely. As soon as their backs are turned, Rehvana wrings her hands and bites her lips until they bleed. Then she pulls herself together—chin up and clear-eyed—bracing herself to face the blue eyes of the ruddy man with a Marseille accent, and the smile forming under his fine moustache hairs.

Her innocence is only partially faked, since Enryck never tells her anything on his brief visits home; she's never had the nerve nor the need to ask a single question. Still, she'd swear that Chabin has women working the streets for him in La Savane Park, on the route des Religieuses, or at night, by the beach, next to the offices of Air France. Rehvana gathered as much through some snippets of conversation, worried words and loud bursts of laughter every now and again, over a rum punch. Of course they've never said anything to her but she's almost positive it concerns prostitutes. At times she'd even been a little afraid for herself . . . She's never liked Enryck's friend—overweight, chubby-cheeked Chabin with iron-grey eyes with nothing of value to say to her . . . She'd always suspected that all those television sets and stereo systems were procured by dubious means, and she was even sure they were all stolen goods, but what could she do without implicating Enryck? The only thing she fears right now is that the police officers will find it strange to see all this equipment in a house without electricity. Rehvana quickly convinces herself they can't possibly know; she forces herself to believe it: after all, she tells herself, it's not written on the door! And these two baby-lones look so dense, so inept . . .

The blond man pulls himself up; robust, with hard thigh muscles which Rehavana can see bulging under the cuff of his shorts, he turns towards her again. This gendarme from the South of France eyes the large, bluish bruises that cover Rehvana's legs. The young woman stiffens; preparing another lie, she hastily wonders what abracadabra fall she's going to have to invent . . . But there's no need: the fellow makes no comment, asks no questions and settles for politely taking his leave, after looking over, one last time, the improbable house with no electricity, where oil lamps and hi-fi systems shamelessly coexist. But since the pretty young lady said it all had come from Paris and belonged to her boyfriend, that they'd brought it with them and so forth and so on . . . he didn't really want to hear anything else and quickly signalled to his colleague to stop snooping around.

Neither of the men displayed any exemplary zeal in their detective work; neither of the two seemed driven to fulfil his duty nor create any trouble for this sweet young lady, so poised and poignant in her regal gauntness.

The two policemen feel ill at ease, and prance about, as if they don't know what to do with their bodies. They know that even if they catch the notorious Enryck Marie-Égyptienne and his accomplice, it would only be to watch them be released within two days' time.

As soon as she'd noticed the police van, without really knowing why, she'd had the presence of mind—or rather an automatic reflex—to race to Aganila's crib and take her into her arms—less to protect the child from an unlikely threat than to use the sleeping little body as a shield. And she'd quickly pulled down a section of the baby's sheet to cover her purple-mottled forearm.

Aganila is now completely awake and doles out smiles all around; Rehvana appears to be obliging as ever. The policemen only saw—or, rather, chose only to see—Rehvana's fiery, magnificent eyes—wide and ringed with deep ochre.

The virtuous and unshakeable epitome of beatific motherhood, and a gracious and perfect hostess, Rehvana politely walks them back to the well-maintained fence, adorned with blooming bougainvillea—a sweet mother, tense with fear but beyond reproach. With an imperceptibly trembling hand, she pushes the immaculate white gate, then courteously steps aside to let the two men pass and deferentially nods in their direction.

Hands on the car doors, they only ask her to let them know if this Marie-Égyptienne guy or his buddy should show up and, their mission accomplished, get back inside the blue van.

Rehvana will never know if she should feel relieved by their giving up so soon; for now, she wonders if she should be pleased with their quick exit or if, quite the reverse, she should see in this a kind of underhanded move—perhaps a trap. She's got no idea where Enryck might be, so at least she hadn't really lied on his account; however, she's not sure she gave the proper responses and worries about having let something slip—through lack of habit or mistake—that could lead the gendarmerie to Enryck. And what if, through carelessness and stupidity, almost dazed by emotion, she'd compounded their suspicions, rather than quelling them?

The gaze of the solid man from the South of France had lingered on the blotches all over her face, and on her unusually elongated ear lobes, overstretched during her time with the sect, from the heavy brass earrings which had been consecrated as ceremonial and auspicious during Abdoulaye's hallucinatory prophesies, and which, one day, had been violently ripped off in Enryck's rage, and where recent scars had formed in a large swollen crater of melanin.

Was it just her imagination or had the honest gendarme—a family man—really been so moved that his red-veined eyes welled up with something akin to sadness?—an embarrassed, almost tender, sadness; a startled, slightly guilty sadness; a mute and meek disapproval; a tacit, timid, furtive interrogation—involuntary, as it were. It was as if the man, in spite of himself, had felt an indefinable pity, a compassion strangely mixed with respect, soon defeated by a sense of duty, lassitude and the call of ti-punch.

From her garden, concealed behind the trunk of a hundred-year-old mango tree, a saddened Ma Cidalise, with a disapproving eye, observes the two police officers return to their car empty-handed.

Disappointed and concerned, she furiously shakes her head.

If you can't even count on the law any more, or have faith in the forces of order, then you have to resort to drastic steps. The old woman is reluctant to involve spirits in this business; until now, she's kept them out of all this, limiting herself to secretly slipping a few 'blessed' parchments of prayers wrapped around three grains of coarse salt into Rehvana's hems, and then, on the sly, into the baby's crib, for it's always best not to awaken the spirits—even the good ones: you never know how far their fancy will go! Sometimes you ask them for a tiny little thing, and they hound the designated victim like the true demons they are . . .

But faced with such a wretched condition, strong measures are required; neither prayers nor rumèdrazyé—the notorious open-air-market sellers' remedies—will suffice to chase the devil away once he's settled inside a body.

Come to think of it, if that fellow gets a good thrashing, it would certainly serve him right! Except there's no time to waste, because he might end up killing that beautiful girl and then her pretty little kid, my God!

'Jail for those tramps, jail I say, that's what they are deservin', and that's that!' she mutters between her loose teeth, frustrated, a nasty look on her face, as if she were talking to Rehvana who's over there shutting her gate.

Have the two girls spoken to each other? Rehvana doesn't know. She believes she's seen in these students a type of latent animosity—impenetrable and icy—both pig-headed, entrenched in their differences, so unalike yet having so much in common.

Christel is subjected to her father's nocturnal visits almost every night, in the presence of her younger sisters and with her mother's approval: the poor woman has already given birth to ten or twelve kids and believes it's completely natural for her to be spared from her conjugal duty at last. The pack of younger sisters who share Christel's bedroom will soon take the reins, just as Christel herself had done, once her older sisters were grown, unless one of the disowned young women rebels—one who can't bear seeing him do to her siblings what she, too, had had to endure—and throws a stew pot of piping hot oil in the rapist father's face, just like one of those many sex-slave daughters in Remorville did last month.

The other young girl hasn't shared anything with the 'schoolmistress' in her essays; she's a bit luckier, if you could call it that. A cleaning lady told Rehvana that, with increasing frequency, the little girl's stepfather now seeks the memory of her mother's once-seductive delights in her tender, young flesh.

And they're also lucky not to be pregnant, like four other girls in the eighth and ninth grades.

Sitting across from the two young martyrs in the lurching bus, Rehvana struggles to think about something else, staring into space, head resting against the window, with a flicker of a sad smile for the tall stalks of sugar cane—the remains of the sugar factory rusted away in the distance—and the high-pitched voices putting her to sleep. Christmas is almost here, and carols are on all the children's lips. 'Come, Shepherds, Come!' follows 'Michaud Was Keeping Watch' . . . and then 'Go, My Neighbour!' and all keep rhythm with religious, Christian Nativity songs as they tap the backs of seats to African beats.

The field trip was a success. Rehvana had entered the mangrove marsh with great joy, guided by her colleague from natural science but, rather than worship the unscathed, age-old dignity of the mangrove trees whose roots are bathed in mud, she'd revered the warm, sticky earth and had happily trudged through the life-giving swamp, where she'd found infinite peace and complete safety in its supple embrace. First her bare feet, and then her legs were swallowed by the warm suction of the swamp; she would gladly have sunk in deeper, but she'd reluctantly let herself be rescued from the mud with the help of a few of her strongest students.

A spigot with non-drinkable water awaited the visitors who were asked to wash their feet before getting back on the bus. With all the splashing and gales of children's laughter, Rehvana had felt some of their happiness rub off on her.

One of the pupils had drawn a child's body in chalk on the blackboard before they'd left school for the trip and, in the naive circle defining the belly, had written in large cursive letters: 'Long live Christmas! I'm going to eat warm blood sausage, tasty pâtés, pigeon peas, pork stew, blancmange!'

On the return trip, why did she have the bad luck to end up opposite those two little girls, forcing her to think about all the things she's helpless to change?

Why must she contemplate, transfixed, the little girl nestled on the seat across from her, who had recently had her earlobe torn after a particularly brutal beating, just like Rehvana? The brown and tender flesh split open when the hand slapping the face got caught in an earring and continued its arc, hoop and all—the delicate skin ripped apart, torn into two bloody shreds which now hang like two withered flaps.

She can't bear to look at these two, nor the others, nor especially that other one, over there . . .

The child is always late on days when Rehvana has given homework, and she's learnt that it's because he doesn't have time—in fact, he's not allowed—to study anything at home: as soon as he returns from school, and even when he first gets out of bed and gets ready for class, he's sent to manage his stepfather's grocery store. He has deep scars on his face and arms—traces of beatings she'd not noticed before, but were as plain as day when she called him to her office. Reluctantly, he revealed that his mother beat both his sister and him for the slightest provocation, with whatever she could grab—scissors, steam iron, belt—to such an extent that their father, long-separated from her, and who saw them once in a while, had resorted to filing a complaint against his ex-wife, which, alas, had only served to make things worse. The child was trembling with fear as he told her all this, remembering the terrible consequences their father's vain intervention had provoked. Neither child had been removed from the home; however, the raging shrew accused of abusing her children had taken revenge on them.

When Rehvana had alerted a social worker, she was simply told a respectable housewife had the right to punish her children.

She doesn't feel strong enough to take on all the misfortune surrounding her or fight back the shame—the indescribable shame that overcomes her—whenever she tries hard to ignore that sacrilegious voice—the other, faint voice, hardly recognizable—which nevertheless implores her to listen, and cries out that she never did anything for her own child and now, with her heartless cowardice, won't lift a finger to help others!

And Rehvana is ashamed, irrepressibly ashamed.

She's in a hurry to get off this bus, and keeps her eyes closed until they reach the school. There, she mumbles an excuse to her colleagues, is the first one to jump off the bus, and she abandons them all, without bothering to look after the children.

She wanders aimlessly through the streets of Remorville until she reaches the fringes of the suburb, then enters a pub where she spots a few seated couples. A blond woman from the Pacific or one of the former tiny French trading posts in India—a pale wreck with a wrinkled face, washed up here, stranded— holds court at the bar and chitchats to drown a dark and dull heartache, telling Rehvana she's travelled the world, and offering her a third ti-punch, afraid she might leave too soon and she'd lose her conversation companion—really her audience—since Rehvana has barely spoken a word.

On the tall bar stool, Rehvana starts to feel the room spin, and Michel Godzom's 'Alamanda' waltzes through her head. The three or four adulterous couples scattered in the chaos of the room sink deeper into their seats, hiding under the leaves of the potted palm trees, and completely ignore her. They've arranged to meet at this spot, right after work, in secrecy, in the subdued lighting of this ill-kept bar, where they rub up against one another before going back to their legitimate and respective homes. Offered breasts venture forth from bras, and hands snake under skirts to discover what they conceal. For some of these pairs, Rehvana only glimpses a shoulder, a bent nape of a neck—here, the strong build of a man who could be Enryck, taller than the back of the faded couch, but no, he's leaning over, it's not him— and way over there, the profile of an amorous madam lapping up the kiss of a mulatto man, amid the confusion of dying potted plants, folding screens, beaded curtains and worn-down small columns.

Her head is spinning. Thin layers of dried mud still stick to her ankles and legs.

She hangs out in this buzz of voices that reeks of rum, including the exotic escapades of the blonde wreck, until night-fall, then suddenly, unable to bear the self-centred babbling of the bleached alcoholic for another second, she gets up, mid-sentence, and leaves. She didn't return to the high school that afternoon. She didn't have the heart to go back.

On rue de la Redoute-de-Matouba, before going on her way, she paused for a moment and, with an impatient gesture, scraped the clumps of dried mud from her skin.

She hurries to get to the taxi stand because she doesn't like to be out after dark. Like the other nights when her afternoon classes end at five o'clock and the last shared taxi to Vert-Pré leaves her in town at dusk, she'll have to proceed on foot, alone in the night, for the four kilometres separating her from home, because at that hour, Anastase has already finished his shift, and shared taxis don't venture into the depths of the Café neighbour-hood that late.

However, she could choose to avoid the walk down to Café: there are still quite a few cars driving by—a few men going home. When Rehvana walks by the roadside, it doesn't take long for her to attract the unwanted attentions of drivers who stop and offer her a 'ride' but she never accepts; she's not interested. Rather than climbing into an unknown man's car, she prefers to continue to push on alone, into the shadows of the unlit, narrow, winding road, even though she knows the revolting Boniface is on the prowl, demonically lying in wait for her near La Charles. Far more formidable than the amorous centaur—the dashing Anastase from her morning commute—the crude, bitako Boniface vows to her his fierce hatred blended with animal desire. Most often seen perched on his anachronistic mule with its huge and quasi-permanent erection that makes him the laughing stock of the town—but only behind his back—this fiendish nègre-congo, upright and proud, belligerent, concupiscent and rapacious like a gamecock armed with murderous spurs on its claws, shoots daggers at her in the dark with his large and yellow wolf eyes.

The fellow isn't old, but he's let his body go, as Cidalise would say, passionately loquacious on this subject while oblivious to her own deteriorating state. (It must be said that she's got a good fifteen years and fifteen pregnancies on him.) The madman had turned ugly due to ignorant neglect, fierce avarice, and disparaging everyone, everything and himself, to the point where he now looks like an 'old man'.

'He was sure the worst of the worst of all those fathers I had for my boys,' Ma Cidalise declares, day in, day out. 'Damn, but that fellow is a clever devil! If I'd known, I never ever would've had three ti-manmailles with that crook. Seven men I've shared my bed with, seven Negro males, one after the next, my bedroom never haven' time to cool down. Seven handsome Negro males, my dear, and the whole lot of 'em with pretty potent stuff lyin' between their legs, not sissies, mind you, seven Negro males, *man di'w* (I tell you)! And I make boys for 'em, all sorts of those handsome li'l boys! But to take me to the altar, not a one who says "here I am" . . . Marriage ain't no picnic, and gettin' married can come back to bite you. Like machine-gun fire, I made some boys for these Messieurs, *manman manman manman*! And then who was goin' to put on fresh butter-coloured gloves to ask for my hand, considerin' I was still a "Miss"? When you put your foot in a nest of ants, you can't never be too sure who the culprit was that bit you . . . meaning that I was the talk of the neighbourhood, and folks were beginnin' to jabber and make jokes 'bout me, 'cause it looked like Ma Cidalise was bein' used for everyone's so-called wife. Those women folks, they're nuthin' but bad-mouths—all those neighbours from Chère-Épice, you gotta beware of 'em lyinliars and blabbersillymouths, and those gossipmadames and company: they're all cut from the same cloth, thick as thieves, and there's always someone around to spread untruths and make all kinds of wisecracks. I let 'em go on prattlin' away, and was raisin' yiches one after the other. If you think I was gonna hang my head in shame and crawl into a crab trap hole *ad vitam aeternam*, forever and ever . . . Me, I'm no shrinkin' violet. And I took my job raisin' my boys real serious-like, oh no, my dear, though I was all alone, more times than not. I took care of ev'rythin' that needed doin' for 'em: shined shoes, ironed shirts, kneeled for *pater noster* each mornin' and ev'ning. You could say I kept my yiches in line by rulin' with an iron fist, and I made sure they got their education. Each mornin' when they left for the school house, they held their shoes in their hands— nice li'l well-shined shoes—so as to keep 'em from gettin' all dirty-like when goin' down Morne-Galba in the mud, and their bellies were always filled, every day that the good Lord made. As for those daddies who were no husbands for me to be sure, and not jus' maybe, but exceptin' the dead ones (now four of 'em) and that mess-up Boniface, not one of 'em was goin' to run off and leave 'is brood without a sou. And even the ones who have passed on, they are watchin' over their yiches from purgatory—'cause I can't say heaven: they weren't no vagabonds, but no saints, either . . . But even if your yiches are a bunch of ragamuffins et cetera, you still got your duty as a parent, good God! Kids, they're not jus' a bunch of little pebbles, my goodness!

'And nothin' but boys is all I know how to make, poor me! A daughter, a pretty, li'l chabine, or a li'l mulatto girl like you,

Rehvana dear, that's exactly what I was needin', sweet darlin', that's what I was wantin' for my old age, now that I'm up in my years. Listen to what I'm sayin'. Boys only come and go, eat their meals whenever they want, plant themselves at the table and go complainin' if the breadfruit's too sweet. You're never gonna see a young man put a torche on his head to help carry stuff, or grab a basin and go fetch water at the spring. But the daughter, she'll always take care of her mama, she's always wantin' to pitch in, even when she's got children of her own. You never gonna see the daughter leave her mama to fend for herself when trouble comes a-knockin' and she's stuck with a heap of hard luck,' concludes Ma Cidalise with the utmost solemnity, resting her case.

And Rehvana is almost as disgusted by Boniface as Cidalise, at least as she is now. (Indeed, it's well known that the Cidalise of old—vivacious and headstrong—wasn't always as immune to the bitako's potent animal allure.) Apart from his banana trees, around which he spends one or two half hours each day twiddling his thumbs in the cool morning and night air, he doesn't have much to offer the world. He lounges around without *joie de vivre* or cheer, and drags himself along, hoping for a nice, destructive hurricane that would enable him to collect compensation and subsidies from the government, from the region, who knows, '*I pa menm sav*,' he doesn't even want to know, because he's here to drink the milk, and not to count the cows, he insolently sneers, and he's sure it'll end up coming, the 'compassation', as he says. His wide maw is nothing but a gaping, putrid hole, except where his rare teeth shine like those of a meat-eating shark, stuck in the middle of a face of unfathomable black with scaly, saurian skin. 'He really looks like a gangster,' thinks Rehvana, whenever the satyr springs from the thicket, making her jump each time, or when, bow-legged, he blocks her way, fists on hips, straw hat worn defiantly low on the forehead, and lifted with a flick of his finger when he sees Rehvana—yes, even from far away—to ravenously scrutinize her from the depths of his cruel, yellow eyes.

'Leave 'im to his business, Rehvana dear! Your own Negro guy has bad manners, but that there bugger is pure evil, on top of all that. Jus' continue to be goin' on your way, girl, and don't even look at 'im. Oh no, don't be even givin' a glance in his direction, or 'e's gonna burn your eyes, 'e will, like someone possessed by hell's fire. That *Mussieur*, 'e's the Devil's son!' Ma Cidalise insisted.

And perhaps Rehvana disobeyed her because some part of her, deep inside, was fascinated by the energy emanating from this character. Their eyes must have met—at least once.

Boniface is the brother of a neighbourhood woman with a tormented look—as if from beyond the grave—the one who is Rehvana's soucougnan from her long nights of waiting and keeping watch.

The terrifying boloko had even had the audacity to come by Rehvana's house one fine morning—swaggering, all spiffied up in suit and tie, belted and stiff—to offer a few yams to the 'great lady from France'. For the occasion, he'd dug up from his worm-eaten trunk a Methuselah suit he only wears for funerals, that reeks of mothballs, eau de Cologne, and mould. We can bet he was making the most of having to attend the burial that afternoon of some enemy—since Boniface has no friends—by paying Rehvana his heavy-handed and boorish respects. He'd thought to kill two birds with one stone, since it was such a chore for him to bathe, confine his huge, blogodo feet in lace-up shoes, and trade the rags he usually wore, stained with banana sap, for a more or less clean white shirt and a frayed, black suit.

Politely but firmly turned away by Rehvana, who'd been warned by Ma Cidalise, he now hates her.

He keeps an eye out for her, and mumbles when she passes by, 'You're a lucky lady . . . '

And his sister, coming out of nowhere, squeals insults at her, calling her a witch!

Ma Cidalise, whose mouth never rests, even on Sundays—to whom Boniface left three sons in three years and scars all over her body—the only keepsakes from their torturous love—implies that Rehvana's youth and beauty are a threat to the monstrous incestuous affair going on between the villainous, toothless sister and her scrooge-of-a-brother: she even swears he 'owns banana plantations everywhere', and never took a wife because of his penny-pinching ways, making do, somehow, with his satyr sister to satisfy his physical needs, ever since Ma Cidalise threw him out, many years ago. He never took care of his three sons, Cidalise maintains with disdain, lips curled into a disgusted pout: it's as if they never existed; he's never spent a single sou on them or on anyone, and his three sons return the favour with unconcealed hate which also extends to their devil of an aunt.

The aunt, for her part, seems convinced that Rehvana has cast a spell over Boniface; how else to explain the generous gift of these three choice yams?

Such extravagance, and all this for a tiny, mulatto woman who any man, even a wimp, would crush as soon as he started handling her . . . even Boniface! And she's got nothing upfront or behind for padding, she decided *in petto*.

She thought she'd die of rage when Boniface sent her to pick the yams and she saw him bring them to that man-stealing woman. But all she could do was spit at his back, 'I know you like young things, but that worthless, little pissecrette!'

She fumed much longer, shrewish and debauched in the doorway of her house, not daring to launch a frontal assault on her brother, who was already far away. The rest of her curses were lost in the banana groves.

Although he hadn't heard her insults, Boniface made her fully pay for them upon his return, by unloading on her, without warning or preamble, all his pent-up resentment suppressed during the funeral service: aggrieved and seething with rage, he took revenge on his sister for the coldness of the 'lady from France' by hitting her with his patent-leather belt and his well-shined shoe, followed, when she fell to the floor, by other attacks no less virile and vicious, with much swearing. The guy exerted himself so much, putting so much heart into it, that he ended up with shameful stains on his special occasion suit, because in his almost-foaming madness, he hadn't taken the time to change clothes after returning from the funeral. The ceremonious, black suit—too tight, under the circumstances, to permit such a display of brutal manliness and epic erections—ended up disgustingly soiled and ripped at the armpit seams, while the hussy was left black and blue everywhere.

They say in all of Vert-Pré, from Zabeth to Rivière-Pomme, from Sabine to Habitation-Directoire, from Bois-Neuf to the Brice neighbourhood, from Morne-Galba to Providence, from Croix-Odilon to Galette and up into the depths of Four-à-Chaux, that the soucougnan didn't fly that night.

Fearless and as if she were sleepwalking, Rehvana walked down the road without really being aware of it. She didn't know if, in all this black, she'd had a dizzy spell, or if the fact of blindly walking alone at night gave her this muffled sensation of nonbeing. Without a glance, she passed Ma Cidalise's house. Numb, oblivious to her surroundings, not even caring about the baby already asleep in the old lady's home, she lay, fully clothed, on the living room's chaise longue, and succumbed to a dreamless stupor.

AWFUL LITTLE SISTER . . . even if you're angry . . . so afraid . . .
ask for your forgiveness . . . police . . . 'missing persons' . . . lie to
Maman . . . Come back to us, Rehvana! . . . Not important . . .
Aganila, you realize . . .

Matildana's letter lies crumpled in the nebula of the bed; it's
unlikely that Rehvana read it in its entirety—she's so tired of sermons. Shrivelled in places, it rests in the mess of the bed sheets,
like some helpless, ancient artefact, reduced to a sorry display of
incoherent snippets, null and void. It hasn't moved since last
night—was it last night? or was it the night before last? If the small
paper wad had moved, riding the galactic ripples of the sheets, it
was only to follow the valleys and slopes that formed from the
random movements of Rehvana's body throughout the night.

Rehvana had made a move to destroy the letter, like all the
other ones, as ordered by Enryck, or hide it and read it later, or
perhaps reread it, when she feels strong enough—though she
doesn't know what could possibly give her the strength, if
Matildana herself and Matildana's letter and Matildana's
strength—which asks only to surge forth and carry her off, head
spinning, on the wings of her righteous anger—haven't sufficed.
She'd suspended her gesture mid-air, transformed into a muscle
twitch. Her hand briefly held the letter, and creased it without
further thought—barely squeezed—then softly closed on it, only
to quickly let it go, because of a more urgent need to wipe away
the sweat on her face, and the letter was allowed to wander
through the sheets. It was such a useless, insignificant, imperfect
refusal to obey—a vague, unfinished rebellion—when Rehvana
postponed the letter's destruction: Enryck wouldn't be back anytime soon . . . She deferred the obligatory desecration—hard to
tell for how long. The blackened, diamond-sharp edges of
lightweight airmail paper probably pricked her a bit during the
night, as if to keep them on her mind, one way or another, as
they roamed beneath her body. But she held on until dawn without relighting the lamp, letting her nocturnal restlessness create
sentence fragments she'll decode the next day, one superimposed
on top of the other on the translucent, filmy, folded page—her
first vision of the day.

In the bedroom, furniture and objects dissolve in the curdled, milky haze where they were trapped for the night by the blurred screen of the mosquito net to which Rehvana still hasn't acclimated herself. Tentative and timid, with one hand she splits apart the worn, grainy gauze, whose dusty folds unfurl haphazardly around her, protecting the secret of the bed with a clouded veil. Before placing her feet on the loose floor tile, she hesitates, eyes narrowed, and checks that there's nothing beneath, since she doesn't want a repeat of her first morning in the Vert-Pré house when she stepped on the upsetting rotundity of a hideous, twisted, roly-poly caterpillar—probably as pusillanimous as Rehvana—adorned with glistening rings like warlike armour which makes it look grey when it's really black—a perfect black, perhaps—immobile, as if half-asleep and unable to flee, indestructible, able to ridiculously arch itself so head meets tail to form a thick, semi-rigid and sickening hoop when you poke it, forcing you to pick it up between two sticks to toss it into the garden, even if it means, one way or another, you have to suppress your dry heaves.

What's the point of getting out of bed in this pasty and wan early dawn that's a cruel mockery of her own state of mind? (But does she realize what's become of her—so pathetic, so fragile she might melt in a fine mist, just like her life, and all she's ever dreamt?) Adamantine and real, the only object in sharp focus in the powdery morning light, Matildana's letter is still there, abandoned, even unread.

Matildana's letter mopes nearby, in the middle of the four-poster bed, close at hand, desperately insistent wherever it happens to land, in daybreak's indifferent rays of sun—sole, true and clarifying presence that's more important—oh, so much more!—than Rehvana herself, with her unreal nudity in this virginal or sepulchral white of the bedsheets, the mosquito net, and the white pages. Rehvana sinks, abyssal and drained, into the jumbled sheets where she lies in sulphurous wait for the one who never came—under the capsizing ripples of the muslin's untruths.

In Ma Cidalise's medicine stash, Rehvana was able to find piles of old, expired painkillers and an assortment of sleeping pills which she discreetly spirited away behind the old lady's back, and indiscriminately takes to get some sleep or at least to numb the pain from her bruises—souvenirs from Enryck's last visit.

Ma Cidalise respects this dented shoebox like a tabernacle, where she stockpiles the triumphal loot she brings back from her trips to the doctor. Even if she doesn't ingest them, she's happy to have this jumble of pills at home, keeping them around like talismans. She doesn't really distinguish between these colourful drugs with hard-to-pronounce names, and those from the conjurer's recipes, since both are bought at the pharmacy through a simple piece of paper. (How many times has she handed the pharmacist both a medical prescription and a list of products scribbled by the seer on a sheet ripped from a spiral-bound notebook?)

For the past three years, Cidalise has dragged along a foot with a gaping wound—an ugly, pus-filled, proliferating infection that has spread to her ankle. Nevertheless, her main concern doesn't seem to be healing or even treating the injury but, rather, providing a blow-by-blow account of the ins and outs of treatment and the progression of the wound. After each consultation, she tries hard to recreate, in a priceless song and dance, the strange-sounding phrases of the man of science. Most of all, she gets a kick out of all the medical jargon, which she does her utmost to mimic and mock each time she returns from the hospital, to Rehvana's delight. But she doesn't completely trust conventional medicine because she's convinced her unhealed sore comes from a neighbour's evil spell. Since she'd pronounced 'spell' without the initial s and slightly changed the e to an ay, Rehvana had smiled at first, wondering what kind of 'pail' filled with what kind of contents could have been directed at poor Cidalise. Rehvana recalled, with a look of amusement on her face, the stories her father had told her—unless it was Ma Cidalise herself, she no longer remembers—anecdotes from the days when people emptied their enamelled chamber pots each morning, when 'caca-guards' were in charge of enforcing the rules; she was expecting the old woman to relate another of her trademark, outlandish tales.

Rehvana quickly concluded it was about witchcraft, when Cidalise, brandishing a scrap of square-ruled paper of dubious cleanliness, quite creased and covered in clumsy handwriting, told her about that skilled and renowned psychic from Guadeloupe, whom she had asked to 'look into her business' and who'd agreed to do it by mail. Maintaining that all the medicines in the world would prove to be useless until the 'pail' was removed, Ma Cidalise had asked Rehvana to read her the letter, assuring her that its author had an extraordinarily powerful gift, and therefore could certainly do something for her and her little girl. Still smiling, Rehvana had taken the magical dispatch—just a crumpled sheet of paper.

'We removed the piece of garbage for you on Monday,' the letter said. 'The evil spirit sent your way was male. He's the one who prevented the children from staying home. His name is Tôtô. He's a man we have killed very slowly; he's a mulatto. The person who had the spell cast is a black woman, of medium build. She talks to you, but betrays you behind your back because she's jealous. She paid 2,400 francs plus a whisky for the work.

'For a cure, go to the cemetery and find an abandoned grave. Pull out a few weeds on this grave and say, "As I clean this grave, let all wounds leave my body, no matter where they may be." After you've said this, while still in the graveyard, light a candle in honour of the souls in purgatory, then leave without looking back. When you're done doing all this, on the same day, go bathe in a river, getting wet from head to toe, then go home. *Do not go home before bathing in the river . . .* '

'In any case, the great Saint Michel is protectin' me, since I did nuthin' deservin' of blame,' concludes a triumphant Ma Cidalise, while a pensive Rehvana finished reading the letter.

Ma Cidalise continues to read the Bible for the rest of the day, waiting for her cure to come.

The Arrogant and Miserable Alliance

RAGING RAINS HAVE RELENTLESSLY BEEN PELTING the closed jalousie windows. Submissive and weak, they've been enduring the water's whipping assault for days. To Rehvana, their glass seems so ancient, so fragile and so ill-equipped to weather the unexpected deluge. How much more can they take?

When Enryck was still coming by, he'd slowly lean over her, and she would tilt her head up to him, docile, while the louvered windows gathered the moist warmth of evening showers and tamed the devouring solar glare of the living God. But Baal has snuffed out his fires; the victorious star no longer deigns to dispense its ardour, and Rehvana now doubts they can withstand the diluvian violence much longer.

She's really afraid they might unexpectedly break.

It's been raining non-stop for days. It rains night and day. It rains through sleepless nights and through lonely days. Rehvana has crumpled up in the little warmth she's got left. It seems she's unable to do anything—neither for the passion fruit, strewn and crushed in the mud, martyred by mighty downpours, nor for her garden's soil, this rediscovered land, fertilized by her determined resurrection and the indefatigable jubilation of her return to her roots, this land on which she lavished attention but now offers her a bloated appearance, streaked with soggy scars: decapitated narcissus stalks, neglected crab-apple trees, mistreated mangoes and apricots. Rehvana stares into space; defeated, listless and helpless, she bears witness to the collapse of her life's work. The poinsettias she'd lovingly planted in the fullness of an auspicious moon have drowned from hostile floods. All her flowers had shortened lives. The evening shadows—friends Rehvana had invited under the veranda—have all vanished in the storm.

Everything has gone under, lost in the never-ending torrential rain. Dejected and expressionless in the contemplation of her destroyed universe, Rehvana's glazed eyes stare straight ahead, until the glossy cement floor beneath her begins to glow—now suddenly reflective, like a cursed mirror—forcing her to close her eyes.

She's cold.

Rehvana is cured of all nostalgia and hope. The one to whom she'd turned for kisses—the chosen one who had escorted her to the threshold of the great Return—has understood nothing of her zeal, and has proven unworthy of her love.

Enryck has ruined her Martinique.

Fruit is rotting in the garden and piling up at the base of the bushes, in a compact swarm of yen-yen and flies.

Ma Cidalise gathers the fruit from time to time, without daring to say a word.

Rehvana doesn't read precautions, directions, contraindications, doses or possible side effects.

She picks at random, recognizes a few brand names, and gorges on everything that makes you sleep, calms you down and kills the pain. She swallows it all: drops, tablets, coated pills, blue gel caps, pink capsules—it's all the same to her. She binges on drugs just like she had gorged on chocolate cream puffs and thick napoleons ten years earlier, on rue Houdan.

In the beginning, Rehvana had chosen according to colour; she was still looking for something then.

She used to create intriguing combinations on the spot, drink water while choking pills down and deliberately count drops.

Now she has no idea where the droppers are; the blister pill packets pierced by her nails point their little metallic teeth upward, a collection of empty pillboxes are strewn here and there, and she is stretched out on top of it all. Once in a while she kicks some packaging out of the way—perhaps partially full—because it scratches her ankles, but she can't be bothered to reach for it.

She's pillaged Ma Cidalise's shoe box. When she'd first started, she conscientiously organized her bounty, just like sick people, after a doctor visit, line up all the drugs bought at the pharmacy on the nightstand, in the order prescribed, and from which they feverishly expect salvation and a cure.

Impossible to say if she's attempting suicide, or only seeking a respite. She no longer fills the carafe, toppled and spilt by a heavy leg, that must have rolled somewhere into a dark corner, she has no idea—it might even have broken. She chews on a hodgepodge of mashed pills, which, whatever their colour—or perhaps thanks to the indiscriminate concoction she makes of them—leave her without revolt, appetite or despair.

Out there, the blue mass of hills kneels in silence against the grey of the sky and the sea, in this cold, post-storm fusion. Then all sinks into the darkness of night, without a trace of light or breath, filled with crackling scratches of nocturnal sounds deferred by rain; the air is heavy with thick secretions all around the sealed-off house.

She remains there, shaking with faint spasms and shivering in fits and starts from the nearby rumbles of thunder, with their furious lightning strikes which illuminate the night with transient light.

The pills with their bitter taste fill her with useless substances, barely able to blunt her fear of the storm or bring drowsiness to her, like that of a punished child. The drugs are stuck in her throat, and eventually, after the rain stops, she finds enough strength to slowly get up to drink, from two cupped hands, the water from the kitchen tap covered in verdigris—always a little too warm. She bangs into unknown masses, stumbles over unforeseen presences with confrontational edges and cruel, unexpected corners—furniture with vicious curves whose location, and even existence, she forgot, unless they've moved on their own in the whirlwind madness of her nightmares, or so she thinks. She staggers, while grabbing onto imaginary, missing supports that elude her, slyly disappearing under her, and from their fanciful failure, she loses her balance. She looks for the hallway buffet, inexplicably lost because the wind has penetrated the glass of the only kerosene lamp, and swears at the unknown folds of the off-centre, raffia rug—good God, what's it doing here!—whose raspy fibres are recognized by her feet but how in hell did it get here? Her path is strewn with hazards, both treacherous and out of control, created by the previous times she ventured around the house, when she'd caused objects to randomly fall in her wake—objects she doesn't recall and which she never picked up. Knocked-over chairs and knick-knacks make an unpredictable obstacle course of the house, with traps everywhere, for in her extremely debilitated state, she can't restore them to order nor keep track of their disorder—the current, maddening and provisional placements, each time more noxious and new.

Only the chaise longue of heavy wood has faithfully retained its usual place in this dangerous chaos. Groping her way in the dark, that's where she returns, cursing the conspiracy of all things around her . . . When she finally prevails over the numerous pitfalls, narrowly escaping being knocked unconscious—or, at least, not totally knocked out—once she succeeds in reaching the chaise longue, though stunned and half-dead, she lets herself fall into it with a deep, hoarse groan, her legs folding under her, as if giving out, and with lolling head and arms loosely coming to rest wherever they fall—passive and unfazed. One arm dangles on the floor, and her face is buried under an avalanche of pillows, while the other arm, inert and totally idle, struggles to obey, or ignores, for several unbearable and oppressive minutes, the order to set her free, now, right now, suffocating, almost asphyxiated and still weakened, despite having drunk some water. She didn't think to fill the carafe; in fact, she didn't even look for it.

At no moment did she think of anything else but her pressing desire to drink, then the urgent need to return, at all costs, to where she started, as if she truly couldn't go anywhere else. She could have ended up in the swarming shambles of the kitchen, or somewhere on the broken tile floor: doubtless a remnant of feeling had blindly led her back to the languid bed where Enryck's odour still lingers—to the smooth, sagging cushions where neither her fever's sweat, nor the sour breath that escapes into the stuffy air as she lets out a moan, can suppress the former scent of love.

BEFORE CHECKING INTO THE HOSPITAL for a skin graft on her ulcerated foot, Ma Cidalise had taken it upon herself to bring Aganila to her godmother in Tartane. Upon her discharge, she'd dropped by to see the baby, since the doctors had prescribed a stay in a convalescent home in Cap-Est, many kilometres away. She didn't dare ask her eldest son—already annoyed at having to leave work to drive her from La Meynard Hospital to Cap-Est, by way of a stupid detour through La Caravelle to visit the baby—to go out of his way again, to Café, where she'd be able to find out what Rehvana had been up to.

'*Po piti malgré sa!*' ('Poor little one, despite all this!') she mutters in an inaudible, reedy voice. 'And what if I said I forgot to put enough clothes in my duffle bag? Like the top of my second pair of pyjamas? Tchip! I know him—he's gonna tell me they have ev'rythin' in Cap-Est . . . '

She racks her brains and can't think of anything that might convince the one whose stubborn profile is outlined in the cutting wind. He's driving fast and masses of air—bitterly cold—blow into the car; she's shivering, but doesn't dare ask him to roll up his window. She sees him so rarely, after all: he's become a stranger. She's intimidated by him. He doesn't speak.

'*Et dire que c'est ti manmay mwen!*' ('And when I think that he's my child!') she cried somewhere deep inside.

She kept it all to herself—both her crying and her thoughts.

She hasn't found any excuse, any reason to have to stop by her house: her son would have replied that she didn't have to worry about anything, that he and his wife came regularly on Sundays to take care of the rickety place, that it was already late and they still had a long way to go. Hadn't he already tried to discourage her from going down to Tartane? She'd had to lie to him, and pretend she had to kiss her godmother . . . And her son had driven her with such reluctance . . .

And the old woman wouldn't have found the courage to abandon Rehvana to her tragic fate once she'd inquired after her state of health. That would have been beyond her strength. A visit to the child had consoled her, but she didn't know what to do for the mother. She'd tried everything though and Ma Cidalise, while admitting her helplessness, still agonized, in her devout simplicity, over what solution, what miracle, could change it all.

In any case, she breathed easier, reassured by knowing, at least, that Enryck could no longer hurt the baby, that Aganila was out of his reach, safely sheltered from that no-good's blows, and that the man wouldn't be able to torture this child any longer, whose sole crime was not being his. But what about Rehvana?

She knew that taking Rehvana's daughter away from her would sever whatever tenuous link still connected her to life, but she'd had little time to act; she'd been pressured to proceed with the surgery since her sores hurt too much, and she couldn't take care of the baby any more. She'd nevertheless refused to leave without first removing Aganila from Enryck's claws, even at so high a price, and even though she'd had the unpleasant sensation that she hadn't done the right thing.

Ma Cidalise didn't have a totally clear conscience.

But no sooner had she kissed the little girl and complimented and thanked her godmother for taking such good care of her than the hurried young man was impatiently hauling her into the car.

The car zoomed straight ahead on the main road to Trinité and, at the Pelletier junction, Ma Cidalise couldn't hold back a long, anxious shiver at the thought of the young woman—alone, up there on the hill. But Aganila is feeling much better now, and she's being fed—even overfed, despite her small appetite—with fresh-caught fish, juicy fruits and wholesome vegetables: it won't be long before she regains some colour and strength and puts on weight, far from the humid and heavy atmosphere of Vert-Pré.

'In any case, she hasn't been askin' after her mommy yet . . .' she thinks, as if to calm herself down.

Ma Cidalise doesn't know that the young, abandoned mother has shut herself away in her state of neglect, and forsaken her students, once and for all, too ashamed to return to the school.

Rehvana feels neither the courage nor the strength to go back. Besides, the substitute teacher job in Remorville was coming to an end.

Rehvana now feels as if she's been bleeding for ever.

She doesn't know how long it's been since the rains began to flow, as well as the bloody streaks down her thighs. Two weeks, several weeks, maybe months . . .

She seldom moves, surrounded by sickening, soiled bed linens and her endlessly trickling bloody stream—the only warm presence her body can still feel. She believes she's bleeding to death; for that matter, she hasn't touched the pack of blue, orange and white birth control pills, useless for so many nights, now. She doesn't question anything and she resigns herself to endure the tireless, crimson tide that stains her skin.

She no longer lights fires to burn her menstrual pads; her blood is up for grabs to anyone who wants it!

In the beginning, Rehvana had counted the days, like a rookie convict from Devil's Island. She thought Enryck was bound to come back since he'd let her stay in his house. But from the time Ma Cidalise had entrusted Aganila to her kinsfolk, Enryck had gradually spaced out his sporadic visits, until he'd stopped coming at all.

The baby's departure—which the young mother had accepted without much grief, and in fact had welcomed as a true godsend because she believed that when Enryck came to visit, he wouldn't be disturbed by the baby's nightly cries and would be grateful to her for it—had curiously coincided with her lover's almost complete disappearance, despite the excessively effusive homecomings and the reconciliation which had followed the alleged attempted poisoning. Rehvana had proved her innocence through innumerable kisses but, soon after, Enryck had met a new, bewitching beauty who seemed less dangerous and less of a conjurer than Rehvana. Besides, he wasn't in such a hurry to come back to the calamitous Circe from Café.

She doesn't go visit her child any more. Where would she find the moral instinct, the hygienic drive, the self-esteem necessary to bathe and get rid of the smell of an unfit lifestyle—the morbid odour of menstrual blood and death clinging to her skin? Where would she find the courage to face the wait in the rain, the inevitable attentions of Anastase and his self-serving, mocking concern?

She winces weakly with irritated disgust at the idea of sitting once again on the shiny, leatherette passenger seat, and handing over her pale self to the clutches of the gallant taxi driver.

Just the thought of having to face Anastase's burning gaze in her weakened state—his smothering gestures and the heady musk of his intense desire concentrated in the sweltering heat of the car with its windows rolled up in the rain, not to mention the memory of emotions she allowed herself, back in the day when she was brimming with boldness—depletes and drains her, making her head spin.

And, most importantly, how to face her little girl?

What does she have to offer the child; what does she have to offer anyone?

She'd need a sudden jolt, an awakening, an explosive forward thrust to make her get up.

Rehvana lies in her own blood; she doesn't even bother with sanitary pads and belts. When she feels the occasional need to escape her sticky listlessness to move about, glassy-eyed, in the chaotic rooms, she leaves behind a trail of scarlet drops she won't think to wipe up, and which turn brown as they dry, staining the dusty and dirty tiles with overlapping, haloed rings she hasn't mopped up in days. The house has been left to itself and to the hordes of pill bugs, spiders or caterpillars, cockroaches and worms that have gradually moved back into the hideaways they'd lost when Rehvana arrived.

You'd never suspect anything's been altered in the house; it's reverted to its former state, before Rehvana tackled the mould and grime, armed with bleach, spray disinfectants and elbow grease. The small figure slumped in a dark corner is so minuscule, so silent, so still, that it seems as if the hovel has been emptied of any human presence—long abandoned by its tenants. Her breath is so weak, her weight so negligible and her footsteps so light, that when she slowly glides on the old, dirty tiles, she no longer scares roaches away. The floor doesn't even realize it carries her; it's been nothing but a broken and ignoble tile floor; it never was anything else and had never undergone any change. It never creaks when she steps on its shattered tiles. Despite her hard work, this place never transformed into a happy home. The entire house—indifferent and unchanging—pays her no mind.

Only a few bloodstains dotting the floor are evidence of the woman's presence. This flow of death is the only proof of her life between these walls.

She'd have to get a hold of herself and snap out of it. But where could she draw the strength to take charge of her body, stand up and run away? She'd need a strong burst of confidence and a full-bodied, running leap towards life, towards her daughter, to drag her from this house, to rush to Aganila—yes!—run to her child, hold her tight, carry her off and be on her way. Days trickle by like her blood and Rehvana has no idea where to find the momentum—the life-saving energy that would wrest her from this den of pain and wounded pride.

Even if Enryck came back to her, it would now be too late. He shouldn't have left her alone for so long; he could have kept up his little dance for years—his fickle comings and goings between Rehvana and his mistresses.

She'd got used to being on the lookout for his returns, and she knew how to be patient, forgiving and docile. She'd learnt to wait.

But never for such a long time—not for weeks!

Over all these days, Rehvana has lost the memory of his warm hands and his tall, beloved body. He's no longer there to confuse her, intoxicate her and soothe her wounds with a caress. He's not there to put her to bed and anaesthetize her with his promises. The only thing she now recalls of the man's strength is the barbaric force with which he struck the sick child. He's no longer there to squash her spurts of lucidity under his virile command, or quash her aborted rebellions under his kiss.

He'd have to be here to quell her revolt, subdue the voice of reason that screams the man is a brute and she's got to leave, escape! Extract herself from this inhuman and shameful submission, take her child away, yes, go get her child and whisk her away.

REHVANA CLIMBS THE STONY SLOPE until she reaches the wèt, the winding shortcut in the middle of the cane field. Her skin scrapes on the rocks on the trail, her frail ankles twist, she walks fast, almost runs, she'd run if the slope weren't so steep, she's drenched in sweat, and its salt mixes with her tears. She cuts through banana thickets and groves, to emerge from the plantation. Cheeks on fire, she reaches the paved road and continues her feverish flight on the steamy asphalt. She quickens her pace, blinded by sweat, and trips over the crushed body of a female opossum—a pregnant one—belly ripped open, where the pup quivers, still alive—pink form coiled inside the gaping womb— who won't survive since its mother has died.

Rehvana doesn't stop; her eyes are swimming in tears. She gets past the bloody opossum without blinking, then robotically moves ahead; the more exhausted she feels, the more she hurries her step, for she knows if she pauses—even for a moment, just to catch her breath, as she's dying to do—if she sits for a second on the cool grass, so tempting to her feverish body, she'll never find the strength to get up again.

Now her feet are simply grazing the ground—maybe even floating above—spurred on and carried by the thought of Aganila, up there, by the sea—her salvation and absolution of sins. She feels neither the truly expiatory pain this frantic rush inflicts on her weakened limbs, nor the agony of the fast; neither fatigue nor fever slow her ascent. She lifts her head high to the sun and drinks the rain, which moistens her chapped lips. The coils of her silky curls, now unstuck from her drenched temples, unfurl and inflate—life-saving sails in the free air. She braces herself and yields to the high wind that hoists her into the air, the shower that soaks her, the trade wind that carries her, and the rainbow's halo of colours that crown her escape.

Rehvana flies towards the child who waits for her, nestled in the rostrum at the far end of the island—Caravelle—which opens with its prow a passage across the salty waters of the Atlantic.

FINAL SONG

Last Alliances

IT SEEMS LIKE CENTURIES HAVE PASSED since Rehvana's venal female friend moved out.

The sleazy, fat lover her friend had agreed to follow to the Canary Islands had been accompanied by another heavyset man, drooling and lewd, who had set his sights on Rehvana and would have done anything, given all the gold in the world from his thick, lustful hands for her, even with her child.

It was both distasteful and sad that the poor devil seemed to be sincerely moved by the little girl and was seriously eager to welcome the two of them into his house in Garches in the suburbs of Paris, the photos of which he'd proudly displayed. He gently explained to Rehvana that he was genuinely willing to make available to them a tidy sum of money left over each month, once all the bills had been paid. From his substantial salary of a dull, small-time CEO, he had to deduct mortgage payments for the house and alimony to his ex-wife and two grown-up sons, whom he'd ditched a good while back for the false eyelashes of a former secretary of his, now long gone, who wore garish make-up, even when going to sleep.

Without being blunt or mean, Rehvana will refuse the tribute of the infamous chequebook. Without being harsh, I say, and even without arrogance. For once, she's not cruel.

She's now less and less cruel.

Was she ever truly cruel to anyone else besides herself?

She only asked her friend from the demimonde to lend her the flat just for the time it took to find a solution, money, a job, who knows? For Rehvana has promised to pull herself together, and the friend took off, trusting and unconcerned, closing the door of her low-income, high-rise home, leaving behind a sweet, young mother giving her daughter a bath. They dug up a large plastic tub for Aganila's daily baths and Rehvana lovingly laid out the well-ironed baby clothes, already a little tight, on the edge of the cracked bathroom sink—the irresistible rabbit-print jammies she'll put on her child before tucking her in, next to her, in the only bed. Her departing friend's titillated squeals and her lover's teasing are swallowed in one gulp by the walls of the smelly lift, where the poodle on the seventh floor can never hold it in.

She'll ask for nobody's help, especially not Matildana's.

She's still got a little money left from what her sister last sent her in Vert-Pré, and what the man from Garches kindly gave her. By the time this money runs out, something will have happened. It's true she could look for work, perhaps go back to Louis Faraud, try to get him to find a few photo shoots here or there—but only freelance and as a stopgap measure—because a full-time modelling career—dream of all the young nitwits she's known—already had nauseated her back in the day when she was living that 'dream', and it's unlikely she'd take to it any better now . . .

Recalling this time before she'd met Enryck or her ageing, foppish beau plunged Rehvana into a bittersweet daydream . . .

Draping his shrivelled old skin in the torn silk of a lady's dressing gown, her suitor, the great Parisian fashion designer whose annual sales revenues topped thirteen billion old francs, inscribed her words—the sacred words the superb young woman, this ravishing stranger had volunteered—on the empty walls of his huge, split-level flat, monastically devoid of most furniture. At the end of a performance of Pasolini's *Medea*, he'd wanted to see in Rehvana all the magic of the cosmos. The man had been handsome, but a bit of sickening saliva bubbled from the corners of his mouth—a ridiculous, frothy, obscene drool—and although he'd offered her, out of pure platonic selflessness, the hospitality of his four hundred square metre flat, the affection of his dogs, steaks from his Spanish housekeeper, and chickens he ordered by phone and which came ready-to-eat, already roasted from the Champ de Mars rotisserie, he had nothing to give. Besides, the luxury meats—maybe filet mignon, she knows nothing about these things, but for sure, first-rate beef—the Spanish woman bought for the dogs. She'd simply bought a little bit more, perhaps, since Rehvana had started living there.

And the indecisive young woman let herself be paraded around for a while by the handler of Medeas—boastful like a circus acrobat, smooth-talking like a hustler at the fair—at insipid evenings at princely restaurants where he presented Rehvana as a prized auction piece for sale, until she got sick of it and fled.

The ridiculous man has left on a business trip for a few days and she's let the place be overrun by a horde of friends. The flat is so enormous, it's too tempting, there's almost no furniture because the fashion designer is, as it turns out, rather off the wall, but it's not important, they're fine with it, sitting on the floor, wolfing down a wondrous tabouleh salad and a tiébou-dien, and they dance, and they party hard, like there's no tomorrow, to the delight of the dogs. They eat with their fingers, grabbing handfuls of rice doused with red sauce which they joyfully knead and roll into little balls. The merry bond between them is sealed with the joints passed around for dessert, the 'horse' that gallops from snort to snort; things get broken in their intoxicated state and wine is spilt on the thick carpet. Rehvana finally kicked out the gloomy lesbian, still swaying alone in the morning, in the middle of the wide empty living room with the maenads sprawled on the floor.

The penny-pinching man probably disapproved. Still, he didn't say a word, too busy playing the part of the now successful, former member of the working class yearning for joys of the intellectual sort. This apprentice baker from Pézenas, who 'left for the capital' on a whim, is still amazed he made so much 'dough' from duping rich Parisian dames. She ditched him right there, busy knocking in vain at the Muses' door with his palette knife.

This narrow-minded partisan no longer amused Rehvana, so she left him where he stood, stuck at the threshold of the sanctuary of Ideas, without being concerned about whether or not he'd managed to get in.

. . . And Faraud's dogs, Xakan and Tchiba, had African priestess names.

She emerges from her memories while bitterly biting on a clove. Her teeth have gone downhill, little by little, since her pregnancy; she can't afford to go to the dentist, and besides, she doesn't feel like it. She chews, pensive, trusting the virtues of a clove tree bud to calm the stabbing pain.

The Other Paris

REHVANA DIDN'T RETURN TO FARAUD'S HOME. With Aganila—from now on they'll never be apart—the two of them feasted on all sorts of scrumptious pastries in cosy tea salons, savoured delicious meals and hailed countless cabs.

Everywhere, covetous eyes pause on this elegant, beautiful woman accompanied by an adorable child.

The young woman knows this strange and solitary idleness with Aganila can't last for ever. She knows she's never seen anyone do this sort of thing before—anyone respectable, that is—it's just not done.

But she feels so lethargic, so tired, so numb from disillusionment and bad luck.

She doesn't want or desire anything, except to escape this torpor that completely invades her being. So she huddles up close to Aganila and softly falls asleep in the child's warmth.

Little by little, the city begins to frighten her; all these people around her make her skin crawl. For a long time now, she hasn't ventured to Paris; now she's practically glued to her adopted suburb where her perimeter shrinks more and more. Anyway, there's no longer enough money to take off for somewhere far, and where would she go?

What would she do?

Poor Rehvana. She didn't know how to make the most of what she was given.

The man who offered her Africa turned her initiation into an ordeal; the one who made her flesh quiver abandoned her for other conquests, ravaging and breaking both her body and soul, and the one who loves her tenderly cares nothing about her return to her roots.

Should she call Matildana, call her for help, complain? Call Matildana to fill her in on her life? More likely her death. Her death from the start. From rebirths to returns, from quests to rejuvenation, from pursuing one's roots to guilt trips—her death when it all began. Matildana would sneer: Terence's *Heautontimorumenos*—the one who torments herself for some unknown offense—mad or martyr—that impudent and ungrateful creature living a half-dead, senseless life. What a pain in the neck, she is, with her Greek and her big words!

Should she call Matildana so she'll interrogate, deride and confess her? Confide in Matildana and let the triumphant older sister do her best to coax out of her whatever tiny truth she hopes to extract from Rehvana's foolish excesses! Or she'd need to lie, and make up things, make up things like when she was little, but how could she fool her vigilant sister with the penetrating look?

With the same cruel smile she now unleashes at everything—every memory and thought—Rehvana recalls that as a child, she'd have these sudden memory lapses as soon as she entered the confessional. Neither her hands, clasped in a crushing embrace, nor the holy balsamic vapours, so pleasing to her nostrils that flared with emotion, nor the venerable, diagonal latticework, which held her intense gaze, nor the religious knee pain from kneeling on the sharp-edged boards, exalting her humble position to one of pious martyr, could help her remember her inconsequential, childish sins, and she fought with all her youthful might, as a member of the 'Valiant Souls' Catholic girls' movement, even though the whispering of the invisible confessor—only glimpsed in the dark, through wire screen and tears—disarmed rather than encouraged her, and overwhelmed her with pain and shame and guilt. Each Saturday, at the end of a gruelling inquisition, without a defence lawyer or mitigating circumstances, she would always declare herself guilty of having nothing that serious to confess and sometimes—oh the horror of it all!—guilty of having nothing to confess at all, so she decreed in her heart of hearts that such diabolical blindness and satanic amnesia had to be the sin of pride, and what's more, she feared she might insult God, or worse! annoy him and waste his time—as well as his representative's time—with the boring catalogue of her weekly silly sins, her piddly childish things and the string of venial trifles she could barely recall most of the time.

And yet, there was no way to escape Saturday confession! Although she carefully compiled an exhaustive list before going to church each week, she could never read her words in the confessional's darkness. As soon as she brushed past the font, as she entered the vast nave, all these minute details dissolved through some strange chemistry bathed in the smooth and divine incense, as if the altar's grandeur only served to highlight how truly trivial they really were.

Nevertheless, she still tried to make them much worse, opting to invent inconceivable, enormous sins which the priest didn't believe for a second, since she was so afraid that when put on the spot she'd forget the small ones that would later weigh on her conscience. Naively, she made sure to obtain one great big absolution to cover all the minor violations omitted from the voluminous veil reserved for the worst of sins.

She magnified and outrageously inflated everything her young memory was able to glean, everything her inexperience could reconstruct from a world that was no longer pure—a world she barely knew. She indiscriminately borrowed a few of her monstrous misfortunes from Ségur's Sophie, her 'love 'em and leave 'em' attitude from Margueritte's Monique, and her libertine ways from Colette's Minne. To top it all off, she ruthlessly made it worse by not forgetting, in the end, to accuse herself of making it all up . . . In this way, relieved, her soul at peace, she could go take her rosary and recite a series of 'Our Fathers' and 'Hail

Marys', assured that none of her real sins had been missed, and this orgy of prayers for forgiveness, worthy of her imagined crimes, would certainly cover her petty pranks—forgotten but still quite real.

Yes, she had to go to confession on Saturdays: it would have been a great sin, and mortal, no doubt—such wickedness Rehvana could never even imagine—to go to communion the next morning with a blackened soul. As for missing mass—the Holy Eucharist and the munificence of the Catholic service and the Latin and the organ pipes, the silences and genuflections, the Cross' message of love, the Christ-King's divine agony for humanity's sake, and the holy odour of incense—it was out of the question.

For now, Rehvana doesn't know what to say. However, there suddenly came to her a kind of allegorical and incomplete vision, a way of looking at things, vague at first, then bit by bit: two halves of a symbol, as in ancient times, that have, like Rehvana and her sister, jagged edges that fit together and, like them, the one incomplete without the other, both of them infinite, and both of them plural in multiple worlds. This is how the one and the other appeared to her, and she said nothing more.

Someone

REHVANA HAS CAREFULLY PLACED HER LITTLE GIRL in the shopping cart's tiny child seat, especially designed for that purpose. Nonchalant, she slowly unwraps a pack of Petit-Beurres she's grabbed from the shelf, and hands it to Aganila, who is delighted to sit atop this funny contraption. Standing straight, dignified and stiff as a board in the middle of the aisle, both hands calmly placed on the cart's handle which is coated in scarlet plastic, the unhurried mother keeps a watchful eye on the child who clumsily removes biscuits from the box.

An attractive housewife has glided next to them: neat and tidy, well groomed, preened and primped, she's dressed in the latest styles from the Vélizy 2 mall; she solemnly pores over pound cake labels and hesitates between pre-sliced loaves, butter or fruit cakes, and off-brand cakes—much less expensive and so enticing—as she sneaks curious glances at Rehvana. Mesmerized and perplexed, she finds this incredible brazenness almost too difficult to accept and believe.

Calm, but growing annoyed, Rehvana detects a series of emotions in the other's green eyes: shocked surprise, then stunned discomfort—perhaps fleeting disapproval—and again, embarrassment. But something new, powerful and real suddenly overwhelms the woman, who abruptly loses interest in the prices of off-brand lines. The meek and good-looking housewife—so diligent in her shopping duties, with a cart filled with groceries wisely chosen for their favourable quality to price ratio, now

217

carefully arranged by generic brand in her cart—is now the lookout for her two partners in crime. It's the first time she's ever gotten an adrenaline rush from buying groceries in the shopping
centre, after cleaning, top to bottom, her two-bedroom flat on
the twenty-second floor, applying make-up to her face to look as
pretty as possible, and before welcoming her lord and master by
granting him the favour of a quick kiss—part of their unchanged,
midday routine.

They're both dying to speak to each other—green eyes,
especially—but nothing will be said.

Under the short, curled bangs as fine as newborn hair and
smelling of silk, baby and milk, the dazzling eyes, limpid and
large, are lost in thought as they study Rehvana's face. The
charming, round cheeks with invisible, downy blond hair, iridescent in the light, blush with shame, reserve and, most of all,
excitement, since seeing Rehvana. She's got so many things to tell
her—heaps of things! But no word escapes her lips. Her eyes say
it all.

She wouldn't know what to say. She won't dare.

Yes, she speaks with her eyes, but the other one isn't looking
at her any more.

What did they behold, what did they see, the perfectly made
up sea-green eyes of 'Miss Maybelline'?

The suburban Minerva is making faces at the adorable
chabine doll with golden cinnamon curls, who nibbles and wrig-
gles in her seat. Aganila doesn't take a bite without first offering
the biscuit to her teddy bear—a gift from the man from
Garches—so herculean, it hardly fits in her lap and whose brown
fur is now strewn with crumbs.

Miss Maybelline, dressed in an emerald green, fake-leather
suit, bends over to pick up the box of biscuits dropped by the
child's small, awkward hands. She doesn't stand up right away:
she remains crouched there, like a temptress, then suddenly raises
her clear eyes—a silent offering—to meet Rehvana's.

Rehvana thinks that a box of Barquettes Fraise, even strawberry-filled, won't be enough for the child. She's got three francs left, and wonders if it might be possible to buy something more filling, more nutritious; besides, she has to put something, anything, into the shopping cart before facing the checkout row—barbaric frontier, barrier of policed civilization, inhumane, voracious—with its icy, metallic clacking already lying in wait.

But savoury foods (cheese or ham) are much more difficult to consume in the store: they're all pre-packaged. And then Aganila takes too much time to chew this kind of thing. Perhaps she could get some milk for her three francs? A quart of milk? She might drink some, as well. A half quart maybe? She's never paid attention to how much things cost.

In all haste, Green Eyes has begun to haphazardly grab boxes of shortbread biscuits from shelves, excitedly throwing them into her cart, where they pile up in a mess; she's eager to destroy the impeccable structure, the perfect order of her purchases, once meticulously arranged, in the heady and harmful anarchy of this unscripted collusion. Rehvana hasn't touched a thing from the other cart; she feels self-conscious eating in front of the other. She feels the pangs of hunger though, and vertigo's tender lull. Hunger bites her and muddles her mind. Her guard lowered, she delays and feels her feet falter. No, the woman's no store inspector; supermarkets are not so sophisticated as to put heavy make-up on a female cop and pass her off as honest Margo from the housing projects! Turning her back on the charity of her green-clad accomplice, Rehvana jerks her cart around and pointedly places the trash of the second pack next to the first on the shelf; both remain there, precariously balanced on the edge—insolent and almost intact. The kind-hearted woman in green automatically makes a move to follow her.

Rehvana pulls her little girl out of the child seat, leaving the useless shopping cart behind, and pays for her half quart of milk.

The woman in green abandons her own cart, filled to the gills, well before reaching the row of registers; she tries to regain her composure, clasping her handbag's shoulder strap to her chest like a life preserver, then makes a run for it and leaves, head down like a thief, through the 'exit, no purchase' line.

Rehvana walks very slowly. Under the awning of the store, she pauses to crisscross and knot the long boubou folds around her waist; in the space she prepared—just like she'd seen done by the Daughters of Agar—how long ago was that?—she carries the child on her back. Her way of draping the cloth is hardly orthodox, but no one really cares. Who's going to look twice at her in these dull, working-class streets? Not one among the worn out, busy, or simply blasé passers-by finds anything at all bizarre about her. Or at least they don't show it. Ahead of her walk a handful of jeering New Wave Iroquois with yellow crests of hair. Behind her will come chalk-skinned, black-clad Goths—girls with charcoal lips and green eyebrows; the one with the wide mouth—voluptuous, outlined in coal-black—will stand out with her disconcerting beauty to anyone who takes the time to look. What does the black uniform they wear mean? What does the ceruse on their faces scream? No questions asked. As for this one walking by, why is she so pale in her boubou robes? Has anyone wondered? She passed by; they passed by; the only difference is that there's always more than one of them—two at least (punks always go in pairs, at a minimum)—while that one walks alone, a baby on her back.

The ones just sitting around, the ones less morose, and those with the time to look see her as truly different; they ask themselves what brings her here, though they have no response.

Their eyes follow this tall, pale woman in African garb, with bare feet in tan leather sandals, despite the cold.

They only know she walked by—beautiful and lean and strangely attired—and that they'd wanted to approach her but had a change of heart once they'd looked into her eyes. A waiter has these thoughts.

The same thing is true for a barber on his doorstep.

He finds her splendid and strange but a bit too thin for his taste. Those waiting for the bus at the exact moment she walked by briefly crossed paths with her destiny, though nothing of her rubbed off, not even a memory, as they gave the driver their boarding pass.

The woman in green has fallen into step behind her. She trails her for a bit, but can't keep up.

The Other Martinique

JÉRÉMIE TRIED TO FIND REHVANA.

After several days of searching, taking pensive pilgrimages as far as the rubble of the squat, as far as the Montagne-Sainte-Geneviève, he easily tracked down the older sister—more a part of the system, more socially stable—easier to find. He was given her phone number, he called, someone told him Matildana was out, and that she'd be back very late.

Matildana has finished her bachelor's degree; she now lives in Fort-de-France where she studies linguistics and Creole, and contributes, in her spare time, to a fledgling Caribbean weekly magazine which strives to report, with all the lucidity and dignity it can possibly muster, all the cultural, political and social activities of the Antillean world.

She's learnt Creole. Not content with knowing some words, she keeps working at learning more, and now approaches it like something more than just her mother tongue—though occult, half-asleep, hibernating in the cold of Paris during her first years—but as a language whose inner workings and richness she's eager to explore. She wants to do everything in her power to protect its future—to keep it alive. The survival of Creole is essential to her life—her entire being thrills to the sound of Creole, penetrates it, surrounds it; Creole inhabits her, and Creole completes her.

With no effort or conflict, she now lives in Fort-de-France.

Besides, she feels she's never ceased to be Antillean—that her many years of exile haven't changed who she really is deep inside. And she had to come here.

Matildana never misses a chance to enjoy a savoury migan of stewed breadfruit and salt fish; she savours the gooey, shapeless purée that sticks to the roof of her mouth with delicate clicks of the tongue, and even asks for more!

Matildana is never surprised to see balaous on her plate— the small, bony fish shrivelled from frying, served in a reverent arrangement. She also adores, without the least bit of effort on her part, the oily mini-mackerels called coulirous, which her people love. She willingly took part in the excitement of the famed pigeon peas, that mythical Christmas delight which everyone talks about two months ahead of time, licking their lips, and which proved to be more bland than garbanzo beans.

But in truth, she prefers Mozart to the throbbing tom-tom of the big ka. She doesn't care much for the primitive anarchy of trempage, nor for the folkloric custom of serving it on large banana leaves, and if she delights in the names 'gueule de Polius' or 'chellou', she isn't charmed by the gamy taste of marinated headcheese or the saggy and soft consistency of lungs, which revolt and disgust her. As for bondas man Jacques and other fearsome peppers, she avoids them like the plague, and would give all the Caribbean pepper-based sauce in the world for a bland veal blanquette.

For her, being Antillean isn't reduced to a Creole palate, ear, legendary 'charming chatter' or swaying walk.

She loves Fort-de-France, the small city and its seven mornes, as much as that other city with seven hills—the Rome of her humanities classes—which still remains close to her heart.

She loves Terence as much as Senghor: nothing human, whatever its colour, whether white, black, yellow or tricoloured, *'nothing human is alien to her'*. Contrary to her younger sister,

Matildana is not like those who punish themselves for a shade of blackness they can't achieve.

Matildana feels whole and complete; she doesn't think of herself as anything other than Antillean, yet refuses to let herself be distilled into artificial essences labelled 'beautiful, languid doudou, always in love', 'black woman, the beauty ideal of the '80s' or 'hip roller for swaying beguines', because then what's left, she wonders, for those born neither beautiful nor tall, who become neither 'pro' nor 'creators', who are neither 'go-getters' nor 'successful'? Yes, what's left for them, besides being black?

And yet, she dances.

She dances just like in the beginning, back in the days of clandestine evening gatherings on former plantations, when behind the béké's back, and in defiance of the whip, slaves used to give in to the nocturnal fever of kalendas, and the unbridled undulations—part lascivious, part warlike—of the once-forbidden rhythms.

Jérémie is still speaking, Jérémie is drowning in words and talks about searching for the lost, little sister; he says they're going to find her and then everything will be back to normal.

Triumphant and unexpected, concluding the nightly broadcasts of RFO-Martinique, *La Marseillaise* drones alone in the dark at the other end of the living room, and Matildana gets up to turn it off.

With a heavy heart, she rises. She feels drained. Her head bent over the receiver, with Jérémie's burning voice—urgent, and so clear and now so alone—penetrating her being, she finds herself visualizing the inopportune, out of place face of her Fort-de-France cousin, a blue-eyed, light-skinned mulatto who fiercely refuses to stand up when the national anthem is played. It's a question of rising or not rising for Rouget de Lisle's war song, in the name of another war, another army!

Jérémie is still talking.

He evokes the troubled times of the squat, Rehvana's enlistment into the equivocal fraternity of the Ébonis, her shifty friends . . .

A sad, forced smile floats on Matildana's lips, tall daughter of the islands, who feels entitled to rise and soar to the sky for 'La Marseillaise' on her soucougnan wings.

He concludes that Rehvana is nothing more than an amoral child, and Matildana, without replying, lets the distant rustle of wings in the pulsating night air resonate inside her, with the voice of eternity proclaiming: 'Like all amoral beings, she verges on the goddess.'

NO, OF COURSE, SHE HASN'T FORGOTTEN JÉRÉMIE, how could she?

No, she no longer gets news from Rehvana.

Oh, it's been a few months already. Rehvana doesn't want to speak to her any more, she finds her too preachy . . . Their last conversation ended on an unexpected note: 'You don't understand me; listen, Matildana, I see we don't speak the same language, I think it's best we leave it at that.'

'The last time she spoke to me, she insulted me. She treated me like rancid roe. She doesn't want to listen, you know, Jérémie . . . doesn't want to listen and doesn't want to speak . . . I don't know what her problem is. You see: that's what's killing me! I have no clue what she's getting at. What she does is nonsensical—it's just a dead end. I've even tried to make inquiries with "missing persons" services but Rehvana is no longer a minor, you see—so no matter what we believe, she's free to do as she pleases!'

'In this case, perhaps we could hire a private eye. There must be a way to track her down. What about your parents?'

'My parents! My parents know nothing about her. Besides, it's been a long time since they've wanted to hear anything about her. For them, it's as if Rehvana's dead. It started a while back, when she terrified them with the theories of the "Sons of Agar" . . . Papa literally threw her out of the house, completely outraged. He didn't even wait for her to become pregnant . . . So, to be a "single mother" to top it off, you can imagine!

That wasn't the best way for her to come back into his good graces . . . They received news from her through me and pretended not to hear. If she were to reach out to someone in the family, that could only be to me. If you knew what they say about her at home, you'd understand that Rehvana has no desire to go back there . . . '

Yes, all she knows is that the man—the last one to date as far as she knows—was apparently still in Martinique. She ran into him the other night in the Savane Gardens: disillusioned, laughing at himself, Enryck had asked after her sister.

She barely could stomach his presence.

'He asked me about Rehvana and told me he loved her . . . cared for her . . . and he didn't understand why she'd left . . . but that she'd put him through the wringer, that she would make scene after scene, that she really was a pain in the ass, too complicated for him, and, at the end, she'd become totally insufferable . . . Crazy what this guy had the nerve to say! Jérémie, I thought I was dreaming. He couldn't understand why she'd "done that" to him, after all he'd "done for her" . . . As he was telling me all this, he was waddling about and almost smiling . . . I couldn't take any more, so I ditched him right there.'

If Matildana had eventually overcome her initial reluctance to speak to him, it was only because she'd hoped, for a split second, running into him by chance in front of the Hotel L'Impératrice, that he could tell her where Rehvana was.

His smug, mocking tone still echoes in her ears. She can still hear herself stooping to ask: 'Did she leave you something—a letter?' She'd tried to find out, without much hope.

'A letter?' he'd crooned in his head voice. 'Rehvana, leave me a letter! But she left my house like a slut, without leaving me anything at all! I was away, uh, for a bit of time. I ran into some trouble, well . . . let's say, with the gendarmes, and anyway, I had other fish to fry, I couldn't stay home fussing over her all day, she didn't want to understand . . . '

She doesn't tell Jérémie everything. The silence is heavy with unsaid things: there are a lot of things she can't share with

Jérémie, as if she feared, somehow, they might reflect badly on Rehvana.

She still hasn't told Jérémie the child is his. What's the point? She's keeping the promise Rehvana forced her to make. She's dying to tell it all, explain everything, clean up and smooth over these butchered lives, if there's still time.

It seems that Jérémie, when he speaks about Aganila, is completely ready to hear what she's eager to reveal . . . She also remembers that he hasn't asked *the* question, nor even inquired about the dates, thus sparing her from having to lie, as if he'd wanted to leave her free to choose . . .

But the little, childish phrase the two sisters added each time they'd swear an oath, after 'cross my heart and hope to die', still shrilly resounds in the far reaches of her memory: 'Remember, Rehvana, a princess must always keep her promises.'

Which princess? Which promises?

The two sisters added these special words as a kind of private joke, taken from a story they'd read together, which the older sister had read to the younger one. Derived from an old, forgotten tale, the little magic words—of a sisterly, indelible magic, deleterious and confused—imposed silence and respect for their old ways. She had never betrayed her sister and she never will.

She'll never be guilty of perjury: this faith in the given word was a basic value, an inalienable virtue. Since childhood, like young Romans from ancient times, they'd sworn allegiance to unbreachable *fides* and the goddess of faith—without knowing what implacable pact they'd made.

But she's going to try to persuade her. Yes, with Jérémie's help, she's going to try to find her; with Jérémie's support, she'll succeed in convincing her. Yes, she's overjoyed to hear Jérémie's voice again. Yes, thrilled after such a long time, across so many ocean waves, to hear Jérémie's serious, deep, calm and warm voice.

Jérémie!

The holidays are near: she'll be in Paris soon. Together they'll manage to find them.

Yes, Matildana is sure they're no longer in Martinique.

'It's such a small place, it's impossible that my sister could hide here without a good soul letting me know. I've already looked around a lot, you know . . . The only person who might have helped me, her old neighbour in Vert-Pré, was absolutely no help at all. When I went to see her, hoping she could provide some information, or that Rehvana might have left her an address, the old woman was of no use.

'She wasn't there when Rehvana left, and the day I went to see her, she was coming back from the cemetery where she'd buried someone named Boniface, her worst enemy, from what I could gather. "He'd had a car acc'dent, and 'e wasn't even drivin'!" she told me, laughing her head off. She insisted on giving me a detailed account of his death, delighted to describe the fellow, proud as a peacock on his mule, brutally knocked down while rounding a bend in the road by a brand-new motor coach driven at breakneck speed by one of Rehvana's admirers, a guy named Anastase, whom my sister had mentioned. It seems he was driving his flashy new vehicle faster and faster, after he'd recently sold his beloved Peugeot 504, to everyone's surprise, saying it brought back too many memories; he'd become a real public menace ever since my sister left.

'The old woman was so happy to assure me that the victim of the accident, that Boniface, had endlessly suffered in horrible torment, crushed by the weight of his dead mule, since he didn't die on the spot: both man and beast were violently thrown from the wreck, landing on the edge of a banana field. The animal collapsed on its master's body, who'd remained there, alive, fully conscious, but immobilized, his legs smashed by the huge, inert mass while someone called for help. That's all this old loon was able to say—that's all she wanted to tell me. I had to insist and interrupt her several times to get a few words from her about Rehvana. She was so jubilant, calling on God as her witness, and going on and on: "There's justice, yessiree!" that I had a terrible time dragging her away from the subject of her Boniface to get her to talk about my sister. But I didn't learn much, nothing that could help me find her. Then the old lady started to babble incoherently: she said now that her Boniface was dead and buried, the guy's sister, who was a witch, would want to harm Rehvana, and we'd have to be careful and protect her from her evil spells. I left her to her trance-like state—I'd had it up to here with her witchcraft tales.

'When I left her, that Cidalise was trembling all over, with bloodshot, bulging eyes, grabbing at my sleeve, and saying in a quavering voice: "You gotta protect your sister, you mus' undo the Devil's work." To think that Rehvana had been spending so much time with that woman! No wonder she got more and more mixed up . . . No, she's probably in Paris, but where and with whom? It'll be hard, but between the two of us, we'll succeed.'

Jérémie has already calmed down. He's going to keep on looking on his own while waiting for Matildana to arrive.

The angelic medical-school student who had graciously tended to Jérémie's downcast soul—for the sake of Rehvana's mental health and Jérémie's lovely, gold-specked eyes—is now pregnant with his child.

Last-born of a wealthy lineage of the upper bourgeoisie from Touraine—ecstatic over their daughter's happiness and thrilled to welcome into their family such an exceptional person, so appreciated by friends—a radiant Marie-Aude was able to wed this magnificent, tall black, at the head of his business school class, and so loving. Her parents are looking forward to having grandchildren with café-au-lait skin—the epitome of amazing, little quadroons, a-do-ra-ble, who'll be so successful, thanks to their father's sharp mind, their gorgeous mother's seraphic good looks and their grandfather's cash. Their big wedding took place in Touraine, under the respectable vaults of a Romanesque abbey, where tender little lambs and suckling pigs roasted on a spit. They were married with great pomp and circumstance, with no expense spared, with the Red Cross and the fire brigade keeping watch outside in the yard, among hundreds of guests. In the group photo, you could see all kinds of people with afros and dreadlocks linking arms with delighted, Chanel-clad lah-di-dah ladies, their hair permed for the wedding; the Negroes from Basse-Terre were teaching limbo and laghia to an entourage of blond pageboys in velvet. Transfixed and quietly sitting cross-legged in a circle around their new cousins, the little angels kept a respectable distance during the dances. Their knees, pink from playing games, were sticking out of emerald-green knickerbockers—in fashion long ago, or perhaps in England—paired with white gauze shirts with tiny, ruffled jabots: what the bride wanted, because they were junior groomsmen. Two of the older cousins from Guadeloupe showed up wearing the exact same thing.

Lately, though, Marie-Aude has developed a nasty habit of transforming into a praying 'mater-mantis', but Jérémie doesn't want to worry about it, and thinks it's only a passing personality change, most likely due to her pregnancy. Yesterday morning she left to get some rest in Touraine at her parents' house, where she'll be well taken care of, and he smiles at the idea that it'll do her good.

Jérémie went back to sit in the pale sun on the terrace. He's overjoyed at the idea of trying to find Rehvana and seeing Matildana again . . .

He's looking forward to her upcoming trip and the timid spring-like weather brightening Paris.

He knows the two of them will eventually find her.

This drab winter drags on, not willing to step aside for spring. At Café Mahieu, across from the Luxembourg gardens, Jérémie stretches his legs. No longer worked up, he watches shy daylight gently radiating over the city, with loving young mothers slowly pushing their baby strollers. Soon Marie-Aude will have her baby, my child, and Matildana will be here, and we'll have found Rehvana again—the beautiful, prodigal child—and all will be well.

He's filled with confused emotions, knowing the Inaccessible One is now so near. Rehvana must have filled his entire being with pain—powerless pain—for Jérémie to feel this way about Matildana.

For him to discover a shared and deep complicity with her.

In just a few short days, Matildana will be here.

The One or the Other

REHVANA HAS EMERGED FROM HER LONG LETHARGY to plaintively murmur confused curses and cryptic rebukes in Matildana's ear, and to Jérémie, who's leaning over her. In an otherworldly voice, she wails a string of barely audible anathemas. Irrational and suddenly verbose, she escapes her stupor only to attack them with words they cannot hear.

In turn she's tender, emotional, truculent or cruel, and her skeletal fingers—lifeless and long—attempt to grasp the absent hands gripping her face.

She can't make out what Matildana and Jérémie are whispering to one another. She tries to sit up—why all these secrets? What are they telling each other, as they exchange knowing glances like partners in crime, and exclude her? They've never spoken together for so long. What's the point of this drawn-out, mysterious dialogue above her head, such a weak head, oh! so weak . . . So weak and also so hard to lift.

She can't seem to hear.

Something buzzes and shifts, something moves inside her head like waves of a huge ocean, and their words come to her through the muted roar of the surf flooding her head.

Matildana and Jérémie have stopped talking about her, but they continue to speak, they're immense, both so tall, so tall she can't see them any more, so tall they've engulfed the room. After nausea, throwing up bile, sluggish numbness and aimless crawling on the frayed carpet, the hallucinations had begun.

Rehvana's vision blurs. Through a halo of cloud, she can barely make out the small, oblong shape that still keeps her arm warm.

'Sleep, my zougoun, you can keep on sleeping, Aganila, daughter of Africa, my African goddess, my love!'

Aside from this little mass of quiet and loving warmth, everything around her is frozen—hopelessly, inexorably frozen. Nothing but useless, threatening or sordid objects surround her: bare walls, empty Formica closets covered with dust, gaping refrigerator door, radiators without heat, lamps without light—because Rehvana couldn't pay the rent or the bills—a sinister, silent phone, since she didn't pay that bill either. The concierge came to complain and threaten her, but he beat a hasty retreat when he saw Rehvana's crazed eyes. Starving, exhausted, she still found the strength to kick out the vicious and vile snoop with the muzzle of a mole, who stood on tiptoe, twisting his long, plucked heron's neck to peer over her shoulder at the inside of the room.

A faint, little smile reached her lips.

'I've never kept much in reserve!'

She remembers, strangely amused, that this, for sure, was always the inexplicable secret of her leanness, so envied by her girlfriends, furious to see her pack away cream puff after cream puff, éclair after éclair, and remain liana-thin, stomach as flat as ever.

'You burn everything you eat, Rehvana, and so fast!'

Rehvana feels the urge to vomit, but she's got nothing to vomit.

'Well, enough talk, but I've got to get up and find something to eat! Who's going to give me food? I'll find something, somewhere in Paris, or I'll steal at the store. I'll go play pauper at city hall . . . Is that still done? I'll beg at social services'

whatchamacallit or in front of Notre-Dame! . . . reduced to pan-
handling, yes, that's all that's left, my poor girl!'

Her body shakes from a barrage of hiccups that won't let her
catch her breath.

'Matildana! Jérémie! Help!'

She calls for help inside her head. Her lips, pallid and grey
from the cold, would be incapable of producing a sound. Guard
lowered, weapons lowered, shame swallowed, pride set aside,
she suddenly decides enough is enough. She admits in a flash of
brilliant insight that she can't get out of this on her own, and
the two people she naturally thinks of—simultaneously, never
apart—are these two. Jérémie and Matildana.

They're also those she's hurt the most, those who love her—
those she loves, who knows?

One moment, she renounces them; she tells herself she's
already caused enough pain, and must leave them in peace, that
Jérémie now has a wife, and perhaps even a baby, that Matildana
needs to lead her own life as a free woman, without having to
always drag her sister behind her, like a ball and chain.

And then she changes her mind. She really wants to see them;
she needs to see them!

Sceaux, Sceaux Gardens, big, ivy-covered house,

rue des Imbergères

Sceaux (Seine)

Old-fashioned street with cobblestones in different shapes,
gently sloping towards the church.

And the garden separated from the one owned by the Orantes
by a simple, peaceable fence of honeysuckle and climbing
bindweed.

The lily pond which charmed her—alluring and mud-
coloured and murky, with its low, oval edge.

How many times had Matildana kept her from falling in?

Marie Curie High School, 'Maricu' . . . blue smock, brown
smock, worn on alternate weeks. Don't get the colour wrong, or

you'll catch hell from Perrachon, the old teacher aide, mean as meanness itself, so ugly you want to puke, as she paces up and down dining hall aisles, white socks twisted and rolled around varicose ankles.

Matildana prepares two separate translations from Latin: Rehvana's and her own. It's not because Matildana took Latin that I have to, as well! I can't stand Greek. No way. I won't compete with Matildana's love of Greek.

Matildana, the gifted, older sister, hunts down the string of small, scared little demons—Rehvana's adorable spelling mistakes—in each text.

Matildana is beautiful. Matildana is the fairest of all: thus has ruled the school-wide beauty contest organized in the middle of a physics class. During experiments in the chemistry lab, the schoolgirls laugh themselves silly, and use Bunsen burners to make tea—but classes with theories are such a bore! So they busy themselves as best they can . . .

Rehvana repeats seventh grade. Things begin to fall apart. She thinks she's a little too black, always a bit too black. She despairs over her hair: it absolutely must be kept straight, and the uncurled locks, falling like leaden curtains, must be restrained with a polyester fabric band—wide and slightly elastic—or a headband of green velour—that's the style—not curls that drive her mad! They all want to touch her hair: oh! it's so soft . . . They don't touch anyone else's hair, why hers? Curls, ringlets, a riot of ringlets! Definitely not in vogue! Hysteria induced by frizz: Rehvana is behind the times. Straight hair is 'in', period, that's all, yet a slew of curls escape from her hairnet that's supposed to confine her chignon, according to this year's rules of style. Everyone loves her hair, except her. Ponytails, yes, but with flat tresses that glide between hairpins, and for teased hair like the pop stars, no kinky hair, or even just waves to start with!

Matildana feels too thin, because that's what Maman used to tell her over and over again when they were small, and she didn't want to buy her low-cut dresses or tiny halter tops to wear on vacation. But Matildana still finds the strength, God knows from where, to feel comfortable in her skin, no matter what.

Matildana dances, Matildana completes her high school degree, Matildana loves champagne, and her eyes shine—no champagne will ever rival the imperious sparkle of those eyes.

'Rehvana is too disgraceful.'

Rehvana is a naughty, little tafiateuse who drains the glasses after the last party guest has left. She snakes her way through corners of the living room like a mongoose, before everything is cleaned up, to stealthily sip the last drops of champagne from each glass.

Aunt Idoménée caught her.

Denounced me in her shrill voice—the fat sow!—and Matildana had laughed.

Matildana sends me to buy her cigarettes. I'm dying to smoke, I cough, I'm ridiculous, I lose face from the first puff.

Matildana silently smokes, but all eyes turn to her. Rehvana sits in a heap in a corner, her eyes full of Matildana. Matildana talks and they listen. Matildana chats, and I speak in her voice, and that crazy old auntie says I'm turning pretty, I'm becoming a young woman, I'm starting to look like my older sister. The other day, another one said I'm beginning to adopt Matildana's manners and moves. I trick her boyfriends on the phone for the first few minutes so they think they're talking to her. (I don't have a boyfriend yet.)

Matildana wears make-up, despite the ban, and I stare at her like a cow. I'm sick of these large, heifer eyes, these lacklustre eyes. I can't wait to use eyeliner—to put that black in my eyes, like Papa says, when he sends Matildana to wash her face. Matildana does it again behind his back and gets slapped, but standing proud, she demonstrates to Papa that using physical violence isn't worthy of him and, according to her, not based on any educational beliefs. Mat does as she likes outside the house, then, on the stoop, quickly removes the make-up from her face before dealing with Papa in the living room—with her naked eyes, slightly lined in soot-brown. Matildana works hard; Matildana fights well. I can't wait to wear stockings, to impudently arch my foot and voluptuously pull on my garters. Nonchalant, graceful, superb. Gentle, gently, my garters—knee halfway bent, foot elegantly arched, silky nylon on my thighs, the imperceptible rasping of infinitesimal electric shocks—and to be so accustomed, like she, to slipping them on, with ease. I'm always too young. When I'm old enough, pantyhose will be what's left . . .

Let Matildana die and let me live!

It's meant to be. Yes, it appears it must be so: Matildana dies and Rehvana will live.

Matildana is living a happy, fulfilling life—or at least, she could be completely happy if she'd received news from Rehvana these past few months. The only thing missing to tip the scales is news from Rehvana—good news, of course.

'No news is good news, as my grandmother used to say,' she ventured, under duress.

What she didn't have the nerve to tell Jérémie, among other shameful things, is that the only trace of her younger sister was a bounced check made out to Air France, which the family, notified by the bank, recently had to cover.

The rest—the child—Matildana would rather not think or say anything about it.

Across the Ocean, Matildana's husky voice has stirred up confusion in Jérémie. Sitting in the sun at the terrace of the former Café Mahieu, now a fast-food joint, he feels a pent-up, intense, volcanic emotion well up inside, emanating sulphur-like steam, almost leviratic and incest-filled.

No One

'I'VE GOT TO GO MAKE A CALL from a phone booth. I'll find somewhere to pick up some milk at the same time; I need to find something for the child—milk, anything, but she has to eat.'

Snippets of forgotten nursery rhymes, songs from her school in Sceaux, come back to her to softly sing to the child.

Let's saw, saw, saw the log,
For mother,
For mother,
Let's saw, saw, saw the log,
For mother Nicolas.

She snuggles more closely against the small, unmoving, limp form.

What has she done,
The li'l blue bird?
She stole from you and me
Three li'l bags of wheat.
We'll catch her,
The li'l blue bird,
And we'll give her
Three little blows with a stick:
One, two, three,
The moon or the sun?

Rehvana is mistaken or wants to delude herself about the deceptive warmth she still feels under her hands—now only her own body's heat.

> *On my way,*
> *I met*
> *The cane cutter's little girl,*
> *On my way,*
> *I met*
> *The wheat cutter's little girl,*
> *Yes, yes, I met*
> *The straw cutter's little girl . . .*

'I'll go soon. It's not that far. Just at the end of the street, at the corner of the second block. Or the third, I don't recall. I'll find it.'

She concentrates on what she needs to do: get up and drag herself to the door. She focuses on this goal: it's not that hard, I think I can manage.

> *Join in the dance!*
> *See how we dance!*
> *Spin, dance!*
> *Kiss who you please . . .*

Rehvana gently pulls her breast from the little, silent mouth clamped on her nipple in vain, since God knows how long, she can't recall. She hasn't had milk in ages, but the last of her secret zeal makes her go through the motions of nursing her child, as if, against all odds, she still could, like the ageless, old Negress, a female slave travelling on a slave ship, who miraculously saved the life of a white infant by giving him milk from breasts thought to be long dried up. The legend goes on to say that the young, white mother had been killed during a pirate attack, and to the surprise of all, at the end of the fight, in the middle of the general panic that ensued, the unfortunate baby, twisting and wailing on his mother's cold corpse, clamoured to be fed, and they saw the old African woman offer an ample breast, the colour of ebony wood, to the famished and pale orphan, to keep him alive, since there was no wet nurse on board. With her divinely engorged black breasts, oblong and full like the best fruit from female papaya trees—her heaven-sent breasts, like two halves of a gourd, and the stretched brown-purple areolas—she nursed the békée's offspring each day for the rest of the voyage, despite the restrictions and malnutrition from which she herself suffered.

Surrounded by concrete giants scoffing at her with their white, windowpane eyes, Rehvana drags herself to the phone booth at the end of the grey street. After painful efforts and a miserable crawl on the threadbare rug, she'd reached the door that opened to the landing, and had broken her nails on the stuck locks. She'd crumbled onto the lift, like a heap; she'd scraped her hands on the stucco walls, looking for support to guide her unsteady gait. The outside air revives her. She feels better. Suddenly, she could travel to the ends of the earth.

Gangling, stunted plane trees are decked out, as if for an obscene Christmas: dirty cotton balls and sanitary napkins waterlogged with rain disintegrate on skeletal twigs, greasy rags hang from limbs, while faded, brown-red tampons twist their strings around the few scrawny buds scattered here and there.

Inane nuptials of damp greyness and desecrated blood surround her. The 'projects' are sodden and hermetically sealed. The guy on the ground floor is yelling because his older son changed channels. If he does it again, his father will kill him. Rehvana catches loud voices, the din of television sets; she pushes on, alone, lost, yet energized by a new strength, amid the dereliction of this wormy town. She walks with an uneven step, at times lifted by a powerful surge; other times, almost paralysed, crushed under her own weight, she's unable to move her legs.

She advances slowly, holding onto buildings, trees, window-sills, then icy handrails of cellar stairs. Courageous and humble, she trudges through blackish puddles, and trips over spokes of a moped and chains from dirt bike locks. She reaches the end of the street, with her last one franc coin clenched in the palm of her hand.

But what's left of the phone booth is a lopsided shell: monstrous, twisted tripod, miserable metallic mass, broken box of steel and glass, which stands—wretched and of no use—on the edge of the vast avenue. The abandoned suburb turns a deaf ear to all distress—shrivelled and dull in its working-class monotony, mortally crushed by modernity without soul. Broken glass crunches under her feet. For a long time, Rehvana squints and stares at the receiver, sadly dangling from its cord. The coin box was savagely smashed, and there's a gaping hole where push buttons should be, above the mangled phone books. Rehvana presses the receiver against her ear, just in case, and forces her last coin into the distorted slot. Leaning against the misshapen frame, she listens intently, fingers clenched in disbelief, waiting for the dial tone that never comes. She presses the cold plastic against her face until it hurts, and softly calls out into the night. Her faint voice swells and grows hoarse, as she bleats into the bottomless void.

And Rehvana finally bursts out laughing—the intractable laughter of wounded Gods. Gods wounded such a long time ago.

The Samaritan, tan-tan
Goes to the fountain, tain-tain
To fetch some drink, drink-drink
In her little pail, pail-pail

Just like when she and Matildana were little, Rehvana sings to be less scared.

Cardinal Richelieu
Cardinal Richelieu!

On their way to school in Fort-de-France, they walked together along a high wall, mysterious as a rampart, behind which hid the man with the menacing kitchen knife, according to Matildana, who enjoyed spicing up their daily route, so she could push the younger one to sing with her at the top of their lungs, '. . . Three flowers of the nation!'

On the way to Catholic school, inhabited by Matildana's frightening creatures, Rehvana clings to the older one's hand.

Odette
Titanic tits
OH OH dette
Titanic tits!

'There's something green in the distance, whatever this green thing is, Matildana, my sister, you've got to show it to me! You've got to tell me what you see; oh no, don't tell me you see nothing coming . . .'

'Aganila, my zougoun, my baby, my African princess!'

Rehvana muses that reality only exists because she's conscious of it—because she perceives it. Closing her eyes is all it takes. Even if they tell her that things can still be seen, she only has to choose not to listen—plug up her ears—and those words would cease to be.

It's up to her whether or not reality exists, since the sole proof of it is her own existence, the fact that she feels herself existing in this world, according to these givens, surrounded or not by these beings. Trying to communicate with this or that being.

But where are the proofs, who gives them, amid the grey dereliction of overcrowded towers?

Matildana bursts out laughing, makes fun of her, teases and pinches her, but Rehvana can't feel anything any more. As if anaesthetized and deprived of all clear sense, she sees the real and the unreal straddle each other and clash—diabolic, apocalyptic, chaotic. The speed with which she found herself moving from nightmare to dream, dream to nightmare, desire to pleasure, foreboding to denouement, has always left her confused; she's back in the bedroom with Aganila, without knowing how she returned. Perhaps she never left. Perhaps she only imagined an unreal walk across grey streets, and dreamt the ravaged phone booth? Now she's not so sure she ever got there. It seems to her she ended up back where she started, in no time at all, alone in the freezing room with her child. For a moment she tried to break the spell, to remember: Did she really go out? Her mind seems dim and confused. Shouldn't she try again? Her consciousness escapes her, she can't remember, she's lost sense of it all. Did she really have the courage to do this, did she really stoop so low as to drag herself all the way over there, did she really push aside her scornful pride and go ask Matildana for help one more time, whimper and declare defeat? Did she walk all the way to the phone booth, way over there, to weakly beg for succour from the civilized world, and the comfort, warmth and benefits that Matildana and a wisely lived life can offer? But none of this matters any more.

It's Aganila, and She alone is the One who holds the power to ward off death. She appeared once before—Omnipotent Africa—to deliver the chosen one from a useless and false ritual, a mutilation She'd never asked to see, a scarification in which She puts no stock in her everlasting life.

But her vast power, spread over Antillean hills, savannahs and mangrove swamps—all her great might has been watered down in the European miasmas of the city.

Nowhere

THE OLD LADY WITH THE HUNCHED BACK whom Matildana had helped earlier by lifting her suitcase onto the carry-on luggage rack, has settled as best she can in the cramped seat. As soon as she's seated, she sensibly buckles her seatbelt even though the 'seatbelts sign' hasn't been turned on yet. With frail, shaking hands she unfolds the newspaper she's just bought. The shrill roar from the rear is followed by a rumbling that goes from a muffled sound to a high-pitched, piercing note, several times in a row, which the old lady hates. The plane is about to take off, and she's still a little scared, although it's not the first time she's visiting her children on the other side of the ocean, in Chevilly-Larue. Meanwhile, each time she breathes, her nose and throat get cold; the oxygen vents are all blowing out unnatural, freezing air.

'Flight attendants, doors on automatic and cross-check.'

Matildana, desperate to check on her sister, didn't need to hear that.

The old lady gives her neighbour a look of gratitude, tinged with kindness and some fear. She doesn't speak; the young woman's preoccupied face doesn't invite conversation. Pleasant but distant, the tall, reserved mademoiselle shows no emotion to either the repeated, elongated jolts or the grumbling of the engines, increasing and intensifying in a brief crescendo into a high pitch, from one piercing trill to another, even more shrill, ear-splitting sound. She doesn't even notice that the plane has pulled away from the gate.

They're on the move; a deep thwacking startles the old lady, who turns around and focuses her attention on her window, as the plane crosses the gutter bordering the lawn.

This decrescendo into the low registers doesn't sound good to her at all; she tenses up, attuned to the slightest nuance of take-off, her hands—bony and with prominent veins—clamped onto her newspaper while the aircraft pivots until it comes to a stop, facing the axis of the runway. She has time to cast a last glance towards the terrace of the terminal, where a jumble of arms are waving and she's unable to recognize those belonging to the relatives who took her to the airport. This sight doesn't reassure her and holds her attention for only a second.

She feels uncomfortable—more anxious than on prior trips—perhaps because of the presence of this young woman who stares straight ahead, and you can't tell whether her expression is sad or serene.

The old lady would love to know what's going on, and gets lost in speculation, her mind distracted from fear by trying to solve the mystery of the delicate profile in which she discerns—and this is what intrigues her—as much sadness as peace.

Never before has the mood of a Boeing seemed so bleak. Because she feels she's bordering on prying and fears she's a bother, she stops scrutinizing her neighbour to observe the wing's edge, which splits in two and then into several shiny, radiant plates, docilely sliding down rails to form another wing underneath the first one.

Where the two sets of flaps meet, one of the ailerons—poorly placed, wavering, as if panic-stricken and lost between them both—stubbornly moves out of sync from the rest, neither with one group or the other. To her, it looks obstinate, all alone, determined to move to its own quirky rhythm, up and down, down and up. She wonders what this is all about, since the harmonious ballet of the rows of plates, on either side, seems rational, organized and calm, while the wild flapping of the aileron that can't seem to make up its mind seems foolish and harebrained.

She sees danger in all this, an anomaly of sorts, and she furrows her brow and tries to recall explanations given by her son, a mechanic at Orly, to try to ease her instinctive dread.

But yes, this part surely must thrash about and throb, it must startle and shake—that's what you need for lift-off; this frenetic breaking up, this fanatic dislocation on the thin edge of the wing—this is how it's done, yes, it must be done, she repeats, so the plane can ascend! Although chaotic and unnerving, these lurches only look out of control, and through these motions that break the order of things comes the imbalance required to change direction, turn without losing speed, and generate, through increased lift, a broader movement—that of the ensemble, the whole.

Now everything vibrates; the aircraft has started to move again; it accelerates with a sudden whistle that beats on the old lady's eardrums. She feels herself slowly but solidly pinned to her seat, and increasingly so. The nose of the plane roughly leaves the ground; she's knocked backwards by a strong force, her sacrum smashed into her seat. She soon feels weightless.

Gravity's gone, she's nothing but air, but her ears buzz—something's not quite right and she feels sick.

The intense rumbling suddenly stops, but after a few seconds, her heart in her mouth from a tidal wave of brief turbulence and muffled, metallic banging below, she peeks at the young woman again.

The aircraft gains altitude; it soon flies over the Lamentin swamps at the end of the runway and begins its climb above the Caribbean Sea. The old lady has a distant yet quite beautiful aerial view of Fort-de-France, though she can only make out the Saint-Louis cathedral. And perhaps that pinkish, small shape is the new city hall.

As the plane dips into a wide left turn, the right wing unexpectedly jumps into her view. Luckily the aircraft soon rights itself, and at last continues its even ascent.

The small woman takes a deep breath and unwinds little by little. She stretches out her legs and moves her arms, without unfastening her seatbelt. Once again, she risks looking to her left, and exchanges smiles with the kind young woman, then returns to her reading—relaxed and reassured—because danger is now behind them; yes, all danger has been averted, now that the 747 glides through eternity's clouds. She's always heard her son say that planes crash most often at take-off or landing. She's got another good seven hours of peace.

Matildana shouldn't have been on this flight. She moved her departure ahead, leaving Fort-de-France much earlier than planned, feverishly impatient, because even the new departure date Air France had offered still seemed too late. She was counting on coming to Paris for Easter vacation—that's what she'd told Jérémie on the phone—but something, like a cry inside her, had demanded she drop everything and leave.

The decrepit old woman prepares to enjoy the long respite promised by the serene, blue sky, spared from more turbulence, and calmly returns to her reading from behind mother-of-pearl, half-moon glasses. But the charming, old-fashioned smile, which had lingered on her lips, slowly dissolves; are those tired, senile eyes misting? The old lady has tears in her eyes, thinking how today you can still meet polite and pleasant young women, much to her surprise—she's been so used to bad manners from the younger generation, lately—but you also see so much misery in this earthly life. She's just read in a corner of her newspaper that a young Antillean woman and her child had starved to death in subsidized housing in the suburbs of Paris. She could have sworn that these days, on the verge of the twenty-first century, you could only starve to death in the middle of the Sahel Desert.

The old capresse from Saint-Esprit shed tears of disbelief for this unknown young woman—on the Other Side, in the Cité des Quatre Mille in La Courneuve—who'd given herself an African desert death because she couldn't lead an African life.

Balata, April–December 1987

TWENTY YEARS LATER—to quote Alexandre Dumas, that other Caribbean mulatto—reality, unfortunately, meets fiction again.

Newspaper article by Laeïla Adjovi
Libération, 5 July 2006, 9.51 p.m.

A MOTHER AND HER DAUGHTER STARVE TO DEATH
IN THEIR AUBERVILLIERS APARTMENT

Doomitra, thirty-two years old, originally from Mauritius, and her daughter, Chana, five years old, were found dead last weekend in their apartment in Aubervilliers (Seine-Saint-Denis). The medical examiner's office concluded it was a 'natural death from malnutrition'. It wasn't possible to establish the exact dates of death. Mystical inscriptions were reportedly found on the walls of the apartment and, according to a neighbour, Doomitra, the mother, who lived on welfare, made frequent visits to African marabouts. She'd worked in a day-care centre for a while, before leaving to care for her daughter. She received assistance from the children's social services. The little girl, Chana, was registered at the neighbourhood kindergarten. Since children are not required to attend school until the age of six, and since no sign of abuse had been recorded, her absence wasn't reported to the police.

TRANSLATORS' NOTES

PAGE *xi*
We have made a conscious effort to honour the lyric quality of Dracius's prose by infusing music (rhythm and repetition of sound) throughout the translation. For example, using a 'sound-mapping' technique for the first line (in French) of the novel, we noted the repetition of the sound [k] (indicated in bold below), as well as the repetition of [f] (indicated in italics below). Both of these powerful sounds serve to underline the speaker's insistence on making her point, as follows:

Je ne veux pas d'une A*f*rique de **c**ontrainte, de **c**ette *f*ausse A*f*rique, **c**ette A*f*rique *f*abri**q**uée, **c**ette A*f*rique **q**ui motile, avilit, dé*f*igure.

Fortuitously, our translation of this opening sentence was able to make generous use of the [k] and [f] sounds:

I don't want any of this A*f*rica of **c**oercion, this *f*alse A*f*rica, this *f*abricated A*f*rica, this A*f*rica that maims, demeans, dis*f*igures.

PAGE 4
Dracius mixes verb tenses, sometimes in the same paragraph, as is the case here, to disorient the reader in time, in order to create the effect of blending the history of her Creole ancestors with current inhabitants of the Caribbean, as well as to celebrate her own mixed ancestry of African, European, Carib Indian, and Chinese roots.

PAGE 13
négropolitain: Pejorative French name used to describe West Indians born in France, combining 'nègre' with 'métropolitain' (pertaining to France).

Malavoi: A musical band from Martinique, which formed in 1972.

Kassav: A Caribbean music band formed in Guadaloupe in 1979.

PAGE 56
Domiens: Refers to people from the French Overseas Departments.

Tomiens: Refers to people from the French Overseas Territories.

PAGE 70

sui generis: Latin phrase for 'one of a kind', 'unique.'

PAGE 76

berlingot: Pyramid-shaped, multicoloured hard candy from France.

PAGE 85

tchip: Refers to a loud sound made by sucking one's teeth with one's tongue, familiar in most Black cultures, including those from the Caribbean, Africa, or the United States; this sound usually communicates disapproval.

PAGE 86

Maminette: Familiar name used by a child to refer to his/her mother.

PAGE 98

blaff: Manner of preparing fish that is popular in the Caribbean, especially in Martinique. The fish is marinated in lime juice, garlic and hot peppers and then poached in the marinade.

PAGE 99

manu militari: Latin phrase for 'with military aid'.

PAGE 115

totor: Was an actual French coin worth 2 sous. The coin featured the head of Italian king Victor Emmanuel III (1869–1947), 'Totor' being a common French nickname for Victor. According to Ma Cidalise's story, a magical totor is a coin on which a sorcerer cast a spell so that the coin given to a shopkeeper would always return to its owner, allowing her or him to keep the merchandise for free as well as any change received.

PAGE 168

'Adieu Madras': Refers to 'Adieu foulard, adieu Madras', a traditional Creole song or lullaby composed in 1769 and popular in Martinique.

PAGE 217

ti-punch: Literally 'small (petit) punch', a rum-based drink popular in French-speaking Caribbean islands, made with white agricole rum, lime and cane syrup.

PAGE 270

'Like all amoral beings, she verges on the goddess': Quote from Lawrence Durrell's *The Alexandria Quartet* (1957–60).

babylone: gendarme.

bagaille (bagay): thing.

béké (békée): white person from the Antilles; descendant of European colonialists.

bitako, blogodo, boloko: rough-hewn countryman; uncouth, uneducated.

bombe: shared taxi.

bonda man Jacques: literally, Madame Jacques' derrière—very spicy pepper.

boutou: large stick.

bwa-bwa: elaborately dressed puppets carried around by revellers for Carnival.

cacarelle: diarrhoea.

cagou (kagou): sick.

cal (kal, koko): penis; also, wand, staff.

calagouaille: gamecock; flame-coloured.

calazaza (kalazaza): refers to a light-skinned mulatto with red or blond hair and very few black features.

capistrelle: scatterbrain.

capresse: half-black, half-mulatto woman with black hair.

cattechiopine: brazen young girl.

chabin, chabine: refers to a biracial man or woman with golden skin and hair.

chappé-kouli (chapé-kouli): term used to describe a mulatto who is part Indian, part black.

chaudière: little hat that is part of the traditional costume of a woman from Martinique.

chellou: Antillean stew made with beef organ meats (heart, liver, spleen, lungs).

coucoune (koukoun): woman's sex.

couri-vini: in case of emergency evacuation.

dégras: Creole term referring to fertile earth in a garden or orchard.

engagé: under a spell, bewitched, or one who has sold her or his soul to the devil.

femme-l'estrade: matron.

gole: wide dress cut out of a single piece of cloth with no defined waist, similar to a tunic.

gros-sirop (gwo siwo): (1) brown-feathered gamecock; (2) nègres gros-sirop (*qv*).

gueule de Polius: name given to pork brawn or headcheese in Martinique.

icaque: fruit of the icaquier tree, a small tree that grows in the tropics and produces a variety of plum that tastes slightly bitter.

ka: refers to both a family of big hand drums and the music played with them.

kalenda: very lascivious Creole dance.

kannari: stew pot; cooking pot.

kayali: bird with very long feet.

koui (kwi): hollowed-out half-calabash used as a container.

lafouka: to dance lafouka is to dance collé-collé or collé-serré—very tightly, close to your partner as if glued to him/her.

lambi: large, edible mollusc.

lélé: cooking utensil used for stirring beverages and stews, made from branches of the swizzlestick tree, which end in a five-finger star pattern.

mabouya: lizard.

madiana: the last musical piece played at the end of a ball.

madjoumbé: fork.

mâle-femme: virago; woman who looks like a man; shrew.

manawa: prostitute.

manman: Creole word for 'mother'.

marakoudja: passion fruit, bright yellow and very juicy.

massibol (masibol): passionate lover.

massoucrelle (masoukrèl): woman who interferes with other people's business.

matador: elegant woman; brazen; often of loose morals.

matoutou: traditional Martiniquan Easter crab stew.

métis/se: mulatto man/woman.

michelin: makeshift shoe made from tyre rubber.

molocoye: turtle.

morne: hill.

nègre-congo: Negro freshly arrived from Africa in the time of slavery; today, a very dark-skinned man or a boorish countryman.

nègres gros-sirop: revellers at Carnival smeared with molasses and soot, like old-time sugar factory workers.

patate-l'ombrage: woman's sex (and surrounding pubic hair).

pipiri: morning bird whose song imitates the onomatopoeic name it was given. 'At pipiri' means 'at dawn'.

pissecrette: a small, worthless woman.

pitt: sandy area where cock fights are held.

potager: draining board; part of a sink next to the basin.

quénette: small, round, green-coloured fruit extracted from its shell in order to suck the delicious juice and spit out the stone.

quimboiseurs: those who practise witchcraft.

rigoise: whip.

roquille: container used to measure a quarter of a litre of rum.

sabador (chabador, jabador): loose-fitting, African ceremonial robe with oversized, flowing sleeves.

sacatra: a term used in French colonies to refer to the offspring of one black and one griffe (three-quarter black) parent; in essence, a person of seven-eighth black and one-eighth white ancestry.

soucougnan (soukougnan): mythical character born of the metamorphosis of a woman who has the power to leave her own skin at night and change into a firebird.

tafia: cheap rum.

tafiateuse: from 'tafia', a drunkard or alcoholic.

tazar: large fish with tasty flesh from the mackerel family.

tchololo: very weak coffee; pun in French for 'lolos', which is slang for 'breasts'.

tchébé-coeur: literally, 'holds the heart'—snack or light meal.

tiéboud-dien (tiebdjeun): Senegalese national dish composed mainly of rice with red sauce, fish, mixed vegetables and spices.

ti-manmaille (manmay): a gang of kids; a child.

toloman: type of mash made with a vegetable powder; edible flour from arrow-root rhizomes, a native plant from tropical America.

torche: small circular pillow used to carry items on the head.

trempage: traditional dish from Martinique consisting of poached cod served on stale bread previously soaked in water, then laid out on banana leaves.

wèt: path, trail.

yamba: hemp, marijuana.

yen-yen: mosquito.

yiche (yich): child.

zachari (zakari): cookie.

zibicrette: frail young woman/girl; short insignificant person.

zorèy (pejorative): white person who came from mainland France.

zougoun: from the author's xenolalia, a personal alteration of azoun-goun, a term of endearment signifying 'my treasure', 'my beloved'.

zouk: party; type of music from the Antilles that is very conducive to dancing.

ACKNOWLEDGEMENTS

Excerpts from this novel have previously appeared in *Drunken Boat*, *Eleven Eleven*, *The Massachusetts Review* and *The New England Review*.

We are extremely grateful to Germinal Pinalie, for his discerning eye in editing the text, as well as to James Davis for assisting with early drafts of the novel. Additional thanks go to Ted Miller and Larry Kellogg for their invaluable help in bringing this translation into the English-speaking world.

Nancy Naomi Carlson
Catherine Maigret Kellogg